Also by Anna Shapiro

The Right Bitch

LIFE & LOVE,

such
as
they
are
. . . . .

Anna Shapiro

Simon & Schuster

New York   London   Toronto   Sydney   Tokyo   Singapore

SIMON & SCHUSTER
Rockefeller Center
1230 Avenue of the Americas
New York, New York 10020

SIMON & SCHUSTER and colophon are registered
trademarks of Simon & Schuster Inc.

Designed by Levavi & Levavi
Manufactured in the United States of America

1   3   5   7   9   10   8   6   4   2

Library of Congress Cataloging-in-Publication Data
Shapiro, Anna.
Life & love, such as they are / Anna Shapiro.
p.   cm.
1. Man-woman relationships—New York (N.Y.)—Fiction. 2. City
and town life—New York (N.Y.)—Fiction. 3. Women—New York
(N.Y.)—Fiction. I. Title. II. Title: Life and love, such as they are.
PS3569.H3383L5   1994
813'.54—dc20   93-28773
                                                              CIP

ISBN 0-671-87114-5

For Alison

Contents

· · · · ·

Part III

Part I

. . . . .

'Twas grief enough to think mankind
All hollow, servile, insincere;
But worse to trust to my own mind
And find the same corruption there.
                    —Emily Brontë

1. Seductive melancholy

The meat loaf looked just like Frank's head. Ella hadn't meant to do this, but now that the resemblance was coming out—she gave the loaf a ketchupy pat—she was quite pleased. In art school her portrait busts had been the only ones that actually looked like the person who was posing. Ground chuck was not, perhaps, the ideal correlative for spectacles, but it would be delicious—slicing into Frank's dolphin forehead, dismembering lip from thin lip as though his were never to grasp hers again, and above all warming the cool slick flesh to something sizzling and yielding its juices up to her.

And of course to Stephen, who would be eating it too.

She considered giving it bacon-strip hair and olives or mushrooms for eyes, but decided it would be *de trop*. This wasn't a gingerbread man. It wasn't as if she had set out to do this on *purpose*. If she had, it wouldn't have worked. Or not if it really mattered to her. "I'm a fuckup," she liked to tell people when they asked what she did. If they pressed further, at least wanting to know at what, precisely, she fucked up, she would insist that being a fuckup was the profession. It was the one thing, she felt, at which she could safely be a success. "I'm thinking of applying for a grant," she might finish, so that her questioner might then have the impression that she was both clever and modest, intriguingly reticent and yet without pretense. Or such was the impression Ella, without having articulated it to herself, hoped to convey.

Luckily, as the meat loaf cooked, its features tended to amalgamate into a generalized lumpiness, so that when Stephen saw it his comment was only, "It looks sort of—topographical. Don't you usually put bacon on it?"

"It's a new recipe. It was in the *Times*." She had become so adept at lying since lying with Frank that it had become easier, almost, to do it than not. She could practice on the inconsequent lies. Though it was amazing how easy it was to tell the whoppers, like "shopping" after she had spent three hours writhing on the gritty bed in Frank's studio, when Stephen asked what she'd been up to. It went down with Stephen like a tasty dinner—like a succulent slice of meat loaf. If he had ever really wanted to know what she was doing, she might not have been doing the first thing in their eight years of living together that she hadn't wanted him to know about. So she told herself.

She watched Stephen as he ate. This is an excellent practice if you should happen to want to detach yourself from someone to whom you have been excessively tied. Though Ella could perfectly well remember a time when this hadn't been so. She could remember a time early in their alliance when a very young Stephen had had a cold and she had brought him boiled eggs and toast on a tray, and she had hunched on the edge of the bed and watched as he had scraped the yellowy goop onto his toast and torn at the toast with the ineffectual teeth and soft, lovable mouth of a small, dear child, as it seemed to her (the only one she would ever have, as it seemed to her). She had felt like a courtier at a king's levee, grateful to be able to sit there and watch the adored personage—semiperson, semidemigod—at his toilette. She had felt every morsel go into his mouth as if it had been feeding her. As it had been, since she felt nourished by Stephen's very existence. The torn knitted pajama top with the pale band around the neck, fraying at a shoulder seam. The pleased, embarrassed smile each time he looked up and met her eyes, so that he had shyly to look down again, his gaze traveling from good fortune to good fortune. That was how all of life was to be from then on.

But as she looked across the somewhat too-small table that was all their apartment could accommodate, another image rose continually between her eyes and Stephen seated before them: Frank, like a ghost floating up from under the table. She just couldn't fix herself on Stephen anymore. Couldn't even hear him sometimes. It was mortifying when he played her something he had composed. When the music stopped, the trance ended: she hadn't heard a note, but had been reliving, moment by moment, Frank mashing her against a wall, his pelvis satisfyingly holding her in place. "Could I hear it again?" Stephen would be flattered; she might manage on its second airing to hear the piece for the first time.

She sliced open Frank's spongy chuck forehead as though she could scoop the brain from Frankenstein's monster. It really wasn't as good without bacon.

Frank's studio was in a dilapidated warehouse on the waterfront, up two flights of locked stairs, which meant Ella always had to meet him outside. It was a place where the wind became almost a solid thing you could lean against, if it weren't at the same time whipping you and burning your cheeks to ice.

This was not a bad approximation of the effects of their affair.

Even if she called from a pay phone seven blocks down on Hudson Street and dawdled on the way, he never got there before her, and she always had to wait, pressed into an archway over a loading dock that offered minimal protection from the harbor gusts. Waves churned up on the water like the tails of silver fish. It was the same river she could see from her apartment windows like a square of mirror at the end of the street. It was so cold the clouds looked frozen, high and compact and cleaving through a sky of opaque radiance. She raised her face to blend with the wind and sky, squinting, wincing, irrationally excited and pleased. A man appeared, head down, swathed in wool like an Arab. He thrust his key into the door with a dark look at her, a rather improbably glamorous woman clenched against industrial brick (hairy boa, broad fur collar, soft leather boots with fuck-me heels, snood of the finest accordion-pleated wool, and not much more of her face visible than eyes heavily outlined in kohl). He couldn't mistake her for one of the numerous waterfront hookers, so high on dope that they didn't bother buttoning their skimpy jackets, and most of them self-evidently men anyway beneath satiny Lycra. It must be written all over her that she was waiting for a yet more illicit if weirdly sanctioned kind of lover, and she wished she could have worn a cloak of invisibility, or at least dressed like one of the artists who might actually be using the building for a more conventionally legitimate purpose. On the other hand, she imagined his dark look contained a note of envy, which she would take for a compliment. She would take whatever she could get.

Ah, there was Frank. She spotted him from a block away by his queer, scuttling walk. It was very fast but his legs, slightly undersized for his height, looked as though they were tethered at the knee. He walks in chains, she thought. His head swiveled from side to side like a mechanical doll's. He is checking for muggers, and humming, was her conviction. Sure enough, as he got near, his big yellow teeth bared in what passed in her sex-aching eyes for a grin, she could hear the tuneless hum as he leaned forward for a peck. At the last moment, as she raised herself for the kiss, he swerved to the side: "Not out here."

"Who's going to see us?" she cried. She could have hit him, if her hands hadn't been too cold to bear removing from her pockets.

His face furrowed, deeply displeased. The man who earlier had passed in with his possibly envious look now burst from the door, checking them out with another quick, furtive glance.

"You see? You see?" said Frank.

"Well, it's no worse for someone to see us together than for someone to see you kissing me," Ella grumbled, falling forward into the chill but mercifully still air of the sordid hallway, where boards and pipes and miscellaneous furniture parts were heaped. "Acting as if we aren't supposed to be together can only make people think we aren't supposed to be together," she continued hectoring as they mounted the first flight. "If you behaved as if nothing were wrong, no one would suspect."

"You forget," said Frank through his big teeth, "that I'm a married man."

"Fat chance. Anyway"—they were at his studio door, reinforced with plywood and secured by a padlock of cartoonishly large proportions—"you want people to forget. If I were married to you, I wouldn't let you go around not wearing a ring for one minute."

The sense this conveyed of his being as dangerous as a full-natured bull flattered him so well that he dropped the fight and laughed. Fighting in any case was for him a form of love play, if not the thing—"love"—itself. Especially when he laughed, people said that he looked like a certain notorious movie star and ladies' man, which is to say that he was cocksure, self-delighting, and elusive. Ella looked at him with annoyance, but laughed anyway. Fighting was, after all, easier than loving. And considerably more binding and addictive.

Still, it was annoying that he wasted any of their stolen time together on the practical and fairly disgusting chores of his studio. Leaving her to stand or do what she would, he contorted himself over a corner of the bed to reach under the flaking radiator, whence he fished up a corroded coffee tin, balancing it with care: orange water glinted at the surface. The radiator was incapable of giving off heat, but it leaked. Halfway out into the studio the linoleum floor had the texture of a frozen river where it had buckled from the creeping waters, and was stained with their rust. Ella sat on the bed, which sank as if it hoped to roll her off, and pulled the butterflied heavy nylon sleeping bag over her legs and coat with a zipping sound. Frank reached down a crevice behind a different corner of the bed, rocking Ella, and pulled out a mousetrap, with the dead creature stiffly jutting. While he was off flushing it down the communal toilet in the hall, Ella amused herself by studying, as so many times before, the instruments of torture and kitschy photographs ornamenting the flyspecked walls. He had spherical African masks like severed heads taken as trophies from a jungle war; leaning in the corner, dangerous spikes were upended, along with other arcane black metal instruments that could pierce, gouge, and tear. The photographs had been cut from magazines and, whatever their original hues, been bleached a uniform blue by sunlight. That so highly self-conscious and austere a photographer should choose to surround himself with bad reproductions of the most sentimental possible representations of his own subject—"nature"—was an ironic contrast that did not lose its charm over time. Clouds glamorized by sunshine presiding religiously over snow-capped peaks. Tips of trees reaching toward heaven. A nimbus of light over a vast plain that suggested, like alleged photographs of auras in books of the occult, a visual proof of the Great Presence Itself.

They were of that class of picture found on calendars profiting conservation organizations that could be characterized as inspirational: they were intended to make you want to take off for the wilds immediately, or at least send a check. Maybe that was why Frank hung them. He had no checks to send, but took off for the wilds whenever possible, or whenever he could get someone to give him a check to do so. To take pictures that would if anything deter any-one else from following him. In his pictures, the world took on the aspect of his studio: raw, harsh decay, unforgiving and unprotecting. In this his photographs were, like all the best art, self-portraits. Their relish for the grit of earthiness accounted for their paradoxical status of fame and lack of popularity. Everyone knew of and admired Frank; few actu-ally wanted him.

As Frank came back through the plywood-sheathed door with the empty can and trap, whistling between his teeth, Ella swished her covering to one side in an invitation for him to join her. But he wasn't looking.

"Frank?" He went on whistling. *"Frank."* His head jerked sideways toward her and back. "Jesus. I get ignored enough at home. I don't need to come here to do it."

That got his attention, sort of. "Ignored? I thought your friend was nuts about you."

"He adores and ignores me."

"I thought you said he thought you were irresistible."

"Well, if I were inviting him into bed he would."

"Not in your coat."

Frank was riffling through some papers from his desk, his head involuntarily shunting to the side every so often as if jolted by electricity or spasm. He pushed his glasses up a nose of impeccable high-WASP nondescription. The twin windows of the studio became four in the twin lenses.

"It's freezing in here!"

"You can go home to your warm apartment and your adoring friend. I don't want you to do anything you don't want to do."

He didn't want them on his head, the things he manipu-lated her into doing, like being obsessed with him. He didn't want her to do anything she didn't want to do but, some-how, those were precisely the things she ended up doing and even, most humiliatingly, wanting to do.

She looked out the window where the sun over the river was just a brighter spot in the generality of cloud, and down at her fingers. One of her first boyfriends had told her she had pretty hands, but at twenty-eight the veins were starting to rise, and this disgusted her. "Obviously I want to sleep with you," she said to them.

"What? What did you say?" Frank said almost as softly as she had spoken—murmured, in his low, intimate way, sinking onto a rattling desk chair and setting the papers aside.

She cast her hungry eyes up to his. "Obviously I want to sleep with you." It never occurred to her to do other than reply directly. She was always amazed at how people found ways to respond to questions without answering them.

"Hey, sweetie. Sweetie sweetie sweetie." Frank was cradling her head, his lips touching her hair. "You just made me jealous, talking about your friend like that."

"I thought you were glad I had a boyfriend. You said it made things more—equal between us. You have your wife." She trusted to his twenty years' experience in clandestine affairs.

"You sleep with your boyfriend."

She didn't answer.

"Right? Don't you?"

"Yes." She couldn't help giving him the clear victory.

They made love, and he was asleep. Poor baby. He couldn't sleep at night, because he hated sleeping alone. She looked at the shiny spot at the back of his head, bare as if worn away by the tramping feet of worry. Horizontal lines marked the dolphin brow; the baron of time, like Frankenstein, really had made rows of stitches. Over the hump of his shoulder, she watched as the edge of a cloud began to be tinged pink. Then the strips of solid vapor turned purple against the sky as the sun fell below them, beaming salmon light over the bed and the aquatic-looking landscape photos, gleaming white in patches along the walls. She would have to get back soon. It became possible to look directly at the sun as it burned red, the withered sky mottling like a bruise around it. The seductive melancholy of winter sunsets! "Frank." His breath erupted in horselike snorts. "Frank. I've got to go." He nestled in. "You're missing the most beautiful sunset."

At once he was alert, blinking at her, nearsighted and irritated. "I've seen enough sunsets."

2. Blue

Is the best over or is it yet to come? Burton kicked a clod of ice all the way down the block, over the curb, and across the street before it bounced into a storm drain while he mulled this horrifying question over. If you were ninety, you wouldn't care, but he was just past thirty and it not only felt as if the best were over, it felt as if it had been for years and years. In fact, life might as well be over. If you thought the best was past, what was left? Nothing to live for, certainly. Yet he was equally certain that it was wicked, evil, unequivocally wrong to think this way. He had no *right*. He had everything going for him—free, white, male, and over twenty-one. Not to mention a solid middle-class education, a modicum of brains, talent; people liked him.

Though most often he felt that none of this was true.

He was walking up West Street, along the landfill. He had always wondered how people managed to drown themselves, if they knew how to swim, that is. Virginia Woolf had put stones in her pockets, but wouldn't you just flail out of your clothes, or pull the stones out, or carry the weight? He was a pretty hefty guy. It would take boulders.

Unfortunately, this image amused him, which broke the practical trend of his thinking.

Okay, stones were out, but that was, let's face it, a girl's way anyway. Guys just swim until they collapse or get a cramp or something. He scuffed along the stony ground to an Anchor fence between him and the Hudson. It figured. There was probably no place in Manhattan where you could face the water unbounded (not that you couldn't jump off a pier). Clearly there was no room to swim until you collapsed. For one thing, some asshole would come along and try to rescue you. For another, unless you swam up- or downstream, you'd hit the other side long before you got tired, much less wore out. If you did it at night, to avoid rescue, someone would probably try to mug you on the pier. Your money or your life: Which would you prefer, you'd politely reply.

But Burton knew that to the kind of poor jerk who'd be a mugger, Burton's life and means would look pretty good. He stood with his big hands curled into the wire diamonds of the fence, looking out over Hoboken or whatever it was, where the big neon clock was like a colorful line drawing of a clock looming over the water. Burton was of the burly type who are slow to feel the cold or indeed to suffer physically, as if their comfortable bodies are so made for sensual enjoyment that they are impervious to what might diminish it. So, though cut by the same wind that had burned Ella's cheeks, what pushed him on was that by the clock he knew he'd be late for rehearsal. He'd have to find not only the method, but some more convenient time to die.

The five flights of stairs were themselves killers. Burton had forgotten about them, and stopped to rest on a slate landing worn to a shallow bowl, to look out a marble-silled tenement window toward the same everlasting river, down a narrow street as inexorable as a bowling lane. He could hear from the higher floor the door opening and closing, Stephen's voice—"Hey, my man" (spoken ironically, as by someone who would never actually say "hey, my man")—laughter, the twangs and honks of instruments released from the velvet dungeons of cases. Lights twinkled on the street below. It was the kind of gloomy day where dusk descends without a scarlet intervention, and darkness is more comforting than the earlier barren glare. Burton turned and heaved himself up the final flight, peeling down to his inevitable flannel shirt.

Next to Burton, Stephen looked even more twittery and birdlike than he ordinarily did. He rocked onto his toes, nodding his head as jumpily as Burton might tap his conductor's baton. He held a sheaf of handwritten music, on which he was pointing out some subtlety to a young woman in glasses who earnestly studied the indicated passage. He looked up on Burton's entrance—the door stood unlatched—and nodded a greeting intended to telegraph a recognition of something comic in their simple mutual presence. "Maestro," he intoned. Then turned to another of the players. After all, Burton was his friend already. Burton stood in the kitchen, unwilling to press his bulk through the circle of players who filled the near end of the living room. He didn't have any real reason to be there. It was just that Stephen had asked him to come.

Once the music started, Burton felt his heart might break. Not from the music (what Stephen wouldn't have given to have this effect!), which Burton no more heard than Ella did in her sex-glazed state. He also was glazed by longing, but for something lost. He was thinking of his old girlfriend, Lisa. They hadn't been together for four or five years, but he found himself lately thinking of her with a new, more acute sadness. He thought of her ponytail, and the softness of the skin on the underside of her jaw, and nearly choked on the immediate, tactile quality of the memory. The best—over!

How could he ever fall in love like that again? He was a dead person; killing himself would be redundant. He hadn't been so sad when they broke up—it was just a college-sweetheart kind of thing, diminishing for years, pleasant, convenient, but long uncompelling. No, in moments of clarity (which were fewer and fewer), he knew it wasn't even Lisa he was mourning: it was himself, as he once was, a person he could scarcely recognize. A person who wanted things. A person who felt things. Who felt connected, even if not satisfactorily.

These thoughts were projected (abstractedly) onto a bookcase. As though the books' different-colored spines had absorbed the salt and sour essence of his thoughts, Burton had to turn away from them, and thereafter could not look in that direction without the beginnings of a treacherous sob rising to the choking point, especially at the wide spine of one pale blue volume mysteriously imbued for him with his sensation of not being loved. And after all, he thought when his eye fell on it, I'm not worth loving.

He deflected his smeary gaze to Stephen waving his arms around in the air. What was he doing? Oh, *conducting*. He was quite a weak conductor. But it didn't matter, it didn't matter. Stephen was loving it. Or rather, he was there. Every beat of the music was his own living heart to him: with it he would compel the world to love him. And if they didn't, he would try harder. Was he not lovable? Was he not his mama's adorable boy, so smart, so talented, kinderleh, boychik? This knowledge came to Burton without his volition. He could look at his longtime friend and see it, as though the gulf separating him from life, and widening each day, were at the same time a magnifying lens or some kind of amplifier of other people's interior workings. He would just as soon not have known, just as soon not have seen Stephen's vainglory, would have much preferred to see him as he had for years, his pal, part of a team, part of a mutual, complementary, happy vanity.

LIFE & LOVE
such as they are

When Stephen asked him what he thought of the music, Burton understood that this question had nothing to do with the aesthetic qualities of sound but with his friend's anxious lovability. "You get better every year," was Burton's honest reply, since the question was not of music, and he had the satisfaction of seeing his friend beam, actually become more lovable under the rays of love, or what seemed to him such. That this moved Burton because he himself had caused it drew tears into his throat again.

The players had left. The two men sat with their beers, Stephen's neatly poured down the side of a glass to avoid a head, Burton's bottle clutched in both fists as though he needed something to hold on to, which he did, big bearded Burt, who looked a benevolent lumberjack, and Stephen with his necessarily ironic macho swagger—a swagger with a figurative crook'd pinkie. "So what do you think?" Stephen said, score in hand, and went through the piece Burton hadn't heard, measure by measure. Some perfectly detached part of Burton must have been attending, however. "You need to mark the downbeat there," he said, pointing, "and cut out, oh, about a sixty-fourth note early—yes, right there—to give the bassoon time to get in." He went on giving praise and advice in his sonorous, rumbling voice. Yes, the trouble was, he couldn't hurt anyone, that was why he hated himself.

Burton had no idea where this thought came from, or what it meant, and it did not get in the way of what went on to be a pleasant, matter-of-fact conversation—Burton's choral conducting, for which he was actually getting paid these days, though not enough for him to quit altogether as a pit musician on Broadway; the musical Stephen was writing and the great genius he was working with, how inspiring it was. *Yes, I can't bear to hurt people. This is why I want to kill myself.* It was comforting. In his moment of release he relaxed. Then a spasm crossed his face, and he got up from the couch to move to the chair in front of the black window, where there was always a draft at this time of year.

"Hey, you're in the cold spot, maestro."

But from this angle Burton's eyes could not possibly fall on the book with the pale blue spine, pale and cold as the river, that told him there was no reason in the world why anyone should love him.

3. Fuckola

Ella had known when she was twenty that the best of her life was over. That was the year she had fallen in love with Stephen. Far from despairing, she had faith in the following paradox: that since Stephen was (as they say) the best thing that had ever happened to her, then the best would in some sense keep on going, because she would be with him forever. She had not doubted this on the many, many occasions Stephen had given her cause to, and she did not doubt it now that she had generated some cause for doubt, or rather now that Frank had erupted into the bliss of that steady unity that was the basic fact of life, the basis of her life. But she couldn't make sense of this eruption. For this she turned to her friends.

"Fuck-ola." Ella flung out her hand as though trying to shake something from it.

"What?"

"My fucking fingernail just—ouch—ripped."

Ave emitted a low snigger. It was a rare happiness to her to see her old old friend Ella—proper Ella, lucky Ella, good Ella—so loose and layabout and corrupted. Deceitful. Messing up. She had entered Ave's camp.

LIFE & LOVE
such as they are

Ave's camp was decorated, fittingly, like a gypsy's. It was just a camp, since Ave had no fixed dwelling, and even the possessions with which she renovated her constantly temporary surroundings changed with kaleidoscopic speed, since she gave away as freely as she acquired. She stood by the mirrored closet of the borrowed apartment, in what was the daughter's bedroom, in the daughter's antique kimono left open to reveal Ave's breasts and the encapsulated lower part of her body in sheer-to-waist pantyhose that suggested a bank robber's sinister mask for the crotch. She pulled out a blouse and held it on its hanger, toreador style, between her body and her image in the wall of mirror. "Can you imagine having all this money and buying shit like this?" Ave sounded the *t* in "shit" with emphatic viciousness and let the hanger and blouse drop soundlessly onto thick carpeting the studied no-color of modernism.

Ella, in the window seat, looked out at the park to avoid her impulse to pick the blouse off the floor. A woman in a riding habit, blackly silhouetted against the remains of snow, cantered by. A slight figure with his hands tensely jammed into jeans pockets that barely accommodated them approached another man, head down, under the twining lavender bark of the bare wisteria pergola. "That's Lovers' Lane, isn't it?" Ella had heard of it from the "genius" Stephen worked with, who preferred the baths, himself.

"That's another thing. I wouldn't live where I had to watch faggots tricking under my nose."

"Hey, some of my best friends," said Ella, who tried to maintain a cool pose with Ave, not without twinges of disloyalty to her own point of view, whatever that was. She liked Cameron, the genius. What she didn't like was Stephen's fealty to him, which was not unlike her helplessness in the face of Frank's wishes. She looked out at the park again, blinking. The two men were walking off together. When she turned back, Ave was lying on the carpet trying to seal a pair of pale jeans over a stomach flattened by gravity.

Anna Shapiro

·····

She puffed her cheeks like the east wind. "Ugh. The only good thing about getting your period is how fat it makes your tits," Ave commented, small pads of flesh springing up against the cruel tightness as she sat.

"Your breasts are always beautiful," said Ella, feeling the teary pinpricks that accompany generosity toward a person one distrusts.

"They are nice," said Ave to the mirror. Ella remembered how it used to be when Ave came over to the house when they were girls, when Ave—then known as Maria, as in *Ave Maria*—would disappear after going to the bathroom or calling her mother to say she was staying over. "What happened to Maria?" Ella's own mother would ask, thumping a casserole onto a tile set on the Formica tabletop. "She's caught in the mirror," Ella would say, dutifully retrieving her friend from in front of the hall mirror, where Ave would be lost in an intent, nearsighted gaze. "I knew I'd find you here," the stolid child would say, and Ave would laugh. Ave was three years older than Ella, which had counted for so much in those days that Ella hadn't entirely outgrown her awe at being accepted by one of the big girls. Not entirely.

Ave, who was too vain to wear her glasses and too uncomfortable in lenses, was staring from inches away at a black shirt from which with a crackle of static she had pulled the dry cleaner's clinging film. With great care she began blotting stray cat hairs from it, using a piece of masking tape wrapped around three fingers. This was her own shirt. "You would think things would come back from the fucking cleaners clean." She looked over at Ella drooping on the window seat in what Ave had to see as an awful thrift-shop dress. Well, it was awful, it had holes, but not awful on Ella, who loved what was used, faded, bruised. Not unlike Frank, when you came down to it. ("Those pictures of his," Ave had complained when Ella showed her his work, "so brown rice.")

·26·

Ave had the black top on and swiveled before the mirror to check the hang of the fabric, the flatness of her tum, and whether any cat hairs lingered on the back. She turned to Ella for comment.

"Fine." Ella had long resigned herself to a Hollywood-suburban, nouveau-riche element in Ave's taste.

"You're right, it doesn't suit me at all. You take it."

This really made Ella feel like crying. "I hate getting hand-me-downs," she managed as Ave pressed the garment into her limp hands.

"You do? Oh, yeah—Suki." Suki was Ella's fat wealthy cousin whose expensive oversize clothes Ella had worn until she discovered the anonymous hand-me-downs of thrift shops.

"Suki!" Ella laughed. "I haven't thought of her in ages. How great of you to remember." And she felt a rush of warmth.

"I always used to think of Suzuki Bean and wonder why this rich cousin didn't have more fabulous clothes." Ave noodled in the wardrobe, not wanting to make too much of this moment of warmth and thereby make herself too equal to Ella.

"What are you going to do when you have to leave this place?" Ella asked.

"You mean when they come back? I can stay."

"But would you want to?"

"Oh, something else will turn up. It always does."

Ave, having settled on a striped sweater with puffed sleeves and a peplum, allowed as how she had better do some blow, as a kind of preventive measure, in case something brought her down. You never knew what might be out there. She shuffled across the carpeting, her nylon-girded toes making sparks, to pull out of her purse a mirror and dollar bill. There was also a vial with a spoon attached by a chain around its neck.

The spoon reminded Ella of the ones her mother put out

in saltcellars for fancy dinners. She watched as Ave folded the bill, pressing the crease in a manner that stated all dealings with the material world were alien to her, as if her very fingers wished to protest their helplessness. She tipped a bit of powder onto the mirror. Ella had sunk onto the canopy bed and leaned on one elbow, watching. "I've never tried cocaine," was her mild comment.

"Oh, you've got to." Ave had the zeal of an evangelist. "You haven't—well, I won't say you haven't lived until you've tried it but, Ella-bella, you don't know what you're missing."

This was not unlike Frank's take on adultery, or whatever you should call it if you were only living with someone and not married; adultery. He seemed to feel it made you a better person, a stronger person, more conversant with the complexities of life and therefore in closer touch with truth, in some devious way. But cocaine—that was just silly. Ella had tried drugs in high school, like everybody else, and basically thought the whole thing was a drag. She rolled onto her back, hands behind her head. The ancient dress ripped slightly under one arm. "No, thanks."

"Oh, don't be uptight. Once isn't going to hurt you."

"I wasn't worried!" Ella was offended enough at this imputation to take the dollar bill and hold it so that the edges slightly cut into her nostril. "Wait, wait." She motioned the mirror away, then let loose her bottled laughter. "I'm sorry, this is so stupid. This is like—nostrils, for God's sake. How can something be glamorous that you put up your *nose?* All right, all right." She thought she had control of her laughter until Ave held the mirror up again like a dish of caviar, and Ella was off again.

"It's really good blow." Ave was miffed. "I get it from a guy who gets it right off the boat. It's uncut. Fine, be like that. More for me." She lowered her face to the bill and the bill to the line mounded like sand on the glass, and vacuumed. She sniffed delicately, pressing the side of her nose with the back of a finger.

Ella watched, feeling sorry for her. She was supposed to be impressed by the fancy apartment, by Ave's boldness in answering the door half-naked, by Ave's ability to procure uncut dope; how pathetic, anyway, that Ave needed to impress, and her of all people, little Ellie.

Ella supposed the affair didn't help any either. At first it had made them closer than they had ever been, conspirators, and what was more, Ella always had news, if only in the nature of a weather vane: Frank was being mean to her this week, they'd had a fight; Stephen was giving her strange looks; and then there was the endless, mutually gratifying loves-me-loves-me-not analysis. But it was hard on Ave that Frank was famous. Ave knew lots of famous people. But she couldn't keep people in her life any better than she held on to possessions or places to live. While Ella always had Stephen; always always always. And her one real boyfriend before that had also stuck like a burr. And whatever kind of shit Frank was, he obviously took Ella seriously. No one took Ave seriously. Ave looked troubled but intent as she vacuumed a row an ant might have trenched. "Okay," said Ella, sitting up.

"Forget it. You're too high on life. You're getting fucked so much you don't need drugs."

"Oh, come on." Ella was surprised to hear in her own impatient peremptoriness an echo of Frank. Or rather she felt like him, felt she had appropriated something of his power. If she were married to him, maybe she would feel this all the time. People would do what *she* wanted. As if by magic, Ave held out the mirror, her pillowy lips parted in startlement and delight. She gave instructions abundantly, abusively, as though Ella were an idiot. Ella found it hard to follow with good grace. Ten minutes later Ave asked wasn't it fabulous. "What am I supposed to be feeling?" Ella replied. "It doesn't feel like anything."

• • •

The two friends Ella had confided in were two extremes. Ave she had believed safe to tell because she wouldn't, couldn't possibly be shocked, and besides, Ave had encouraged Ella in the first place to go ahead with this affair. Ella sensed that Ave had never wished her well with Stephen, not because of any visible incompatibility but because of the opposite, because they were so much together, because by comparison with Ave's, Ella's life was too smooth. Ave, Ella felt, would overlook the tragedy of such an affair, pooh-poohing the romance of the sublime from the outset. "He talks about *marrying* you? What a dingdong. Guys like that *never* leave their wives."

Cynthia, however, was another story. It was precisely to the romantic pathos of it all that Cynthia would vibrate. She would see immediately that this was a contest of the fates: Which man embodied True Love? And what was it that Ella and Stephen had up to this point if not True Love? She saw that, for Ella, there had been only one man in the whole world—Stephen—and now there were two. And that she must be with only one of them, forever. Cynthia would vibrate to the potential tragedy all around because Cynthia was a tragic figure. Ella wasn't sure why she was tragic, but it was one of the many things she and Stephen had always agreed about.

On the way back from one of her free-lance jobs in midtown, Ella stopped off to see Cynthia in the depressing Chelsea studio that had once been Ella's and Stephen's more than cozy nest.

"He said that?" Cynthia sank onto her ugly couch with one leg under her, balancing a teacup on a saucer, moving with unconscious grace. "He's seen enough sunsets?" Her eyes, which had the odd appearance of being upside down, being more rounded on the bottom than along the lid, widened to their fullest extent, and the budlike, crinkled baby-mouth, with its pronounced cleft, opened like a chick's.

Ella had repeated Frank's statement for its shock effect—it had shocked her—but felt a ground swell of irritation at Cynthia, who was clearly only showing shock because that was what she thought Ella wanted. This was the problem with people who were too eager to please. And then there were people like Frank, who felt obligated not to.

"Well, don't you see?" said Ella. "I mean, can you imagine, a *nature* photographer . . . Just think if people knew. I mean, one of the things people are always going on about about him is, oh, what did I read? 'The air of uncompromising honesty his work conveys.' Oh yeah." Ella herself didn't realize what the words told her, that he just might be too sick of life, too sick of himself—sick of nature and sick of his own nature—for her or love to save him. Or put another way, that no matter how much she meant to him, it wasn't going to be enough for him to rouse himself on her account. "I mean, you might as well say that you're sick of, I don't know, orgasms."

Cynthia, who had never had one, smirked at the idea. With her eyes fixed to watch for her cues, she buried her face in her tea. "Maybe he was in the middle of, maybe he was concentrating on you, or something . . ."

"Well, he wasn't concentrating on me, but I was interrupting him," Ella conceded, experiencing again in imagination the weight of his head on her chest, the slight scratch and tickle of the short hairs around his ears, and the way he had nearsightedly squinted at her as he woke to what she was saying. "But no," she went on, as the feeling she'd had came back, like stage fright: "it's much worse. It's like saying there's no reason to live at all." Naturally she wanted to believe that she was enough reason.

At this, Cynthia unexpectedly laughed. She put down her cup, which let her clutch at her diaphragm as she rocked sideways. Wisps of straight blond hair escaped her bun and floated alongside her compressed, distorted face as she gasped. "Maybe there isn't," she finally got out.

"What?" Ella waited in perplexity.

"Maybe there isn't a reason to live." A last ebb of laughter escaped like a marble rolling into a corner. Cynthia straightened her sexy long legs to reach for cigarettes and lighter, then folded back, drawing. It gave her face a tough look. Again Ella felt herself becoming Frank, or a particular aspect of how he was. After she had let Frank kiss her the first time, she had asked him a question about his work. It had seemed to her inconsequential, but to him, invasively ardent. "Don't ask for my *heart*," he had said, and pushed her aside. She had managed an ironic expression: Your heart? Why, it's the very *last* thing, it said. "I like that cool look," was his response. Looking at Cynthia looking tough, Ella understood his relief, because she saw Cynthia look as if she were in control and could take care of herself, despite the eruption. She knew how crazy Cynthia could get, saw it just held in check. This is how Frank feels with me, Ella thought. And: I'm becoming a monster. It made her feel stronger, though, and she rose to the occasion by asking what had happened.

"What do you mean? Nothing's happened." Now Cynthia wouldn't meet Ella's eyes at all, but watched herself rubbing the side of her thumb along the back of the other hand, cigarette held clear. Ella studied her friend's face, the cheeks childishly round despite her thinness and pink without benefit of makeup.

"No," said Cynthia in her most New England, noblesse-oblige tone, "tell me what happened with Frank." Her changeable pale eyes once again settled on Ella; only her small chin hesitated in following the upward motion, and her eyes slewed sideways as she pulled smoke in. She waved her hands back and forth. "Really. I was just being silly." She made the face that said You know Silly Me, and upended her cup. It reminded Ella of the way men drink liquor in westerns.

Ella accepted Cynthia's masquerades of reasonableness, of sanity, hoping they weren't just masquerades. Eager for the relief of expression, for reassurance, for sympathy (because it all made *her* feel crazy, almost like something she'd made up or that had happened to someone else, if she couldn't share it with someone, especially couldn't share it with Stephen, to whom she told everything), Ella went on.

4. Flooey

Cynthia knew she shouldn't have invited someone, with so little time left before the rehearsal. She should have said to Ella, Some other day. Well, as long as she was at it, at thinking of *shoulds,* what she should have done was, she should have practiced, before, that is. She leaned in her doorway, listening as Ella's feet went down the four flights of marble steps, until the door downstairs squeaked and thudded closed and the dangerous silence took over once again. It was amazing how a staircase could be made of marble and still look so gimcrack, so tacky; maybe it was the red flocked whorehouse wallpaper, stained black over the radiators, or the wrought-iron banisters painted in flaking cream. Cynthia continued her contemplation of the hallway until the baroque pattern of the wallpaper superimposed itself on whatever else she looked at. She could feel her own apartment behind her like two stern hands upon her shoulders, waiting to make her *face the music.*

Reluctantly, she turned around. There it was, the depressing Chelsea studio, the find, the deal—the kind of apartment you can never move out of. Stephen and Ella had moved

out. But then, they had each other. What was more, they had
to, it was barely big enough for Cynthia alone, though practically luxurious by New York standards—there was an alcove
for the bed that was almost a room. It had the only window,
toward which Cynthia drifted, though the time when she
would have to go to the rehearsal, when practicing would no
longer be an option, was only getting closer. She looked out
at the wall of windows that faced her, some of which were
lighted and illuminating the low roof that separated the
buildings, with its forest of bowed aluminum ducts. She
could see a pair of hands lifting the lid of a pot. Le Creuset.
A light went on elsewhere; a figure briefly occluded it, passing left to right beyond the scrim of curtain. Cynthia listened
to the horsehair sound of her knee pressing the mattress.
The corner of the wall against her cheek was cold. Her violin
was under the bed, on top of piled shelving and suitcases
filled with out-of-season or out-of-favor clothes. In a case, of
course: she didn't want to look at the violin, but she didn't
want to hurt it. The sound of salsa music started up outside:
a beat, a faint distant chorus, and the distinct piercing flute.
Oh, well, she thought: I can't practice with that going on.

Still, she pulled out the case, the old-fashioned hard
grainy kind, and blew on it. A fine spray briefly thickened
the air. She could feel the grittiness of the dust on the plastic
handle like a measure of time. It's only been *days* since I've
played, she told herself, as if to reproach the dust for so
quickly condemning her. She rubbed her hands along her
jeans and exposed the red velvet viscera in which her instrument nestled. It was an expensive one, though not the most
expensive you could get, by far—the price of a modest car,
say, not a house. You could go somewhere with it, but you
couldn't live in it. She had made the same discovery with the
piano; she didn't know why she'd thought the violin would
be any better, any different. Wherever you went, you ended
up in the same place.

She'd been one of those tots who can sit on a piano stool twirled to its tippiest height and, if not write Mozart, play him, complicated, difficult pieces. And she'd been *good,* not just technically proficient, not just facile. She'd gotten better and better with the years, and had loved practicing, loved playing: it *had* been a house she could live in, she'd escaped into music, when she was playing she wasn't there. In high school they'd talked about her being concert material, and then she went to the conservatory. And that was where it went flooey. At first it was hard to figure out what *it* was. When she thought of this time she saw leaves blowing across one of the campus quadrangles. It had been November, a potentially depressing time anyway, gray, short days, living in the unwelcoming embrace of an institution, where there was little of even the physical softness of life—bare scuffed floors, hard chairs, walls in shades of green and urine no real human being would choose, and if there were pictures on them, they were posters, taped or tacked, their corners coming apart and rolling back as though trying to escape from one's gaze, often announcing some festival long passed. Meals were agony, not because of the bad food, but because of always having to be someone in relation to this mass of strangers. You had to sit with, select among, be selected by, or avoid, and be seen to be avoiding. Cynthia didn't have Ella there, as she had at Blithedale, as a buffer against the critical mass of public expectation. Like the posters, she curled herself away from its gaze, and indeed, had stopped going to meals, her meal ticket going unpunched while she tried to live on Wheat Thins and boysenberry yogurt from the vending machines in the basement of the dormitory, hoarding quarters and running out altogether in between the checks intended for "extras" that erratically arrived from home.

Those buzzing practice rooms, cubicles, oysters into whose shell you were sealed with a deathlike pneumatic suck as the faint tinkling from the other shells was violently expelled. Cynthia would sit and look at her hands until they were detached beings, like words repeated into meaninglessness, ugly and red on the unstained high-tech-plastic white of the Japanese keys. She went back to pieces she knew from memory, shutting her eyes, and at moments the music carried her as it once had done and she was safe inside it. But new pieces she had to learn, new fingerings, and even without looking her fingers were worms, slugs, so that the instrument became repellent, beslimed.

It was when she could no longer get out of bed in the mornings that she took a leave from the conservatory. She would sit up against the pillows, thinking about getting up, thinking about nothing at all, and then it would be dark outside on those mercifully, dangerously short days and then she didn't get up.

She returned after a term off and took up the violin, making swift, astonishing progress, and everything was fine. For a while.

Cynthia put on her loden coat with the toggles, picked up the unlooked-at music and dusty violin case, and set off down the tacky marble stairs, her hands bare and red, into the cold.

The rehearsal was at the Church of St. Luke in the Fields, an old building, one of the oldest in the city, with a squared-off Age of Reason steeple and a nest of parish buildings around a brick-walled garden. Cynthia entered through a wrought-iron gate under a tree of a size rare in town, along a paved path. A hand-lettered sign said ALCOHOLICS ANONYMOUS, with an arrow. A picture immediately presented itself to her mind's eye, a stemmed glass glinting with yellow liquid, a picture of loveliness itself. Cynthia only drank in the normal way, at dinners with company. Which were rare enough. Funny, she thought, continuing around to the rear door. The picture had come with a taste that made her tongue ache with desire. The sudden light inside the church made op-art of the black and white checkerboard floor.

Her fingers were so cold she could barely unclasp them from the case's handle.

Old straight-back wooden chairs and metal folding ones made a ragged circle closed by a battered upright piano. A flutist blew, fingered, and blew again, her lips forming the chipmunk smirk the instrument demanded. People folded their coats over the backs of chairs or tossed them on furniture piled at the edges of the room. The bearded conductor struck chords on the piano, repeating single notes for the instrumentalists to tune to. A singer, one of the pros brought in to augment the crack choir, a young woman, walked leaning heavily on a cane to a seat.

"Cynthia Johnson?" said the conductor. Cynthia ducked her head as though trying to hide and smiled at the floor. "Violin over here," he said, pointing at a chair. She came to the spot without looking at him, her shoulders hunched under the green coat. The case made a clatter against the metal seat. It seemed her fingers wouldn't work. It took both hands to undo the toggles on her coat. Her head still turtle-like between her shoulders, Cynthia moved a heavy black stand into place. Holding the unread music between the two flattened palms of her hands, she let the folios drop between them onto the stand's narrow ledge. Turning away from the conductor, she blew on her red fingers, placing them in her mouth. When she turned back, the group was seated, so that she felt them an audience. She ducked onto her seat, hugging the violin case. Gossip and laughter faded until only one voice was caught: "He *didn't.*" The conductor smiled. It was unusual for conductors to be kindly.

They began with "O Seigneur Loué sera." Cynthia knew it well, from high school when she had sung it standing next to Ella, she at the edge of the sopranos, Ella at the edge of the altos so that they could be together. It was harder to sing than to play. Lots of sustained notes, luckily, and Cynthia's ear was even better than her sight-reading. At the end of the first run-through, the viola next to her said, "You must really have been *practicing*. What a bitch!" The piece, she meant. Cynthia risked a tiny, downward-sloping smile that cut deep dimples into cheek and chin. Again the image of the crystal glass floated into her mind, and as if she tasted its contents, she felt a warmth loosening her from within. Her neck, always a problem spot for violinists, uncricked, though she hadn't felt its tension until it began to disperse.

There was a rustling of pages. Burton—it was Burton, of course—announced for the Handel. Opening the pages, she saw them black with sixteenth notes. Cynthia breathed in deeply and let the breath out through her nose. A teacher at the conservatory had promoted yoga exercises. She could hear the rolling *r*'s of his Czechoslovakian accent: "Out of great relaxation comes great concentration." But the Handel—the sixteenth notes were a blur to her eyes, and her fingers stiff and cold against the cords of the instrument hit one perhaps out of four. Burton tapped his baton—retractable, pulled from his jacket's inside pocket—against the music stand. The players and singers straggled to a halt. He asked for a repeat from several bars back. Burton sometimes wore glasses for rehearsal. He looked over the top of them at Cynthia, hard. She looked at the music. The bar numbers seemed to be swimming in something. Out of great concentration comes great relaxation. Her fingers tightened on the neck of the violin, a stranglehold she felt in the cords of her throat. They went through the piece. When she had sung with Ella at school, the two of them, more in tune with each other than with the chorus, used to mouth the words when they lost their bearings, digging each other in the ribs and trying not to giggle. She was not tempted to giggle—and there was no Ella with her, nothing to bolster an ectoplasmic self—but she played on the strings lightly, skating. "Hold it," said Burton, not even bothering with the ritual taps. "Violin," he said. Cynthia knew she had to look at him.

"Cynthia?"

"Excuse me." The violin would have fallen from the chair if the violist hadn't steadied it with her hand, preventing seven-thousand-dollar splinters, as Cynthia fled. Cynthia got to the hall just ahead of the volley of tears, running before the storm. Her hands were quickly covered with slime and tears, her stiff, useless, hateful hands. She rubbed them on her jeans; the storm burst forth anew. The salt rising like sap, tasteable through the nose. The resistance to the convulsions, and then the convulsions, like nausea before vomiting only sharper. I'll stop now, she thought. Then the page of Handel rose in her vision. I could play music like that before I was five! she thought, and the great hand shook her and shook her, wrenching her insides until they yielded up cries.

The world returned little by little. She could hear the Handel in its endless repetitions and silly twitters, the grandiloquent pause before the finale. The raps of Burton's baton came through with distinct clarity; she heard a murmur of voices; a new piece took over, something nineteenth-century, churchy-whiny. The music's unfamiliarity gripped her in a new forlornness and an aftershock of dry sobs. She slid down the wall to collapse, cross-legged. She couldn't leave without her violin.

By the end of the rehearsal she was blessedly bored, tracing the edges of the checkerboard tiles with a fingertip. She had her cigarettes, thank God. The butts were lined up standing on their filters, next to a mound of ash brushed together with the side of a match. Cigarettes were styptic pencils for tears.

When the double doors burst open, releasing their horde, Cynthia scuttled to her feet. It was useless to wish to disappear. Head down, she fought the crowd. Someone put a hand on her shoulder and she felt her face crumple. She dipped her head twice to acknowledge the gesture, using her own hand like a fan to hide behind.

Burton was waiting for her. Though she went directly to her coat, and began stowing the violin in its red velvet womb, pressing the bow into the clinches on the inside cover, she could feel his eyes like fingers against a tender place on her back. She wished she could put herself into the case, hidden from the world, away from *herself.* Snapping the case shut, she turned to face him. Face the music.

He was leaning on the top of the piano. He pulled off his glasses and pressed thumb and forefinger to his eyes. "Cynthia Johnson." Had she ever heard her name spoken so flatly, as if read from a list? Yet it was oddly comforting, despite a snake of fear swiveling upward in her belly. A recognition. He shook his head, with a deep breath, as will a man who, having tried everything, admits defeat. His eyes were tired. The hand with the glasses dangled over the front of the piano. He pushed his fingers upward through his beard, looking to the ceiling whence cometh his help. She felt the sensation almost in her own palm, that beard, like a soft brush.

"So?" he said.

"I—" Her shoes were of immense interest, sleek green suede loafers. No, she couldn't speak, she could feel the salt stinging the back of her throat. "I'm sorry." It was a frog's voice, but that words came out at all made it possible for more to come. "My hands, on the way here. I didn't have my gloves." She met his eyes. They were an intelligent blue. She held out a hand, as if for paddling. "See? They're still red." The lie gave strength. She smiled, a little, to make it easier for him. She was going to be fired. She would never work again in New York. She would be a bum on the street.

"You have a very good reputation," he said. She was stunned, though she knew it perfectly well to be true. "That's why I hired you. So look—wear gloves next time, okay?"

She nodded, a good girl. Turning, she picked up her case. At the door she heard, "And practice." A direct hit. But at least he couldn't see her face.

Outside, the cold air was bracing. She found the lumps in her pockets that had been there all along and put on her gloves. She heard someone on the path behind her and turned. It was Burton, shambling along, not looking up. As he passed, he put up one hand by way of acknowledgment. She would have liked him to stop, to walk with her. Then she remembered the gloves. She clasped her muffled fingers as though she could make them disappear, now that it was too late.

A triangle of light opened out on the path ahead of her. The AA meeting was breaking up. Silhouettes of men, a glimpse of a face with the abstracted look people have on their way from a shrink appointment; a pair of men holding hands: it must be gay AA. Key rings clanked against studded leather and caught the light. Cynthia hoped she hadn't made them uncomfortable by staring. How nice their fellowship looked. They stood by each other. They could call on one another anytime. There was nothing like that in her life.

Outside the bucolic confines of the churchyard, Hudson Street stretched darkly toward the gorgeous purple neon of a sign on a restaurant. In the black air, the frozen traffic lights made loud clicks as they changed. Cynthia peered into windows where couples held hands over tablecloths, and hated the men for looking at her, as if it were her hand being neglected inside theirs. It was so cold outside that a thin sheet of glass seemed hardly enough to protect those within, unimaginable that they were warm on the other side. Outside a Pakistani deli, the last of the day's papers rested under weights with cigarette logos on them. A man leaned on the counter of the liquor store next door, smiling directly through the windowpane into her eyes. Her upside-down eyes, which blinked.

She went in to the delicious warmth. To thaw was painful after a minute as life re-entered muscle and bone, but she had to stay the minute, she had to find a wine that was the exact, the exact color of that yellow in her mind's eye.

5. Tricks

Surely this wasn't love. Wanting someone every minute, thinking about them obsessively, first thing a.m., last thing p.m., that wasn't *love,* that was—obsession. She was obsessed. It was an illness. It would go away. It was an illness just as Frank himself was an illness. *He* would go away, God knows he talked with sickening-enough eagerness about getting his grant, where he would go, not even mentioning the possibility of taking her, as if that were, as if that were not even possible, she could tell Stephen something, she could leave Stephen for God's sake if Frank would *have* her, how could he prefer, no, he didn't prefer his wife, that wasn't about preference, but who could resist *her,* Ella, I mean (she thought), you have this wife you fight with, you hate, who hasn't slept with you for years, and this sexy, sympathetic twenty-years-younger woman comes along who will do *anything,* and you're eager to light out for the Territory?

Ella didn't feel like a beauty, what she imagined a beauty must feel like, powerful, pleased with herself—lovable—but she was surprised these days herself when she looked in the mirror and saw that, indeed, this more or less ravishing creature looked back and that she could claim it for her own and present it to the world as if she, Ella Vaporsky, really had a right. Frank had fallen in love with that image from the mirror. "I've known women as smart, and I've known women as beautiful," he told her in his inimitable mix of flattery and dispraise, "but never have I known a woman as smart *and* as beautiful." He gaped as he said it. Mouth open, staring.

Amazing what contact lenses, eyeliner, and the right hair-style could do. The loss of five pounds had made her former merely average figure glamorous. She wondered if she would have remained satisfied with Stephen if she hadn't suddenly and inadvertently outclassed him this way. The image in the mirror told her she could have anybody.

No mirrors in the churchyard, however. It was fucking cold in the churchyard. Not that it was ever properly winter in New York. A few sad roses continued blooming right up through Christmas. Now they hung, their necks cracked by a hangman's noose of frost, brown, shriveled. The grass crackled, frozen. The hedges had thinned until garden furniture and patios showed through like scalp. A dog tried to lick someone's iced-over little pond. The sun came at an acute angle that sliced vision. Ella had the garden all to herself, more to herself than she wanted. She checked her watch; just two. She studied the stained-glass windows, murky from the outside, opaque except where a window showed through from the building's other side.

"I miss you like crazy over the weekends," Frank had murmured into her hair. His wife was home on weekends; Ella couldn't call.

"Could we arrange something?"

"What do you mean?"

"Well—the church garden? Why don't—if we have the chance to get away—we'll just meet there at a certain time."

"I hate to think of you waiting in the cold."

I wait for you in the cold all the time, she thought. "I don't mind." She gazed at him all wide-eyed, the dependence that so gratified and annoyed him. He drew in his turkey wattles, his aristocratic lips smooth, his brows drawn together. He grabbed her and thrust his mouth into hers, his arm digging into her back to press her as close as might be. She was will-less, unburdened of herself. How happily she would relin-quish that burden permanently, be his aide, his shadow, be relieved of thinking about her shapeless, meaningless life and shape herself entirely to him and his; be his breath when he couldn't speak.

At the same time, she always felt herself to be better than him.

"Don't wait too long," he had left her with, planting fish kisses all over her face.

Only five after two. She should give him at least fifteen minutes to get there. He might just now at the last minute be listening to his wife as she told him what to pick up while he was out, a distant, irritated expression on his face, saying "Fine, fine" and "No, of course I won't forget," or getting into a fight just because of the skeptical, critical expression on Maxine's face, which at that moment Ella could almost feel on her own. Or maybe Finch was demanding to come with him. He'd be standing at the bottom of the stairs, his parka on (olive green, fur-trimmed hood), his shoulders hunched, jerking his head up and down impatiently like a bridled horse.

Finch. Ella had seen her. The perfect child. Straight black hair, pink cheeks, the protected, nervy air of a child who knows herself to be special, who glows because she knows it is her role in life to be happy. Though it was impossible that she was. Finch had told her father that her best friend told *her* that if she answered the phone and the caller hung up it meant that Frank was having an affair. Ella had hung up once when Finch answered. That was when Frank told Ella what Finch had said. Finch was nine. So the next time, Ella made sure to identify herself to the girl. "Daddy. It's *Ella Va-porsky,*" the little girl had said with lewd emphasis. Frank said that now, when any woman asked for him on the phone, Finch always told him it was *Ella Vaporsky*. Frank got a kick out of this manifestation of Groucho-like sophistication. *Ella Vaporsky* was a family joke. Finch, on the other hand, was why Frank stayed married.

Ella wished she were Finch.

Sitting on a garden seat, Ella fell into a daydream. She and Frank were married. She was mistress of the big apartment by the river and oh, it looked much better, so much softer and brighter, and there was delicious food. Frank mooched around the top of the stairs, asking when dinner would be ready, boy did it smell good (he was given to anachronistic golly-gee expressions). And there was Finch by the four-storied dollhouse against the wall where it had always been. No, she'd be older, of course. Just verging on puberty, wanting to know the secrets of an older, attractive woman, someone just enough nearer to her own age than her mother's to be glamorous.

Ella was putting on makeup in the bathroom next to the master bedroom, where she slept every night. Finch leaned in the doorway, watching. Ella held her breath. Their eyes met in the mirror, Ella's brown ones, Finch's baby blues. Ella went on, stroking on eyeliner, afraid to smile. Finch stepped forward and picked up the eye pencil. "What is this stuff?" She leaned toward the glass. "Can I try it?" Ella told her one shouldn't share makeup, but she cleaned the pencil tip with a tissue, showing Finch how to stretch her eyelid to get it on smoothly. Finch stood back to see the effect, pulled her hair back, tilting her face. "Now I look like a whore too," she said before turning from the room.

This was not the fantasy Ella had intended.

She paced the garden, whose paths made a quincunx. Around the perimeter, across the X to the center, back around a long corner. Dried stalks, wispily clinging last leaves, small brown birds hopping along the bare twigs, fluttering up at her approach. Over the top of the brick wall she could see a corner of her building down the street, the tops of other buildings, one with a colorful mosaic. The windows of her own apartment were just out of sight. Luckily.

"I miss you like crazy over the weekends."

Ella stopped dead in her tracks, passing through a wall of heat. She would have fucked Frank right there on the neat little paving stones and rotting crab apples. For minutes altogether she was transfixed by the assault of this fantasy. He couldn't help himself. It didn't matter that they were outdoors, in the cold, in view of hundreds potentially, and that Ella, unprotected, could get pregnant. He wanted to get her pregnant. He wanted to connect with her absolutely. He wanted them to be part of each other. Ella played this part of the fantasy over and over. She saw her pale bare thigh between the brick and the edge of his overcoat (it did have to be an overcoat for the fantasy to work; he had one: Brooks, of course). She felt him inside her, felt the wet and thrill. No one seeing the thin girl on the path of the cold brown garden could have guessed. She felt the crab apples sticking into her back and the cold damp earth. She felt the cold zipper and the chafe of his pants. The concentration of his face and the grim lips. The fierce and tender kisses. "I have to have you." Spoken between teeth.

The little wire gate at the back of the garden moaned and clanged. Ella walked down the path in its direction, her heart tripping. Him, him, him! The passage to the gate was narrow, between the back wall of another garden and hedges. A man indeed appeared around the turn, but it was not Frank. In a gray stained raincoat with a paper bag in its pocket, the lip of a bottle protruding. His stubbly face cracked into a gap-toothed grin at the sight of her, and he flung the thin coat apart and started pumping with his hand. The outer gate to the street, behind her, was locked. The short wide man, with his preternaturally red cock like a stupid sluggish beast in his active hand, extended from hedge to wall. She looked directly into his radiant face. At the glaring snouted organ. Down to his shoes. Holes were cut out. The toenails showing through were long and ringed in black, rippled and thick like mollusks. "Get out of my way." She looked back to the face, no longer grinning but lost in private ecstasy, his glassy yellow eyes still dead-on ahead at her, like the rest of him. The snout emitted a mucilage that hung before spinning down, curdling lumpy white like cottage cheese on landing, making a soft wet sound on the slate in the silence the world had fallen into. She could hear the sky tearing with rushing clouds above what glistened at her feet. Traffic started up with grunts and wheezes after a light.

"Die," she said.

The gate clanged again. But it was the church's vicar, a woman with thick hair down her square back, in her collar of office. "Can I help you, sir?" she said in her fruity voice, approaching him, ready to minister. Ella pressed herself into the hedge, its obdurate twigs grabbing at her hair, and scratched her way past to the muddy parking lot, where she paused a second before charging home, her body shaking like a pebble in a truck bed.

6. Intergalactic mermaid

Burton sighed, deeply. His father used to sigh that way—come home, set down his sample case in the front hall, and heave a deep one before slumping into the dining room for the evening cocktail—filling Burton with longing to ease his father's lot. "I'm not doing much better, am I?" he said to his cat, who lay like a brown pudding against his thigh. She opened her yellow eyes, then dug her nose back between her stretched front paws as Burton stroked her head and neck. He heaved another, as though his heart wanted to squeeze out of his chest, into the world. It did, but where? What part of the world, who, would receive it? Idly he watched the lights on the hypothetical river, its presence made known only by the lights' movement. Black boats, black water, black night.

So funny how you could live for years and years and it seemed as if everything was okay and then this trapdoor opens and you look around and don't recognize anything, and it is only when you notice the ringing in your ears, that pummeled feeling at the back of your skull, that you realize you've dropped into a world you were never really separated from. Boom. The old stage props, hideous, exposed as fakes; masks, wigs with tufts unplugging, lace stiff with dust. The masks bear your parents' faces, serene, smiling, bland, gritty in the creases.

In fact, his father had been dead since Burton's second year of college, and his mother he faithfully saw at least once a month in the house in Weehawken where he'd grown up, with its burnt-orange shag carpets and the Huckleberry Hound jam jars used for lemonade with gin. She had white hair in little curls, though there was still ginger at the nape of her neck. Her hands shook. They always had. The mask she wore had flabby lips that looked too wet for cigarettes, and powdery skin.

Burton shifted, the cat dug its claws into the brown corduroy of his legs, and Burton came out of the trance looking at the actual mask suspended between the windows, Indonesian, with its smooth grin and oval sockets as blind as his abstracted gaze. The boats still twinkled like fireflies, and he got up to pace the perimeter of his neat room fitted up like a ship's cabin, a stateroom perpetually moored above a passing world. Everything had a place, and was in it. A wall of books and scores in alphabetical meticulousness, the couch like a captain's bed with fitted drawers, shutters on the window that folded into recesses in the molding, a broad wooden cabinet with shallow drawers for sheet music, with cast-iron slots to hold labels, a desk that folded outward or closed over pigeonholes, keeping their secrets, drawers in it with keys that he never had to use because he lived alone. He derived great security, but he was also stuck, held fast. He would like a trapdoor to open, to let something *in*. He thought of the sad, self-defeating violinist at the rehearsal; of her long legs and odd eyes. Surely someone that sad would be letting you in only for trouble. He came to rest at the cold window just as the doorbell rang. Squeezing his burly shoulders past the window frame, he called down. A woman on the sidewalk, hunched into a tiny leather jacket, looked up. "Who are you looking for?" he asked.

"You," was the perplexing answer.

"Burton Shumlin?"

"Yeah."

His name was on the bell. She could just be one of the waterfront whores, looking for—what? The waterfront whores congregated farther uptown, in any case. The way she had materialized, as if from his thoughts and the river, made her something more like an intergalactic mermaid. He went down the two flights of uneven, slanting, rocking steps and opened the street door to an icy blast. The woman dashed in. "It is *freezing* out there. How do you stand it?"

She looked like a whore, though she didn't talk like one, not that Burton really knew what those ladies sounded like. She was wearing a skirt that looked improbably like what girls used to wear to go skating, and the jacket was not leather after all but metallic silver. "I'm sorry, but—"

"You don't remember me? I'm really insulted." He watched her ass sway deliberately as she went ahead of him up the stairs. He shook his woolly head, and followed.

"Oh, thank God," she said, "warmth."

The cat had run to the bedroom at the sound of the bell, and now sat in the doorway between the two rooms, paws tucked, looking about the way a cat would look if something half-human, half-fish appeared. "A Burmese!" the woman cried, and knelt toward it. The cat darted away.

"Look, I guess I should know who—"

"Ave O'Shaughnessy," said Ave. "We met at Stephen and Ella's. Don't you remember, we had that great conversation about Cole Porter?"

"Oh!" He remembered a woman with frizzy reddish hair, and something else was different. "Did you, do you sometimes wear glasses?" The woman standing in front of him was blond—or was her hair silver?—and the hair stuck up with that plugged-into-a-socket effect. She dug into a voluminous shoulder bag.

"You mean these?" she said from behind oversize spectacles of Hollywood proportions. "I'm doing Dorothy Malone in reverse," she muttered, lowering lids over enormous pale eyes, dropping the wide-eyed stare only momentarily.

"Okay," said Burton. "But what—"

"Oh, I'm so embarrassed," she said, falling onto the couch, grabbing up the plaid blanket folded there and tucking it to her chin like someone surprised in a French farce, but with perfect complacence. "I wouldn't have come if I hadn't thought— Do you have tea or something? Anything *hot*." Automatically he moved toward the hot plate. "Or if I just got into a hot *bath*."

He turned to face her, a hand on one hip. "I don't have a tub."

"How barbaric. In California, where it's never cold, everyone has a hot tub. You come east where it's fucking freezing, and they have these pathetic drizzly showers, and you have to keep adjusting them the whole time. I've been living at the Majestic, in a million-dollar apartment supposedly, and the plumbing was like something medieval. The Romans had better plumbing. Thank you," she said, taking the steaming mug.

"It's herbal. No caffeine."

"You angel! How did you know? I haven't slept for days." She sipped, keeping an eye on him.

"Do you want honey?"

"I hate tea with honey." She leaned back, both hands around the mug. "Oh, that's much better."

He had a chance to gaze upon her once she had her eyes closed. Silver, definitely, and not so much electroshocked as upswept. What on earth did she want from him?

She opened one eye. "I caught you," she said, "I caught you. You were looking at me. You're checking me out." Her gum-exposing smile had the innocent delight of a child's. Whatever it was she wanted, it would be hard disappointing her.

As she warmed up she threw off first the plaid blanket, then the gleaming silver jacket that matched her hair. One couldn't help noticing her breasts. He couldn't help noticing her breasts. He was meant to notice her breasts, he could tell that, but he noticed them anyway. Not gazanga garbanzos, just beautifully shaped and unusually firm and clearly unbound. It would have been impossible not to notice them. Her sweater was pale pink. It ended just at the waist, gapping there so that, with nothing beneath it, it was like an invitation to put a hand up it and squeeze the fruit on display. "Oh, I've gotten so fat," she said, pressing her palms down her ribs. "I hope you don't mind."

"Look—we may have met before, we may have had a conversation— No," he said at her look, "I do remember talking to you that time at Stephen and Ella's."

"We talked about movie music. I told you Vangelis plagiarized Josef Suk."

"That's right," he said thoughtfully. "That was where I

heard it. But never mind that. You're making me feel like—I don't know—did we have an affair I just happen to have overlooked?"

"Oh, that's great! Oh, I love it! Did we have an affair I overlooked, oh, I love it. No, no," she said when she had her laughter under control. "Not unless *I* overlooked it too. And I'm sure I wouldn't forget," she added, looking him up and down in a meaningful way.

He blushed, hoping it didn't show. Sweat prickled.

"Look," she said, unconsciously picking up on his mannerism—already she was adapting herself to him, nestling, figuratively. "It's not like I'm in the habit of walking in on strange men."

He shifted his stance, leaning an elbow on the arch of the kitchen alcove, his forehead against the back of his hand.

"Help me out here." She affected a slight stutter.

"How?"

"Sit down at least?" He moved toward the chair. "I mean," she said with the shyness of a young doe, and barely audibly, "next to me."

He sat stiffly at the far end of the couch. She had removed the glasses long since, and now bent upon him the full force of her pale nearsighted eyes, her full lips parted. Some dim idea about looking gift horses in the mouth passed across his inner field. Oh, what the fuck, he thought.

He was never sure which one of them it was who made the first actual move.

He was the first to wake in the morning. Not that he had slept so much during the night. The strange woman kept resting her arms on his midriff, curling against his back, his chest, and he felt the weight. He felt the strangeness. His cat kept to his side of the bed. It was just getting light, that tentative winter dawn, gray, in which objects emerge as clumps of shadow and deeper shadow. He wished he had a cigarette, though he was only the most casual of smokers, not even keeping a supply in the house. It got lighter. The cat, excited by his being awake, began to knead his chest with big purring moon-eyed stares in hopes of breakfast. He petted her to keep her from mewing and waking the strange creature next to him, who would do who knew what.

She stretched in her sleep, uncurling onto her back, opened her eyes, and looked at him as though she'd been awake the whole time. "Good morning," she said, radiant.

Despite himself he was gratified at her happiness, as though it could possibly be his accomplishment. "Hi." He couldn't help saying it warmly, or accompanying it with an affectionate look. Her lips curled in a cat-who's-swallowed-the-canary smile, eyes modestly lowering.

"Oh, it's so nice to wake up here," she said, closing her eyes again. She brushed the quilt with her palms, studying it. "This looks like something someone's grandmother would have made."

"My grandmother did make it."

"You're kidding. You're like a real WASP."

Laughing at this was another thing he couldn't help, and she joined in. "I am a real WASP, but I'm not what people mean when they say 'WASP.' Not eastern establishment mandarin. I'm white trash."

"You have the greatest way of putting things. No, I mean it, you do. You would think you were a poet or something and not a musician."

"And what are you?" Oh, for a cigarette!

"What do you mean?"

He felt like an idiot for asking. Of course, he wanted to ask her everything, like what she was doing here in the first place, and why him, and so on, but somehow this was impossible.

"I'm a woman, for one thing."

"I noticed." He couldn't exactly call her an intergalactic mermaid, could he? Though who knew what she would like?

His response, however, seemed to be the one she wanted.

"Are you big on breakfast? You seem like the kind of guy who would have bacon and eggs for breakfast."

It was alienating to be called a kind of guy. But then, she was alien. "I'm a vegetarian."

"How sixties. Do you feed your cat soy?"

"Does she look like a hippie to you?"

In Ave's lexicon of laughs there was a low one that sounded like "ah-hah," which in this case meant touché. "Oh, I'd like to give you a big breakfast in bed," she said, yawning and settling decidedly under the covers. Burton threw his covers to one side. The cat leapt down and began chirruping at his feet. Ave, her eyes closed, flung out an arm, laying a hand on the soft hairy area between Burton's belly button and penis which, annoyingly, began to rise. "I have to feed the cat."

"Oh, let me."

"You don't know where anything is."

"I want her to be friends with me."

Ave scrabbled at the bedclothes and stood pinkly up, her eyes half-closed, like a sleepwalker. Burton, on his edge of the bed, pulled the blanket over his lap. As she shuffled toward the kitchen, he saw that she had stepped into her shoes, high heels squashed by her bare feet at the back. Fuchsia suede.

She ambled back in, carrying a can and the opener. "I haven't been up this early since—I don't know. Elementary school," she said, holding out the can and opener. It reminded him of the way Lisa used to hand him jars she wasn't strong enough to open. But he couldn't imagine not being able to use a can opener. He looked at a line of jagged triangles around the edge of the can, and up at Ave's face.

"I'm just not one of these people who're good with their hands. I'm not."

It was pleasantly domestic to hear noises coming from the

kitchen, but various crashes and clatters did not bode well. Burton, standing, felt his body to be as furry as his mother's burnt-orange shag carpet, felt his shape to be approximately that of a pod, felt as exposed as a statue, and took from the closet a Christmas-gift bathrobe almost never put on.

"Bad boy. You're supposed to stay in bed."

Ignoring his perplexing guest, Burton used the closetlike toilet. As he viewed the splendid trajectory of his piss, he considered the range of diseases he might have contracted in the course of the evening's activities. He examined himself as though scrutiny might tell him something. The incubation period for herpes was two to twenty-eight days. Syphilis and gonorrhea were, thank God, curable. So long as you noticed the symptoms in time. They said if you were male you could not fail to notice them. He hoped this was true. He did not intend to fail through lack of vigilance. He contemplated the Ryder-like picture of a boat at sea above the toilet. Murk and storm.

The living room looked as though it had been hit by that storm. How could one person, in so short a time . . . ? The silver jacket was on the floor, an address book, a hairbrush, keys. As he lifted the plaid blanket to fold it, Ave's glasses hit the couch. Her underpants were draped over the mug, and he had to look away. The keys, as he pushed them into a pile with the other things, flipped over, revealing a label on which he recognized Stephen's handwriting. If only this creature would leave, at least he could call Stephen and Ella and ask them—but he wouldn't want to tell them, so how could he ask? How long ago it seemed that he was looking out at the black river in peace. The water today was choppy and gray and winked at him with a silvery leer.

7. Her side of the bed

Men were saps. There was no doubt about it. Just let them have a whiff of flesh. Just the trappings—send an aardvark down the street wearing garters, would they know the difference? "Nice titties," said a prosperously suited gentleman out the side of his mouth as she passed. Ave was old enough, however, so that if men hadn't made these comments, she would have been as offended as she was by their making them. "I'd like to be inside that silver jacket with you," said a tall, handsome young black man, meeting her eyes.

She couldn't help but laugh.

Well, she was feeling good, there was no doubt about it. Burton, what a sweetie, though he didn't know it yet. *He* wasn't a sap. She respected him for that. She hated men she could push around. Though he was spellbound, she could see that. She laughed again, and another man passing on the street looked hopeful, since her eyes were absently cast in his direction. Oh, he was luscious, the way he had felt inside her . . . She hugged the jacket around her.

The intense cold of the night before had abated, and as she walked from the diner, gulls screamed and glided over the landfill euphemistically known in the area as the beach. The diner had been just right, the perfect contrast to his tidy, adorable little apartment. A little too little—she wasn't sure what she was going to do about that. But anyway, like him the real thing, the diner, where real truckers ate, not those dreadful SoHo types. It was too bad she'd gotten coffee grounds on the ceiling but how was she supposed to know how that tricky lid fitted? And the cup handle had just slipped. She could tell it was his favorite cup, it just had that look, that was why she had chosen it. She would get him another one. She knew an antiques dealer who would know where she could find one, an oversize British nineteenth-century porcelain with a pictorial history in blue and white, couldn't be too difficult. Next time, tomorrow, she really would make him pancakes, feed a man and he's yours for-ever, they really were such big sweet doggies, more loyal than women when you came down to it. So sweet the way he'd come out of the toilet and put his big reassuring warm hands on her shoulders and said, "There's a good diner up the street." She had turned inside his arms and kissed him. He was surprised, she could tell, the way he jumped back, but it had turned into a delectable kiss until the coffee erupted. He wasn't too badly burnt where the grounds had scalded him, just a little patch on the wrist. And that tiny speck of his cheek. What luck it wasn't his eye! And she had been able to play nurse, holding an ice cube against the wrist, insisting he stay still and let her hold it, though the ice had dripped and ruined that velvet cushion on which she propped his hand. She couldn't have known it was that kind of velvet you can't get water on. She would go back to the apartment now and make it all all right. She would give him a happy surprise, have dinner waiting for him when he got back, no, he would be home before then, but something. She fondled the key in her pocket, warm from her hand, coming from his hand, detached from an impressive collec-tion, he was so responsible, people must trust him with everything. Just the way he had an appointment felt so—im-portant. Yes, she was in good hands now, she was sure of it. You could have too much of excitement with men. Excite-ment wasn't so exciting after a while, really.

For a moment the bitter memory of Claude, the man she'd left in California, who had left her, actually—so cruelly!—marred the current of happiness, the sharp glare off the river under a white sky, the few dollars Burton had insisted on leaving her with when she had pulled out her translucent chic plastic bag (Neiman Marcus) and he had seen her distress at finding not a bill left, What if you get mugged, he'd said. This was the man of one's dreams! The image of Claude's face—an exquisite face that fed on well-off women and drugs—contorted with contempt for her, snapped into obscurity, and with it the stab of pain. The gulls wheeled, greedily gorging on garbage.

As she struggled with the external lock, a sharp wind nipping in from the river, she had the strangest moment, just a moment, of wondering what she was doing there, holding down her tiny skirt with one hand, the keys clanking against the dented metal door, her hair, moussed though it was, lashing her eyes, until she fell into the sad musty hallway. It was just a moment. It passed.

It was undeniably a comedown, after the Majestic. But never mind. Ave swayed up the uneven steps. Everything was a little *brown,* she thought, surveying the living room, despite the decorative flowered underpants, which she snatched up with a reminiscent grin, and the myriad contents of her bag flung here and there—a trailing scarf, paisley address book, gold pencil, makeup bag from which plastic capsules and lozenges and clamshells poked; the mirror of an open compact made wavering circles of light near the crust of dried grounds. The cat looked alert, then nestled with the hairbrush it had appropriated. "Give me that, you beast." The cat fled to the top of the shelves, using Ave's shoulder as a springboard and leaving a bloody gouge. They glared at one another. Then the cat shut her eyes. "I *like* cats," said Ave. "Bitch."

She couldn't decide where to begin, picking up her things or cleaning up the coffee? But how would you clean off those grounds? What would you use? She decided that there were phone calls she had to make.

"Ella? Guess where I am. No. No. No, I have not been sold into white slavery. No, I am not in the antipodes with the flutist in a salsa band. I like your choice of instrument. No, I have not had a sex-change operation. Okay. Now you're getting warmer." High-pitched noises of excitement and incredulity emerged from the earpiece. "I told you he liked me. Why do you think that's unlikely? I'm really insulted. Yeah, well, that's true. I'm not generally fond of hippie vegetarians. I can so trust someone who doesn't eat meat, what do you mean? I never said that. You're always telling me I did this or said that that I can't remember ever possibly saying or doing. Anyway, he's really great and—oh, I feel really shy about saying this—I think he likes me, um, a lot. So anyway, you and Stephen won't have to put up with me on your couch anymore, and thank you for the nightgown. Would it be okay if this afternoon I come pick up my stuff? Okay, wait a minute, don't hang up. Yes, I promise I'll tell you every detail when I get there, you filthy creature, I know what you want to know, you just want to know that he's hung like a horse, slut. No, what I wanted to *ask* you is, how would you get coffee grounds up, like if they had dripped somewhere like with the coffee attached? You know what I mean? You're brilliant and I love you forever. I'll see you around—what time is it?"

She thought of calling Claude in California. Just to tell him she was in love. One little phone call wouldn't hurt, she thought. But she knew that one little phone call would hurt. He would be nasty to her again, and she didn't want Burton to come home and find her in tears. For that matter, she didn't want to be in tears. She stopped dialing two digits past the area code.

After she had found the letters from Lisa that made it clear it was a relationship long over, and seen that his checking balance was comfortable, she got to work. By the time Burton returned, the spot on the ceiling was no longer brown, but slightly green from Comet, with a chunk missing where the plaster had gotten soaked and plunked out, and the roll of paper towels had been turned into a soppy wadded mountain on the floor. Ave's hairbrush was next to the sink, and her makeup, lined up by shape and brand, beside it. Her vivid scarf was draped over the lamp in the bedroom, and the fuchsia shoes neatly under what had clearly become her side of the bed.

8. Deliverance

*A ship upon a rocky sea
was never half so lost as me*

Ugh! Nobody knew Cynthia wrote poetry. Nobody knew anymore, rather, since she and Ella used to scribble together, sharing results. Ella used to say that her poems were adolescent effusions, but that Cynthia's were really *poems.*

Cynthia wasn't so sure.

And how much worse, how much more embarrassing, were adolescent effusions when you were in your twenties? In fact, wasn't the poetic urge supposed to dry up with the regulation of hormones? Well, at least no one knew. At least Cynthia hadn't decided to be a *poet.* She played the fiddle better than she wrote. That is, at least she didn't have to make it up as she went along.

The feather pillow felt delicious against her bare feet. Cynthia stretched, her shoulders sore from leaning on her elbows, and lay her cheek against the quilt, spying on her neighbors. Someone was reaching up to water a spider plant. That guy who never looked up, but looked sort of cute, who always read sitting on the windowsill, was sitting on the windowsill reading. In fact, he always wore a yellow tee shirt. Cynthia wondered why he always wore a yellow tee shirt. Maybe it was his favorite one, and so the one he put on when he got home from work. Maybe he was one of these people who believe in the spiritual effects of color and owned a dozen chrome yellow tee shirts.

A woman who might be Asian or Spanish came to her window, saw Cynthia, and snapped her curtains together in ostentatious reproof. Cynthia smiled. She laughed, and happily exxed out her poem, enjoying the roll of her ballpoint pen. She would see Burton again tonight. He was so nice! And she had been practicing and practicing. Much more than a musician of her caliber needed to do for pieces like this, but musicians are not of that caliber with that attitude. She treated work with democratic intensity.

She rolled off the bed, ready to get ready. Blue eyeliner, blusher for her perpetually pink cheeks: just as she didn't believe that she was slender, or talented, she did not believe that her cheeks were pink or her skin smooth and creamy. Though tonight maybe she did, a little. She was afraid to admit the thought, in case she should be punished for hubris. But she did not altogether dislike her upside-down eyes, dark as the sea in their circle of blue. She changed into a thin antique sweater beaded around the neck. It was so soft, and cast such a glow onto her smooth cheeks, she had to hug herself. She let out a nervous laugh like a sob. What a good thing no one could see her, what a fool she was being.

There was no dust on her violin case, and her gloves were fuzzy and warm.

> *Chantez à Dieu chansons nouvelles*
> *Chantez, ô terr' universelle, universelle*
> *Chantez, chantez, et son Nom bénissez*
> *Et son Nom bénissez!*
> *Et de jour en jour annoncez!*
> *Sa délivrance solemnelle,*
> *Sa délivrance solemnelle!*

Cynthia, at least, heard the lyrics with these exclamation points. His deliverance, yes; deliverance of her. Cynthia was not at all religious, was almost immune to spiritual overtones in Christian doctrine, but the message she was hearing this night was not precisely spiritual in any case. They were rehearsing in the choir loft for the first time. As she came back after break, walking across the checkerboard floor, past the empty pews, the singers and instrumentalists up above, with their mundane faces—the wonderful voice with her cane, faces tainted by familiarity and the experience of working together that turned music into skills, techniques, competition, and a chore—were invisible to her, and you could believe almost that the music was celestial, disembodied, floating down from the mind of God (though awfully vain of Him, if so, to chant an order to sing His own praises, not that God the Father was well known for His modesty). How truly transporting music must have been, Cynthia thought, not for the first time, in the days when you rarely heard it, maybe only heard it in church unless you were rich, when it wasn't in every elevator and car (when there were no elevators or cars). She thought this, forgetting how transporting it had been for her, in the days before it became a duty, a job, and the measure of her worth. She paused by the font, where she was out of sight from above, singing along in a small, high voice, until the spell was broken by Burton cutting in with a call to begin again at an earlier bar.

Sa délivrance

"Eh, *eh,*" said Burton, pronouncing the accented *e.* "I want it sharper, harder, and then *deep* diminuendo—" He sang the word by way of demonstration, in a light, undistinguished baritone. Was it her imagination, or had he looked sad when he came in, setting down his briefcase as though it were full of rocks?

As she emerged into the loft, he looked at her and quickly

away. She felt a stab of fear, and a prickling in her eyes. Was it the embarrassment of liking someone that made him turn away, or the shame of having changed his mind? He couldn't have changed his mind! Not that—not that it was as if he'd made some commitment or statement. They'd just had coffee together after rehearsal last week, it was no big deal. But she could tell when someone liked her. It wasn't the kind of thing one made mistakes about, and besides, it wasn't something she was quick to believe. They had had such a nice talk, and she was so sure—no, never sure, but so hopeful of a repetition of the experience. She didn't ask more than that. Just another decaf cappuccino at Maurizio and further exploration of mutual likes and dislikes and expositions of personal history. And walking her home. And maybe— But she tried not to let her imagination run away with her, though her practicing all week had been mixed up with the most florid fantasies, so that as their recollection flooded her mind she felt the tight heat of a blush. She had tried not to think of him that way. She knew how fatal it was, seeing someone after that sort of fantasy, as though you had been spying on him unawares. The very thought, however, spurred a surprisingly accurate picture of him naked: his furry podlike trunk and an erection like a gift.

"From the top now," he was saying.

They got through the rehearsal. It went, in fact, well. Good. He would be in a good mood. Not that he looked pleased. Various members of the ensemble stopped to talk with him as they packed up, or he called this one or that one over to confer for a moment on scheduling or some other point. Burton kept taking off the glasses he used for reading music, and rubbing the bridge of his nose, nodding heavily, not smiling. Cynthia packed away her instrument slowly, keeping a watch out of the corner of her eye. If he didn't come over, she would just have to leave. And finally she had her coat on, and started across the room, slowly. Muffled farewells from downstairs and the clatter of feet on the steps were all that was left of the others. She had her gloves in her hand, new ones, pink, with a frivolous sexy band of marabou around the cuff. Just as she passed closest to him, afraid to look, "Hey," he said in low tones.

She offered a brilliant smile and brandished the limp fuchsia hand in her hand.

"Whoa! Let's have a look at those." He took one of the gloves tenderly, stroking the downy surface. She felt a tingling in her toes. "These can make you warm just looking at them," he said. She laughed. She wanted to say something clever, something funny in reply.

"Are you, do you have to be anywhere right away?" she brought out.

She couldn't interpret the woolly lowering of his head, like a bison or ox squirming in a yoke. "No," he said with apparently sudden decision. "No, I really don't." And his face lightened, the way it had last week when they had so unexpectedly struck up a conversation.

Maurizio was just across the street, and they managed to get there on pleasantries about how the rehearsal had gone and Burton's concerns about how they would manage a certain bit of Monteverdi next week.

"The best cappuccino in New York," he said when they had pulled off the heavy woolens they had just dragged on and set their cases on the chairs next to them like well-behaved pets. They had agreed on this point the week before, looking affectionately at them rather than each other. Cynthia felt reassured, and beamed.

"Why am I so stupid tonight?" she said. "I shouldn't have dragged you here. My head is empty." She knocked on it, to demonstrate the hollow sound. "See?"

"Then I envy you. I wish mine were."

"Why? Oh," she backtracked, "I guess it would be much easier to be a dolt. You know, I sometimes think intelligence is a total evolutionary mistake. I mean, what good is it? We're not supposed to be this smart. I mean, not that I'm some genius or something. But it's counterproductive, don't you think? I mean, it just creates all this sort of dangerous extra voltage."

Burton threw his big arms up. "You know, I love talking to you!" He said it as though he were contradicting someone.

She drew her hands together over her sternum, where a pain had erupted.

"That's a compliment," he said, leaning forward. He lifted her hands from their distressed clasp and put them on the table. The waitress appeared. "Same as last week?" he asked Cynthia.

She felt protected. It was almost the same as being loved. She looked at the intimate place where the warmth of Burton's solid neck disappeared inside his blue chambray collar, where a vein ticked. She looked at his wide pale fingernails. She looked at the gleaming copper espresso machine, the girl in sullen black who expertly poured the frothing milk into cups, the odd assortment of pretty little tables, each with its sprig of freesia and wineglass containing sugar, the slate posting specials, all turned into a swirling paisley by the loudness of opera music broadcast to the room that disorganized all thought. The cappuccino was the best in New York, rich, warm, sprinkled with chocolate. Why isn't life like this, she thought, and at the same time, It is like this, it is this. She was experiencing that paradoxical emotion, envy of herself. Her eyes met Burton's with an electric jolt. They looked, looked away, looked again. He heaved a breath, as if about to make some terrible confession. The opera tape abruptly ended, and new music came on. "Oh," Cynthia breathed. "I haven't heard this since Ella and I used to sing it in chorus at school." It was a madrigal.

"The organ of delight," Burton sang, and they both broke up, blushing anyway.

"They're doing a whole spring cycle," Cynthia noted as the next chirruping song began. "Spring seems so far away now, doesn't it?"

"Not really," said Burton, and she would have been surprised to know that he surprised himself saying it.

"This part has always seemed really funny to me," said Cynthia as the voices ascended to *and rejoice in their happy happy loves*. "It's so funny the way at just what should be the happiest moment of the song, it goes into this minor key and sounds completely miserable and hopeless. Don't you think?"

Of course it was what Burton thought, what he had always thought. He began to talk about his hopes as a conductor, how he really preferred choral music though he felt that the respectable ambition was opera somehow, that he ought to be grandiose but when it came to that, what he loved was madrigals and the country, and he didn't know why he bothered living in New York in the first place.

"Neither do I!" She hadn't realized how fervently she felt this until it jumped out of her mouth.

"No?"

"The only times I've ever really been happy have been in the country." Except for now, she might have added—though that couldn't really be true, could it? And they proceeded to have the kind of conversation rarely indulged in past adolescence, of fantasy lives led in ideal landscapes, comparing Cape Breton to Vermont, the Canadian Rockies to the Alps, Dorset, the Lake District, Scotland, and places they had read about or seen in movies. As it emerged, they both hated to travel. Burton's ultimate ideal was a job that required he do no more than walk across the street, though often enough he had had to take choral groups on tours. Cynthia simply failed to see the point; she had been dragged around enough by her rich parents the first eighteen years of her life.

"You could be Neville Marriner," Cynthia pointed out.

"I think he's already recorded every piece of choral music ever written."

"That's true," said Cynthia. They had long since finished their cappuccinos. Would he walk her home? She didn't want to leave, but caught his distracted look at the clock on the wall.

"I have an early appointment tomorrow. I'd better ask for the check." They had a small battle of manners, but he wouldn't let her pay for herself. She was pleased. The question of his walking her home did not arise. He simply turned uptown with her when they left.

"I know it's late . . ." she said in front of her building, invitingly, she hoped.

"It really is." Still, he didn't make a move to leave. They stared at one another until Cynthia had to regard the pavement, where mica glinted. They stood next to a rank of battered garbage cans. A man from the rooming house across the street lurched through its gate, singing something mournful in Spanish. Burton looked as though he wanted to kiss her; was dying to. "Well," he said. And was gone with a wave.

It was so cold out. It wasn't, after all, the season to fall in love.

9. Meteorology

The forecast had been wrong every day for weeks. If Ella went out in heavy boots against a predicted snowstorm, it turned out to be an unseasonably balmy day; or she would be caught in a downpour in her ancient sealskin, which did little for its further longevity. The announcers of these predictions did not acknowledge their errors (well, could they be held responsible? Still—), but smoothly spoke of rain mere hours after promising days of unremitting sun. And the weather itself seemed to be perversely wild. "Must we go through all four seasons every week?" Ella complained, sweltering in an overcoat. Whatever the weather, it was for her a season of complaint. The triangle may be the most stable form in geometry, but in the geometry of human relations it is notoriously precarious. I ought to be happy, she grumbled to herself, hoping the water creeping through her soles was not ruining her shoes, with two men to love me. But a moment of honest reflection, something she could not well afford, told her that Stephen's love made her feel guilty, while Frank's—well, if he loved her, he certainly wasn't using the word. At least he listens to me, she assured herself; at least he loves to look at me and hear me talk, neither of which could be said of Stephen. Which might lead one to consider the nature of love, anyway . . . Stephen's couldn't be doubted, could it? Though often enough it seemed as if he loved whatever "genius" it was that he was working with—there always was one—and she was just some kind of necessary evil he had to keep in his home. But this thought itself seemed like something evil, self-justifying and therefore unfair.

She had arrived at the midtown office where she did layout and pasteup a day or two a week. And where, not incidentally, she could receive phone calls from either of her lovers with impunity (if not without self-consciousness, since any number of her fellow workers could not help but listen to her end of the conversations).

"You got a phone call," Arlene greeted her.

"From who?"

"He didn't say." Arlene, whose unfettered breasts flowed interestingly over an equally unfettered and opulent belly, uttered the words with corresponding heaviness. It wasn't

that she suspected Ella of being up to no good; she just
wanted to be in on anything, and from Ella's eagerness,
judged that there was something to be in on. "Problems?"
said Arlene, so that Ella practically jumped.

"I'm just waiting to hear about an appointment," said Ella,
which wasn't entirely untrue. As much as possible she kept
an element of truth in the lies. It made them easier to tell
with conviction, easier to remember, and almost possible to
believe in. Such had become the practice of this person who
had previously wondered how people conversed in a different moral mode from the one in which you might fill in a
doctor's questionnaire, or vote.

Arlene dragged on a cigarette, her eyebrows pulled up
above her glasses in a manner that managed to convey both
hurt and forgiveness, and shot smoke through her nostrils
with a vocal sigh, turning heavily back to the slanted board
that held joggles of print and picture over the turquoise grid
of the page dummy.

Ella sat down at the table whose up-tipped end normally
met that of a woman named Harriet, who Ella liked to think
of as her conspirator. Not in the affair, about which Ella did
not speak at work, even though she and Harriet were nominally friends. But they liked to joke about the others in the
graphics studio and, especially, the secretaries or big shots
wandering in from other areas of the company to pick at the
food always plentiful in the art department, or throwing their
weight around, respectively. But Harriet was coming in late. A
sub had been called, someone Ella had run into a few times
before, a gaunt lady in her forties, whose incongruous speech
was boarding-school lockjaw, who wore splashy silk dresses
as if dining at "21," and who neighed inappropriately a brittle
laugh that tinkled with her lost millions—a gentlewoman
fallen on hard times, in short. Mona was her name. Between
themselves, Harriet and Ella enjoyed referring to her as
Mona-and-Groana. Not because she complained, particularly,

but just because, as Ella delighted to say, "we're bitches."

Mona-and-Groana's voice *carried*. "Oh, Ella," she cried, spotting Ella's plaid dress, "you look like a little *school*girl."

"Dig the stockings," said Arlene, who retained from her youth if not the waist, the waist-length ponytail and the kind of hipsters' slang that once went with it.

"Aaaah!" shrieked Mona-and-Groana in the piercing tones of one who's been knifed, so that someone passing in the hall peered in with a worried look. Ella's stockings also were plaid. "Too wonderful! *Where* did you find them?" And Mona actually bent so close Ella almost expected her to bite, one long hand flung out with cigarette ablaze.

"Watch it," said Arlene, waving the hot tip away with her curiously delicate long-nailed fingers.

But nothing could affect Mona's blithe obliviousness. "Lord Redingote is in town. I must have him buy me a pair."

Arlene rolled her eyes. "You're still seeing that creep?"

"Who's Lord—Ridingjacket?" said Ella.

"My beau. Oh, he is married, all right, but Lady Redingote is just not a consideration. For *me*. Anyway, she stays over *there*." She disdained to regard Arlene.

Ella looked at Mona with new consideration. "How long have you been seeing him?"

"Too long," said Arlene with disgust. "She's been letting this asshole string her along, what, seven years now?"

"He's not 'stringing me along.' The impossibility of divorce was always understood."

"The impossibility of divorce was always understood," mimicked Arlene. "Feh. The dance he's led you—no one should have to put up with it. Why can't you find a nice guy and settle down?"

"We can't all be you, Arlene. He is a nice guy. Did you see my fur hat? I'd say seven years was pretty settled."

"I say it stinks," said Arlene, and subsided, thwarted on all sides.

Ella had hardly known anything of such magnetism to happen in the studio. "Let me see the hat," she said.

Mona presented and then modeled it. "Bergdorf's," she said. She looked as though she should be chairing a meeting to plan a charity ball. With a look at Arlene she added, "Four hundred and seventy-five smackers."

"As in kisses or dollars?" Arlene growled.

"Arlene!" said Ella, who at little more than half their ages expected everyone's skin to be as thin as her own. Not to mention that the word *prostitution* had not failed to register in her own mind before Arlene spoke. Then again—Frank didn't exactly give her things, did he? "How do you manage not minding when he's not with you?"

"She's got her hat to keep her warm," said Arlene.

"I used to mind," said Mona in fruity tones. "But I've got used to it."

At this Ella saw an image of herself at forty-something, waiting for a phone call, and understood the expression about someone walking on your grave.

Arlene heaved herself down from her work stool. "Anyone for the Joy Fuck?" Joy Fok was the Chinese restaurant downstairs that served liquor. They understood that she would come back plowed. "All right," she said resignedly, and draped herself in a hairy poncho.

"Mind your own business. Elephant," said Mona when Arlene was safely out of hearing. "Maybe if she weren't so happily married she wouldn't have to eat and drink the entire gross national product."

"How *do* you stand it?" Ella said. "I mean, if it's okay for me to ask."

Mona's face contracted as though she tasted lemon. She pulverized her cigarette. "Well—. For about the first seven years, I thought I would die."

Arlene had said the whole thing had been seven years.

"But isn't—? Oh. Oh. Oh no. Oh, how awful. Oh shit, I

can't stand it." Ella had her arms around her ribs like a junkie suffering drug withdrawal.

"It's not *so* bad. I've just squandered my last marriageable years, that's all."

Ella wanted to hear all the details. And she could not help but respond with corresponding details from her own current history. This is how low I've sunk, she thought. I'm on a par with Mona-and-Groana. She reminded herself that even the glamorous Harriet had first met her husband when he was married to someone else.

"Have you tried to break away? I mean, have you seen other men?"

"Naturally. But no one else—"

"I know. I know. That's what's so awful. What is it they *have?*"

Mona shook her head. "Oh, I don't know. If I could do it over again—I'd do it over again. I just haven't ever met anyone else as—"

"Compelling."

"So exactly right for me in every way."

"Except for one minor detail."

"One minor detail. But what about your young man? After all, I was *single.* I was vulnerable. And he was living here at the time, she was in Scotland, so it *felt* as if he were single, he was so *available,* and it was a whole year like that before— But you have your young man, and you liked him all right, or is that—?"

Ella's mouth was open to answer when the phone rang. She dove for it, with a significant look at Mona. But it was only Stephen.

He didn't have to say more than "Hi." The way they knew each other's voices it was as if they were weather radios, always tuned to the same frequency, a soothing, never-ending report, with hourly updates. Since becoming a couple they had never gone for more than twelve hours without an update; intervals of longer than three hours were rare. He told her of the morning's work on his musical—a drag version of *Othello.* Sometimes they called it *Ottilie.* Sometimes *Mrs. O.* And sometimes *Othellette.* He was working on what he called the linchpin of the piece (though what was not?), and told her some of the latest lyrics his genius had come up with:

> *I want you to meet my future ex-wife*
> *She someday will become*
> *The ex-great love of my life.*

The idea was for it to be a kind of country-western tune. "But you hate country music," Ella inconveniently pointed out. This is the trouble with wives, or spousal equivalents.

"I don't *hate* country music."

But spousal equivalents also know when to back down. "No?" she said, resisting the temptation to cite chapter and verse. She would not get between him and his musical, him and his muse, his genius, who was, as she had dared think, as much Stephen's great love as she was. At least as much. Stephen hung on Cameron Driscoll's every word. But then, Driscoll was famous. Like Frank. As Stephen expected to become, by working with Driscoll. As Ella sometimes had thought she would be, for her paintings, not that she ever showed them to anyone.

Ella told Stephen she was afraid her shoes were ruined, that she was sitting there in wet stockings; "I don't know why I keep believing the weather reports." This was a concession to him, who scoffed at them. She could hear him tuning out, as though the station had started to drift. "They're the stockings you gave me." It almost caught his interest. She could hear him turning pages at his end; probably studying his score, or reading Driscoll's script. "Hm-hmm," he said when by her silence he realized he was supposed to say something. He said he should get back to work, asked when she'd be home, did she want him to pick anything up at the grocery store? It was the easy, familiar exchange of two people who know exactly what to expect of each other and therefore hardly bother to listen. But after they'd hung up, with kisses that registered over the line like the click of the phone being hung up, she felt their talk was unfinished. There was something she had wanted to tell him, discuss with him. Something that would really interest him. Oh. Right. Of course. The one thing it was fatal to mention. She, Mrs. O. Why did they have to be working on that play? If you were reading a novel about a woman having an affair and her husband were working on a musical based on *Othello,* you would groan at the improbability of the coincidence, the bad taste of it. I hate hearing about that play, she thought. "Telephonus interruptus," said Ella out loud.

"Oh?"

"It was Stephen. My 'young man.' "

"What interrupted you?"

"Nothing. I just feel like it was incomplete."

"I must say, you sound very loving when you talk to him."

"I do?" She heard Mona's comment as if it were the ultimate weather report.

But Mona-and-Groana was crazy. Everyone knew that.

The phone rang again. Just from the way he cleared his throat before asking to speak to Ella Vaporsky, she knew it was Frank. "Frank," she said reproachfully, "it's me."

"You always sound funny when you answer the phone at work."

"I do?"

"You sound like you have a cold."

"I do?"

"You have a cold?"

"*No.* I didn't know I sounded that way. You mean sort of nasal and froglike?"

"I thought maybe the rain . . . You always sound a little

nasal. You could have voice training, that would fix it."

"*No* one has ever told me . . . Voice training!"

"See, your friend doesn't tell you the truth, he adores you too much."

"Thank you!"

"Well, look, sweetie." He was laughing so he could hardly speak. "I'm helping you out."

"Thanks a lot."

He was in paroxysms.

"And I'm a comedian too."

"You are. You are a comedian," he choked.

She waited. Perversely, she felt extremely beautiful. Extremely beautiful and extremely sexual. Turned on, in fact, though whether by a sense of her own attractiveness or something else it would be hard to say. It was just *talking* to him. She stretched out a plaid, shoeless leg, pointing the toe. "Frank."

"Now, c'mon, sweetie, be grown-up. It's not enough that you paint your teeth white, that you make your hips like a weasel's, that you make your hair like a cloud?" He spoke through clenched teeth. Ella didn't understand that her virtues, always, would be held against her. She thought that if she just *tried harder* . . . "Your voice is like a woodwind instrument. An oboe."

"Like the duck in *Peter and the Wolf.*"

"Now, don't set me off again."

He was laughing, but it was all right. The string of compliments had done their trick. He'd complained before of the whiteness of her teeth, the slinkiness of her hips, said she did it to torture and lure him. Polished up her eyes. His voice became low, seductive and murmurous as he told her about having imaginary conversations with her until he could talk to her again, about his day so far. He had gotten an assignment from *National Geographic* that he was happy about. Ella listened in silence as he exulted. He would be away months. "I don't know how I'll get through it," she finally said.

"Oh, you'll be long gone by then. Long gone."

"No I won't!"

"Sure you will. Sure you will. Either you're having this affair to get away from your friend, or you're having it as a preliminary to marrying him."

"I am?"

" 'Course."

Ella noticed some loose white skin around a cuticle to pick at. "You'll still be going to your house this summer?" she asked irrelevantly. She had an extensive fantasy life around this house, which Frank's wife refused to visit. It had no running water.

He began to fantasize out loud about having Ella there.

"I think about that too," Ella said, and "I'd love to do that," and "I wouldn't mind that," and so on. His voice became lower, more seductive and murmurous.

"It just might be possible," he said. "It just might be possible."

They made kissing sounds, and Ella hung up glowing. It was the first time he had admitted this possibility that so preoccupied her. It wasn't an invitation, but the fantasy ran away with her. She swam back from the green bluffs of Maine, from twisting naked in the pond he had just had dug on his land, and awakened to the studio, the underbrush of black-vinyl–upholstered stools and the drawing tables whose slanted surfaces were like peons' backs, the linoleum floor littered with butts and scraps of paper and fallen pencils. Traffic rattled by on Columbus Circle outside, around and around, muffled by plate glass in the corners of which various obscene doodles and pictorial jokes had been painted and taped. Drops made patterns on the glass, and the sad fountain in the circle looked drenched and redundant. She turned toward Mona, resting her hands over the back of the stool and her chin on them; she certainly had polished up her eyes. "Well?"

"That was your married man?" Mona took a cigarette, lit it, and puffed, her eyes contemplatively on the pocked ceiling tiles and hornet's-nest fluorescent-lighting fixtures. "You certainly sound more loving when you talk to your young man."

Ella understood nothing. No, Ella absolutely understood *nothing.*

Harriet made her entrance, shaking her brilliant hair, swirling in a shiny golden raincoat, and elegantly tapping the wet from a compact umbrella. "Everybody talks about it, nobody does anything about it," she intoned, sliding the coat from her shoulders and hanging it on a hook.

"What?" asked Ella, who did not know this old saw.

"The weather," said Mona and Harriet in unison, then looked at each other with dislike.

Ella got home that night at around eleven. Stephen was lying on top of the covers watching the news. By the time she got under the covers, he was ready to turn off the set. "Wait. Don't," she said. "I want to watch the weather report." He rolled his eyes and shook his head, enjoying the ritual nature of his scorn. Why do I have to *ask* him every time, Ella wondered as he left the room.

She sat through a car ad, an ad for soda, and one for a medication that showed people looking pained and then relieved, with the sound off. Then the weather map came on. Clouds inched across a surface that looked like a map only it was, remarkably, photography of the northeastern United States. The clouds moved like stop-action images, stilted and jerky. Nothing like the paintings she was working on, which were of sky, or of the atmosphere itself, something photographs couldn't capture. She turned the sound back on. ". . . and an unstable front moving down from Canada, right about here. . . ." The weatherman could have been chosen for his resemblance to a cartoon, as if he had been constructed for the purpose of two-dimensional representation. If he put on Groucho glasses, the kind that came with mustache and nose attached, she thought, you wouldn't even notice. Then came the part of the report where they showed a chart of the days of the week with the sun on each one, either frowning under clouds or under slanted lines for rain or, absurdly, grinning in sunglasses. It was like something from nursery school, the networks' way to send you to bed with cocoa and marshmallows. "So look for that clearing trend sometime Wednesday, with a little lower temperatures—don't put away those winter coats yet!" *You* look for it, she thought. Unstable front. Clearing. What a bunch of cheap metaphors! She heard the crackle of the set settling down for the night as she plowed her head into the pillow, her eyes closed hopefully against every image.

10. Venus flytrap

Burton, whenever he let himself, had been feeling moments of excruciating embarrassment all day. All month, really, but this was embarrassment in a new key. Mortification, humiliation—being in a false position. He would like to be wearing a sign with an explanation, a disclaimer. A little announcement before the dinner party that would say, "The following does not necessarily represent the views of the sponsor." Ave had invited Stephen and Ella to dinner. That was bad enough. But she told him it was a celebration of their anniversary, hers and Burton's—their one-month anniversary.

Among other things, he hadn't realized he'd let things drift that long. He had to tell her. He had to tell her it couldn't go on.

She'd sprung it on him that morning. She woke him up—for a wonder, since normally she could not be dislodged from the bed before noon—with a breakfast tray, having mastered the intricacies of the espresso pot. Hot milk in the long-handled metal dipper and flowers on the tray. His favorite blue and white cup, which she had very expensively had mended on the Upper East Side. One of the little embroidered things she seemed to accumulate from nowhere dipped its corners over the edges. "What's this in aid of?" he had ungraciously asked.

"It's our one-month anniversary." At his dumbfounded look, she added, "That's why I wanted flowers."

She had asked for them. "You never bring me flowers," she had complained, and he had drifted into a florist's on the way home from a rehearsal, not St. Luke's, and seen these—freesia, the woman had said. White. He had bought them thinking of Cynthia. They had a delicate scent, barely there, and their buds, long and fluted, were closed lips waiting for a kiss of sunlight to open them. Committing floral infidelity, he had them wrapped, and really didn't want to be reminded of them.

Ave curled herself against the pillows, of which there were now a great number, encumbered with ancient lace and other materials irritating to the cheek. She had her knees tucked up, and had arranged her kimono to fall down. He wanted to pull it up again, to her neck. He wanted to tell her she didn't have to look sexy all the time. She had a habit of dropping her mouth open and doing something snakelike with her tongue. She poured coffee into the cup.

"Please. Let me do that." He couldn't keep the irritation out of his tone. She plucked her fingers from the vessels.

"So I wanted to tell you—now, don't be mad, I wanted it to be a surprise—I invited Stephen and Ella."

He'd been surprised all right. It had been clever of her to blanket him in precarious, burning, liquid-filled porcelain, though had he been a different kind of person—someone able to inflict hurt, for instance—he might have broken the cup all over again. "For God's *sake*, Ave!"

She blinked, her face pulled into her neck. "Okay," she said in the icy way she had whenever she saw she'd offended. "I'll call them up and tell them to forget it."

"Great."

"I thought you said you liked having people over. You're such a great cook."

"I'm supposed to cook?"

"Well—I'll need some help. With the shopping." The kimono slipped. Any normal person would have pulled it back up. It was drafty in the apartment, especially in the mornings, when the heat was just coming back on. He yanked it to her neck.

"And you don't have to seduce me all the time."

"I don't?" Ave was looking down. Ave was looking sad. Ave noodled a finger around in the cooling milk until he whipped it away from her, sending a spray over the antique lace.

He would tell her later. After. "What do you need for me to get?" Had Ave been able, she would have seen a man defeated not by her wiles but by his own niceness.

As it turned out, she was still in the menu-planning stage, and it was she who ended up going out, not he. She needed his muscle for the miraculous table, the width of a shelf, that could open to seat twelve. It was like the dream almost everyone has, where you find an extra room in your apartment. He worked away at it—she wanted it in the center of the room; had wanted it in the bedroom, but he drew the line—kicking from his path an assortment of very-high-heeled shoes, magazines, and take-out coffee containers. (He was usually out of the house when she got up, and it

was easiest for her to get takeout at the diner. In his overcoat, with the kimono trailing below. She was convinced that
the Dominican counterman was in love with her—and
maybe he was. She gave him a big gummy sexy smile and almost blushed as she asked for *un café con leche, por favor*.)

He considered putting away her things, but no, let her do
that, he thought. He had a score he should be studying, had
planned to be working on that afternoon. But he would do
his bit. He got the greens from the refrigerator and set about
rinsing them in the salad spinner. He still went to the green-
market every week. His life hadn't changed in any essential
way, he assured himself. It was as if he were merely shelter-
ing a troublesome stray for which he had yet to find a suit-
able home. He laid the leaves out on a towel, rolled it, and
placed the salad-ready package in a plastic bag in the veg-
etable bin just as Ave returned, carrying nothing more than a
tiny paper shopping bag, the kind overpriced cosmetics
come in.

"Here," she said, holding it out. "I got you a present."

It was a plant whose flanged jawlike leaves looked as
though they would like to swallow him whole. "What is it?"

"It's called a Venus flytrap."

"You're kidding."

"No, that's what the lady said it was called. Isn't it fabulous?"

"I can't believe you got me a Venus flytrap. Do you know
what these things are?"

"It's a plant. I mean, it's green. What do you mean, what it
is?"

"You just managed to buy me just about the only veg-
etable-form carnivore in the world."

"You don't like it."

"It's not a matter of liking or not liking. Look. Stick your
finger in there." He pointed with his broad finger to the jawlike flanges.

Ave shrank back. "I don't want to." But Ave was not one to

let herself be put on the defensive. "I don't know what you're getting all bent out of shape about. You have a cat. You can feed it cat food."

"So you did *know.*"

"Oh, great. You got the table set up." She went into the other room and came back with her arms full of a big lacy white tablecloth, shuffling on stocking feet she had just slid out of her shoes. Burton kicked one, stubbing his toe. "You were such an angel to get these," she said, lifting the vase of freesia and setting it in the center of the white cloth, from which she fussily smoothed a wrinkle.

Burton took the plant, delicate and miniature in his big hand, set it on the windowsill, and sank onto the couch, leaning back with his eyes closed. "We have to have a talk." She wasn't a cat. She was responsible for herself. She could find her own home. When he opened his eyes she had her shoes clutched to her chest and was kneeling before him, her watery blue eyes filling much as his mother's did after the requisite number of gins with lemonade.

They served gin. When Stephen and Ella arrived, the bottles were set out as he always had them for guests, vodka, sherry, whiskey, gin, and a set of glasses from the thirties striped in different colors, on a tray. Burton turned to see Ave and Ella embracing, and was somehow comforted by the sight and irritated at the same time, especially when Ella, after a wind-chilled social kiss on his cheek, said with her searching look, "Burton—are you okay?"

"Why wouldn't he be okay, bitch," said Ave, coming up behind them. "He has me. What do you want to drink?" She had put on a gown whose flowing sleeves came to long witchy points on either side. It was white, with small salmony blossoms, demure pearly buttons up the front, and a neckline that provoked anxiety as to what might pop out. It was also slightly sheer.

"That's quite a dress," said Stephen, mock-leering, and asked for whiskey.

It was going to be all right, Burton thought. They were his old friends. They were Ave's old friends. Why was he getting all bent out of shape? Why indeed? And he took a glass for a whiskey too, Ave stroking his hand as he did so. He noticed for the hundredth time how her hands, like her feet and ankles, were blunt and thick.

"You are going to be so proud of me, Cinderella," she said to her old friend. "I know you don't think I can cook—no, it's true, I never pretended I was good with my hands like you—but I made this completely by myself." And she bore aloft a quiche she was serving as the hors d'oeuvre.

"Even the crust?" said Stephen, who watched with fascination when Ella cut away the long clothlike strands from around a pie tin and crimped a pattern of ridges along an edge.

"Oh, frozen crusts are perfectly good," said Ella, evidently recognizing the commercial provenance of the crinkled aluminum dish. "Delicious," she said, taking a bite. "Perfection salad."

Stephen, who hated to have praise demanded of him, gave a cursory, "Good." He was in any case spoiled when it came to food.

Ave looked anxiously at Burton. "Yeah," he said. "Great." The whiskey spread in his chest as, he remembered, love once had. Ella and Stephen had it. He looked at the two of them, side by side on the couch. They even looked alike—sort of—with their brown hair, almost matched heights, skinniness. Ella had once confided that she sometimes wore Stephen's pants, and Burton wondered if the navy blue corduroys she had on were his. When the three of them had shared a house for a while in college, Burton and Ella had joked that they never could have made a couple, because they would have battled over who should have command of the kitchen. "Ella," he said, "are you looking unusually gorgeous?" Ella's mouth popped open. She looked as though she wanted to make an excuse.

"It's wonderful what *love* will do," said Ave.

Ella smiled vaguely and sipped from her glass, looking at the river; Stephen watched her.

Almost eight years they must have been together, Burton figured. At least seven. Obviously it wasn't true about the seven-year itch. When everyone else had been fucking around and miserable and searching—as he still was, wasn't he?—Ella and Stephen were already settled for life.

"I just want to announce that there's a reason for this dinner," Ave began. "Not that it isn't enough to see my favorite people in the world all together in one place. But this is Burton's and my one-month anniversary." She stood behind him, running her hands possessively down his chest. Where was that trapdoor? "And look what he got me," she went on, shuffling on the balls of her feet to the table and leaning into the freesias.

"Gee," said Stephen, "I thought you were about to show us a rock." Your tits, Burton thought he had been about to say.

"Ah-ha," Ave's triumphant laugh, and now she leaned toward Stephen to hit him on the knee. He was wearing blue corduroys too. Ave's smile was its most radiant and gum exposing, her up-standing hair gleaming almost white in the lamplight.

With what seemed to Burton great kindness, Ella changed the subject. But it was not an improvement. It was not even, in the secret recesses of Burton's mind, a change, exactly. "Oh," she exclaimed, "I think you must know this friend of mine. Cynthia Johnson? Violin? She told me she was doing that gig at St. Luke's."

"An obvious slut," said Ave, edging onto the arm of Burton's seat. "Who is this hussy and why haven't I heard about her?"

Ella smiled tolerantly. "If you knew," she said.

"What?"

"I think she's trying to say," put in Burton, "that this girl could hardly be less slutlike." And knew he had said exactly the wrong thing.

"You mean not like me." The pretense that Ave's aggressiveness was humor was wearing thinner than her dress.

But Ella laughed. "Ave, I think you've met her. Remember my roommate from high school?"

"From Blithedale? I thought she lived in Oregon."

"The other one. The one from my freshman year, who ran away with me that time."

"*That* girl? The one with the chipmunk cheeks and weird eyes? I thought she played piano or something."

"She was really good," said Stephen, who once or twice had coaxed Cynthia into playing piano four hands with him.

"Is the water boiling?" Burton asked, looking toward the hot plate as though its opinions could rival them all for wit.

But Ave couldn't drop the topic, even once they were sitting over their spaghetti at the candlelit table. After she had solicited compliments from each of them on every dish, she was on the attack again, asking questions. Burton was fascinated to hear Ella let down her guard and say there had been a period when Cynthia slept with anyone who tried to get her to. "She just—it's like her piano playing," said Ella. "She just thinks so little of herself."

"I never buy that self-esteem shit," said Ave in her definitive way. "You fuck people because you want to fuck people."

"*You* fuck people because you like to fuck. I don't think Cynthia dares like—well, practically anything."

"Not a problem you have," Ave shot back.

The conversation at this point became a mystery to Burton. And Stephen looked alert, which was rare on these sorts of social occasions, when he tended to roll his eyes a lot, or joints. "Toto," Burton said to him, "I get the feeling we're not in Kansas anymore."

Ave turned to Burton, putting both hands on his beard. He hadn't been thinking of Ave's fixation on the Oz books, all of which she had in a carton at her mother's. "You fabulousness, you."

11. An exchange

"**B**oy, has she got him under her thumb."

"I can't believe it. I mean, Burton— I don't know. I mean, they can't actually think they'll stay together."

"I think that's how it is these days. The women have the upper hand."

"We do?" Ella stopped and fixed Stephen with an exaggerated look. They were just a block or two from Burton's, in the icy wind that prevails on West Street. Stephen had wanted to cut over to Hudson, but Ella wanted the river.

He backed down. "Maybe he loves her."

"Huh!"

Stephen's lips curled with a strangely grim secret pleasure.

"The food was good." Ella did not sound convinced. "I've never known Ave to cook before."

"I hated the way you had to praise every goddamn thing. I'd rather eat a TV dinner."

"You hate praising people."

"I do not." A look passed between them.

"Anyway, the food wasn't *that* good," Ella added.

"I thought it was pretty good."

"She put sugar in the peas."

"The peas were fabulous."

"Then why not praise them?"

"I did. Sheesh." A particularly icy gust struck. "It's fucking freezing out here."

"You lose twenty percent of your body heat through your head."

"Famous Sylvie Vaporsky sayings." Sylvie was Ella's mother. Ordinarily, to express hostility to her was to express solidarity with Ella.

"I'm not cold," said Ella defiantly, trying to shield her face, her only exposed skin, from the flaying wind by ducking into her collar.

"You're not even looking at the river." It was true, she could not duck into her collar and turn her head.

She charged on, looking depressed.

He kept pace, giving little sidelong looks, ducked into his collar. His nose was red, eyes running. "Let's get a cab."

She stopped, again fixing him with a look, but he had run to the curb with his arm raised. "You can see the view from the window."

They were totally mismatched. He didn't look at things, the way Frank did. Besides, he didn't care what she wanted. He never wanted to do something just to please her. It had to please him.

In the backseat, he took her muffled fingers in his own. He held them to his lips through the wool. Pressed them. Drew his breath in sharply, let it out in a terrible sigh. His eyes weren't running. Those were tears.

She looked frightened. She looked out at the heaven of lights and liquid night, her hands in his lap separate from the rest of her.

"Maybe it's just sex," he said.

"Burton wouldn't do that. Besides—what's 'just sex'?"

"People can be attracted to each other without being in love."

"That isn't necessarily just sex, though."

The skin pinched so sharply as he pressed her hand that

she just stopped herself from crying out. His profile faced his lap, their hands, his full lips so tightly pressed inward that only a line showed, his eyes squeezed.

"Are you okay? Stephen—are you all right?"

"You're right. I should wear a hat."

12. The last good time

Sitting up in bed and counting on her fingers, Ella was trying to figure out the last time she had really liked sex with Stephen.

There was that time in their old apartment, the place Cynthia now had. Not the last good time. Ella was working for a movie company and someone had passed a joint so powerful that Ella had gone home: she had been worried that she would be unable to speak when she next had to speak, or move when she next had to move, and that she would speak when she shouldn't speak and move in ways she might not necessarily be able to anticipate. When she got home the strange paralysis had given way to what all those boys in high school had plied her with the stuff for, to no effect then. She lay writhing on the bed, waiting for Stephen to get home. But when he got there, he had treated her with distaste. "What is this?" he had asked. Maybe she hadn't forgiven him. Not the last good time.

The last good time, she hadn't forgiven him for. Wearing high red leather boots and her pants down around her ankles. They had been dressing to go out for dinner. Two of his friends were meeting them. They had looked at their watches and decided they had time. So they hadn't fully undressed, and it had been the last of the truly transcendental sex. But why the last? Because the doorbell had rung just as she was starting to come. He was coming. He pulled back and she tried to hold him, but, "Ella!" he said reproachfully— oh, a girl who had her priorities very badly arranged—and went to get the door, zipping, while she died on the bed, her feet in the red boots, with the pants around one ankle, still on the floor.

Well. She had always known she came second to his work. But second to everything? To a gay couple with whom he was moderately friendly? But those gay men, they were his work. That couple, they were composers, and the theater directors and all Stephen's geniuses, they were all gay men, almost always. Men, anyway.

Her fingers moved—one, two, three, four years ago? Jesus. That couldn't be right. She moved her fingers again and it was.

And yet. Well, it was much more complicated, really. That may have been the last of the truly transcendental sex but what came after wasn't bad. Entirely. Anyway, you could keep moving your markers back and back and back. God, she couldn't even think of the college town where their romance had started without the most painful, pleasurable nostalgia, nostalgia and *vividness,* as though she had never been so alive since. Well. Maybe that was true too. Romantic poetry, it turned out, was accurate in a perfectly literal way, and all those mushy songs—yes, it could happen like that. Amazing. And it had happened to her, to them, so they had both been awestricken at their very selves. Those markers could be ticked off on the fingers too. A vista stretched that included their first intimate conversation, her glimpse of his chest hair, his of her red underpants, the way he'd held her hand for sympathy, the degree of horror he'd registered at some troubles she'd had—all that before anything sexual, much less romantic, had been broached.

Those markers moved back and back too.

Nothing with Frank came anywhere near even the bad parts.

Oh, autumn, that was the time to fall in love, the season of rebirth, whatever anybody says—when the blood quickens, the pace picks up, the air sparkles, everything and everyone stretching and awakening from the torpor of August, and the delicious welcoming yellow of the trees, an encouraging softness in the air, and you wear a suede jacket and feel that your life is finally beginning. And that year it had, it was.

She had been on her way to a job, an apartment, a room-mate. She had just stopped off to visit. He was still in school, his last year. She had never gotten to the job, the apartment; the roommate never wanted to talk to her again.

"Just go to bed with me. Just once. We don't have to do anything, just sleep in the bed with me. Don't leave. I swear to God, I'm going to have to rape you if you say no."

She had loaned herself to the project in the spirit of ut-most skepticism, and wearing a tee shirt and underpants. In college, not a big deal, the sight of firm young bodies, get-ting in and out of bed with them, it was usual, it was ordi-nary. But.

"Do you—?"

"Yes."

"This is incredible."

Their hands clasped, but they didn't hug, they didn't kiss. It was morning and they still were covered by the thin cotton knits neither had so much as considered removing in the course of the night. Well, Stephen might have considered it.

"So you feel it too."

"It's—I feel as if I've been waking up with you every morn-ing all my life."

They were young enough not to know what a bad feeling this could be. At any rate, they got up, put on the rest of their clothes, had breakfast together, met again for lunch, for

dinner, joking, chatting, no eye gazing, no mysterioso won-
derment, got into bed again together that night like children,
with mischievous smiles on their faces. Lay side by side,
silent. "I can't stand it," Stephen said, and hurled himself
upon her. She let him. She must have gotten up to get her diaphragm, she was extremely careful about such things, but it
seemed as if it happened in one smooth motion, without
preliminaries, because certainly he was the least loverlike of
lovers, no smarmy talk, no "technique"—he hardly touched
her except lip to lip, arms clasped to her back, and then
crotch to crotch. But, oh, when those met. There was no
preparing for that. Or else their whole little lives to that point
had been preparation, though not preparation enough.

"I love you," he said, grabbing her, pressing her to him
again and again. "I know I shouldn't say it, but I can't help it,
I love you," while she said Shh, shh, and Don't, as though his
words hurt.

Stephen was a small, thin man. His hair fell thickly over
his pale forehead, thick and brown, so that he was forever
pushing it back with chewed-looking white fingers. His lips
were chewed too, and immense, presenting a pink wet bal-
loon netted with torn triangles and old ones curling like
crisps. Sensuous lips though withal, kasha lips, Ella had
been taught to call the type growing up. Stephen was the
kind of dark-haired person who is really fair, with his blue
eyes, skin dotted with beauty marks that emphasized an air
of fragility. Yes, it was an oxymoron, his appearance, so delicate, and then that very hairy chest, and an exaggeratedly
masculine way of moving, a sort of swagger . . . but the exaggeration wasn't very masculine, was it? He was making fun
of being masculine. But that was appealing too . . . Oh, these
boys who went to Benton, they were pussy boys. He was a
trog, really; but then, so romantic! You could see him as
Chopin, in one of those blouses with big sleeves, with that
chest hair swirling at the open neck. God, she used to melt

seeing him at the piano. Yes, it was true, melt, it hurt to watch him practice, she loved him so much: him; and making those sounds. Beethoven, one late piano sonata in particular, one passage of one late piano sonata in particular. She couldn't hear it too much. Which was a good thing, because in practicing he played it, had to play it, over and over. Over and over. First in that funny apartment with the piano someone had painted a pale oleaginous pink, and then in that house over the winter, there especially the sonata became mixed up with the snow-covered landscape and that feeling of something literally tugging the heartstrings, as if there were heartstrings, almost a kind of sickness, almost a kind of sadness, homesickness, nostalgia, but for something she'd never had, never had before, anyway. This, it seemed, was happiness.

Sometimes he broke off in the middle of his playing, feeling her presence, smoothly slid from the bench to fly to her, grasp and cling to her, nuzzle her neck, and then go back to playing, his back to her, without having said anything. So much did they feel each other's necessity. Once they'd given in to it, that is. Once they'd given in, the thought that they might not have, might have foregone this agonizing bliss, made them blink and shudder and hold on to each other and say Let's not think about it.

In those days she had lived for bedtime. They'd forced themselves to stop going to bed at all hours of the day. A doctor to whom Ella had gone about an infection asked how often she was having sex, and when she said three times, A week? he said, No, a day, the doctor had looked at her as though she were an animal. They were animals, they exulted in it. We fuck like animals, Stephen said, lying winded and smelling of sweat, his arm under her neck but the rest of them untouching, not able to bear it after all that, and too hot besides. But only for a little while, sometimes not even a minute. Possibly not even animals fuck like that, or maybe cats do, but they don't seem to like it. Masters and Johnson should use us, they said. It seemed so miraculous each time that they wanted something to measure it by, or to grant to them the extraordinariness. It made the whole world tender. Being turned inside out like that.

Too tender for work, that was when Stephen got stern, said he had to get back to work. He was in a panic, remembering suddenly as if waking from a sleep and finding himself in a boat halfway to where he was going, on his way to a concert for which he had yet to learn the music, and only the rest of the boat ride before he had to perform.

For a moment he looked at Ella as though she might be the enemy.

He who had said that he hardly needed to work, didn't need to practice, he could not play a wrong note, he could not make a wrong move, not in that state soggy with love, not in that tender world. And had in fact given a concert, played as well as he ever had, better; conducted his pieces; Ella in the audience melting. Leaping out of herself to feel his every move. What about that? Ella asked. Yes, but now I have to work, he said, and she felt humbled, she felt she'd been greedy, she conceded the precedence of his own importance to himself, of its being more important than his importance to her. Okay. She loved him.

It was a sleigh bed, in that house they had for the winter—thick mahogany buttery curves, a little too high; you had to hike yourself up to achieve it. The house was underheated, with ice double-glazing the corners of the windows, wet and liquefying under a touch, and the sheets would be cold, taut and rejecting. Sometimes Ella was first to bed and lay listening to the sounds of Stephen brushing his teeth across the hall, or clenched her hands under the covers, over her ribs, as his clothes swished to the floor, wide wood boards with slippery little rugs hooked out of rags. And still there were no preliminaries, they fell on each other as soon as they were under the tent of the bedclothes together, as though they'd been straining toward each other all day and finally been let off their leashes.

In later years as she lay under other men, the name of the road that house was on would float up like a signpost for sex.

It was different in the house than it had been in the funny apartment two flights above the local tavern. Out in a field, a huge field that arced away to the mountains, with only a thin line of trees here and there against the snow; there was a sense of the house floating in space, and they in the big bed high off the floor with the scary darkness underneath; and she in an almost metaphysical state where it wasn't Stephen floating over her, or corporeally anything at all, but pure transport, something that took her somewhere else. Whatever it was he was doing to her, and she didn't care, images began flashing like the screen made of lights in Times Square; maps of the country in trickling colors, dazzling stars, images that transmuted from one thing into another so fast that they never quite registered, clouded like dreams on first waking, like cotton candy on the tongue, that is, not completely, but confusing the senses, like an ice cube that has dissolved to a sliver between the fingers, which, anesthetized by it, still feel it to be huge. Always she felt she was holding on to something that was disappearing in her very arms, that was there and not there, that holding on to made disappear but that would disappear if she didn't hold on to it.

Yet never had she felt her own immanence as something so substantial, she felt so material, her breasts seemed to well out, lift themselves to him, and never had she understood so completely that she was female, and what a blessing that was. She felt that nothing more was required of her, nothing ought to be; that she was there, at the secret center of life, and it was owing to him, and she clung to him.

Yes, the practicing was good, because it was more of the same. The chords crashing down and retreating in that characteristically Beethoven way, shy and echoing then pursuing and infuriated, yearning, stomped down—then miraculously allowed to come together, though again it was some dark kind of bliss. There was male and female in it. But not her body. Moreover, she was supposed to be doing something.

She had no interest in painting at all. Let him be the artist. She just wanted to have children that looked like him, milky, hank-haired, half shy, half cocky. Oh, a terrible blow for women's liberation, but she couldn't worry about that. But "I couldn't be with someone who doesn't do something," Stephen said. "I don't think I could be with someone who wasn't an artist." And she hadn't ever thought she wouldn't be, really. Just not right then. But she lacked the choice. She set her paints up in the bedroom, when finally they got an apartment together of their own, she found a terrible part-time job of the sort that she had had ever since, he finished his courses and graduated in glory and immediately got paid in the exercise of his art, albeit in the theater, albeit he cast evil glances at former classmates off to Rome with the *prix de* or swimming in some plummy commission or getting performed in whatever chic showcase was hot at that moment (BAM, Composers' Forum, the Kitchen; Peter Serkin at Carnegie Hall). He was jealous, but she was too humble even for jealousy, so shut out did she feel.

Until that party thrown by some arts commission, very stuffy, giving Stephen an award. He got his award. And she saw two famous middle-aged artists talking to each other at the reception, Frank and a painter, she could identify both of them, Frank in whose tortured pictures she recognized something of herself—maybe not something she liked. And boldly went up to them. The reception was supposed to be so that the younger artists could meet the older ones. Stephen was off talking to an old teacher of his. "You two shouldn't be talking to each other," she said. "You're supposed to be talking to us." And Frank had looked delighted.

Became asthmatic, in fact, with delight, barely able to wheeze out the excited words, which she was able to guess and supply for him. And so it was that with a stranger's words in her mouth, eight years after accidentally, half accidentally, falling into bed and in love so deeply that she hadn't wanted to look around or come up for air, she looked around, breathed the air, saw that there might be a place for her in the world, and wanted it.

13. A pig

Her skin. It really had the texture of a flower petal, roses, and he had to stop in the explorations of his hands and look. Pink. Pale pale pink. He pulled her shirt up some more, kissing as he went. Fine blond hair, a beauty mark, the faint shininess of an old scar from a small bite or scratch. She lay in a stillness that was not passive, that was expectant, her hands lightly resting on his hair. Other men had mistaken her for passive, and she had been passive, but he had the sensitivity to know otherwise, and he was therefore the recipient of something convulsive that had them grappling again, mouth to mouth. He hadn't expected this, he hadn't intended this. He would have to tell her that he wasn't free, that that was why he'd held off—but he would be, he would be. He took her earlobe into his mouth, the soft kernel with its taste of metal and the sharp little stud at the back of her earring pricking his tongue to salt; the white beating throat. They twisted in their clothes. "Oh. Cynthia," he said as if saying the words were the only way he could come up for air. She laughed her breathy, nervous laugh, her mouth, with its pronounced central bead, a chick's open beak. They lay on their sides, fingertips resting on each other's exposed patches, looking at each other, breathing. She kept smiling. He kept smiling. He took one of her hands and brought the skilled fingers to his lips, which felt the square cool corners of her nails. The hand was shaking. They had both stopped smiling. He wanted to protect her. But really, what he should be protecting her from was himself.

"What's the matter?" she asked in that uncanny way girls have of knowing.

He drew her to him. Afraid that his belt buckle was digging into her skin, he pulled away to undo and remove it, but she misunderstood and put her own deft fingers to work on it. She unzipped his zipper. She reached in and pulled him out, all pulsing and ready to pop at the touch of those fingers, so that he had to put a hand on her hand to stop her. She got up on her knees and began unbuttoning her shirt. Her movements had an almost teasing languor—like a stripper's—but it was only later, in memory, that her look came back to him to be noticed, grave, almost puzzled, with fear lurking deep behind the eyes like a habit. What he was noticing at the time was, under the butch shirt (a work shirt, like his—the congruence had seemed significant), the ornate ice-dream-sundae frilliness of her low-cut brassiere. With a clinking of her belt buckle she pulled her jeans and underpants off together. Her hair was gingery, downy-looking, almost straight, the cleft girlishly visible in its cloudy paleness. He wanted to pet it. She let him, holding on to his shoulder for steadiness. Suddenly, roughly, he had to pull the shirt off her, and undo the bra, releasing a wealth of breastwork the clothes must have been concealing, and he was on her and in her, his jeans half hampering his legs, his shirt sweating with him. He did stop himself from coming as soon as he was in her, gripping her wrists on either side of her head so hard she whimpered, but again it was only afterward that he

heard it as pain, at the time he thought it was pleasure. His
balls were so tight it was itself a kind of pain, pleasurable.
Too intense. Too intense. No, he couldn't stop himself, and
he didn't want it to stop, but he had moved deep into her,
clenching her, and then couldn't move, couldn't bear for her
to move, and couldn't believe the sound that came from him,
he who in sex made no noise but breath.

Stilled, he felt her like a wishbone around him, and their
differently textured hairs intermingled like ground twigs. He
felt the soft squish where her thigh met her buttock, thin as
she was, and imagined what it must feel like, walking around
on that, at the end of those long legs, and felt himself already larger again inside her. He half pulled out and went in
again. They both groaned. Again he mistook her look of
pain. He nuzzled under her jaw, into the cleft behind her ear,
took one fat nipple into his mouth, the other between middle and forefinger at the pit of the V, pressing back. Even her
belly button was luscious. He pulled far enough back to
thumb it, slick with his sweat. Then he registered a little cry
she'd let out.

"I'm hurting you."

"No. I mean, no."

"Something's wrong. Something's bothering you."

"Something's bothering *you.*"

With a sigh, he rolled them over, holding her at the waist,
which had a tall girl's solidity, until gravity lay equally dis-
tributed between them. "I'm a bad person, Cynthia. You
shouldn't have anything to do with me."

"Now he tells me." Her eyebrows had the humor; her rosebud lips were puckered with worry. "What's so bad about
you?"

"Really. I'm just a lousy person. I don't deserve to be with
anybody."

"Oh—*deserve,*" she said sardonically.

He eased out of her, and she flopped to her back to reach

for a cigarette. He reached over her to get her matches, to light it, the wing of his forearm brushing her breasts.

"You didn't come." He didn't know he knew till he said it.

She swallowed smoke and then let it form the words "I never come." Then an alarmed look. "Don't make a project of it. I just don't." Then she looked at him with her upside-down eyes.

Now he recognized what it was about the sex, a kind of professionalism on her part, and it came back to him, what Ella had said, about Cynthia's having been promiscuous. That pain in her face—it was pain—had been his not notic-ing. He'd been a pig. But it was because he liked her so much! It wasn't, God knows, as if he was starved for sex. It wasn't *sex,* this thing with Cynthia. Or maybe sex with Ave wasn't sex, because it was just sex. Something like that. Something girls knew about. Girls were much smarter about this stuff. But nothing was just sex. But it had kind of been just sex, impersonal, with Cynthia, to whom he felt so close, not just in his private and extensive secret fantasies, but in their looks at each other, in the things they didn't say to each other, in all the speech of their embarrassed ardent eyes. "Oh, fuck."

"I'm sorry. That's just the way I am. See, *I* don't deserve—"

"No, no. It's not that." He let the breath whistle from his body, letting his spread hand fall placatingly on her flat belly.

"I don't know. Maybe I'm not built like other women."

"Don't be ridiculous." He saw her flinch at the harshness of what evidently seemed to her disparagement. "No, you're not ridiculous. But you're not deformed or something either. It's mental. Of course it is. I mean emotional."

"I've been in *love* with people and not come. Wild."

"But not liked it that much. Sex."

"I have been in love."

"Not so much with yourself. Maybe."

She looked at him a moment incredulous. Then she

slammed a pillow into his head. "Boys are not supposed to be that smart about feelings, dammit."

He thought she seemed pleased.

"Actually," he said, "I'm disgusting. Do you mind?" And he began to take off his sweaty clothes to the accompaniment of her laughter, no more nervous than the high notes of the piano. He flapped his arms to make a breeze. She blew on him, teasing, and pressed her long fingers into the sweet dough of his torso.

Somehow they never discussed why he was a bad person, and he forgot that he was supposed to be. As they talked and kissed, the phone rang. "Aren't you going to get it?" Burton kissed her.

"I've got the machine on."

They listened, still. After Cynthia's voice came Ella's: "Hi. It's me-ee."

When Burton after a while made noises about having to leave, Cynthia looked distressed again, though trying not to show it. "You don't want to—oh, never mind. No, no," she said to his query, "never mind. Really."

"I'd love to have dinner with you. But I can't, tonight." They had run into each other in front of Stephen and Ella's building that afternoon, where Stephen and Ella were taking the sun. A planned accident, on Burton's part; he believed the rest had been unplanned accident.

Cynthia resumed her brassiere. She stood to put on her underpants, the kind that are little more than elastic with a strip of filmy fabric. She held on to a low table as she did this. He clasped her around the waist as she bent, from the rear. He had to dip his finger below the crust of lace and feel the nipple lodged there like a nutmeg pressed into a pillow. And as if he had no mind to think of such things, or think of desisting, his big penis, dark and heavy with all that it carried, pushed the filmy cloth to one side. The elastic dug cruelly into her softness, but the dumb docile animal, her cunt, stared out of its fur, and he pushed on. The little table shook. A matryoshka doll on the table watched with its placid, meaningless smile, rocking back and forth, knocking against the wall. He felt both Cynthia's breasts like a harvest over his forearm. One experienced finger he kept firmly in the forward part of the moist cleft. He couldn't remember sex like this, not that anything so cogent as remembering was going on with him. He went off like a flashbulb.

It had been the first springlike day, prematurely. He had inflicted hurt, and survived. He went out into the newly balmy evening thinking what a pig he was, a pig, a pig. Feeling wonderful.

14. I admit to that

"**S**o? What happened?"

The sense of entitlement to information that girlfriends feel!

"It's not what you think." Cynthia didn't know why she was reluctant to tell. As she shifted the receiver there was in her mind's eye the picture of Ella on the stoop earlier that day, in that first warm sun they'd had, with the whole neighborhood out and a little girl in braids singing "Don't it make my brown eyes blue" and looking embarrassed when caught at it, gay guys with their Abyssinian cats on leashes, "russets" they said of the straining beasts, and a woman with a reflector around her slack neck, holding a wrinkled face to the light. Ella had stretched back on the steps, bringing her breasts into relief, Stephen next to her, trusting, and Cynthia had felt a dart of hatred slash through her. How could Ella throw Stephen away? She must never have loved anybody.

"I'm sorry. Am I being pushy? It's just that after you guys left together, I mean, I didn't think anything of it, but—did you get my message, by the way? I mean, I didn't say my name, so—"

"I knew who it was." We both did.

"Are you okay, Cynthia? You sound angry."

For some reason, Cynthia kept seeing Burton's thumb on her thigh, just his thumb and her naked thigh. "No," she said unconvincingly.

"I thought Burton really liked you."

"Oh?"

"Well, he's mentioned you before, and I had that sense. Well, so did his girlfriend. And I just felt like—I mean, Burton would never two-time anyone, he's much too nice, but I felt guilty or worried or something and I thought I should make sure you knew that he was living with someone. I mean, not that it matters, if you're not interested in him. I just thought you should know. I mean, maybe it's just that I wish you were his girlfriend. I shouldn't say this, it's really mean of me, considering that she's my friend too, but I think Ave's just using him somehow. I mean, she does believe she's in love with him, but I guess I don't believe it."

"Yawh?" said Cynthia in her just-this-side-of-boarding-school-lockjaw way. "Why not?"

"You remember Ave?" said Ella cautiously.

"We thought she was really cool, but sort of an asshole?" Cynthia was surprised she could sound fairly cool herself. She wiped a tear off the table with two fingers.

"Was that when she had her hair sort of à la Jean Harlow?"

"And she wore this great silver dress from Paraphernalia."

"And we both wanted to live in the Village and have dresses from Paraphernalia too. When we grew up."

They emitted simultaneous snorts, and Cynthia flooded

with friendliness like relief. She wished she could tell Ella about it. But it would be too humiliating. What a, what a stupid *girl* she'd been. Well, Ella also thought Burton was too nice not to be trusted. What a comfort. Somehow Ella got to have two men; and a bitch, a cunt like Ave (she had only the haziest sense of her really, anymore, but it did include that hair, that dress) had Burton.

"Do you think Burton loves *her?*" Cynthia asked.

"*That's* a good question. Boy, I've wondered about that one. I mean, Burton's so honest and kind of— I wonder if he's sort of passive . . ."

"Like how do you mean?" If that was passive, Cynthia hoped never to meet anyone active.

"Well—I don't know what really went on between them— I mean, you know, nobody really talks about those kind of things—except of course compulsive exhibitionists like me." Ella paused to laugh at herself. Cynthia felt a twinge of guilt. She had been thinking precisely that Ella was exhibitionistic, looking at those little breasts in the sun under her tee shirt this afternoon, and only just barely under the tee shirt, and Ella's voice in her ear, week after week, trumpeting the latest trauma with Frank, with Stephen, did she think Stephen knew, did she think Frank cared about her, what did it mean that he had done X, or Y, or Z.

"So how do you think they got together? Or why?" Cynthia had always thought it was a kind of hokey shorthand that in movies when people heard about infidelity, they threw up, but she felt something like nausea—or was it tearfulness? Or the rope attached to all her organs that someone was tugging on?

"Search me. She was staying with us—I think she had some of her stuff at the apartment of every friend she has in the city; you know, it was here one night, there the next. You know how Ave is, I mean I've talked about her—I must have."

"I've never had quite this view."

"You mean of a crazy slut."

"Gee, I'm glad I'm not your friend or anything. Who knows what you'd say about me."

"Oh, come on. I mean, you're right, I should be nicer. But she can—"

"You mean, so you thought she moved in on Burton rather than in with him."

"It's hard to know. But yeah. Yeah, I admit to that."

"Then why did he let her? Why does he let her stay?"

"I don't know. I mean, he was really in love with this girl in college, and I don't know what happened exactly, but since then he's never really—I don't know. I've wondered about old Burt. But the thing is, the way he was looking at you—"

"I thought so too," Cynthia said, very quietly.

"Oh, Cynthia. But maybe this could be great. I mean, you'll get to know each other, and Ave won't last—Ave never lasts—and then, you know."

"You've been reading *True Romance* comics."

"Hey, if anyone should be cynical."

"Besides, I wouldn't"—it was hard to get the word past the gasp stuck in her throat that wanted to become a sob—"want to be someone's second choice." Second choice. Those were the really horrible words. Inadmissible.

"Jesus. It wouldn't be that."

"No?"

"Cynthia, you sound terrible. You can't think—I mean, you and Ave—"

"Why not? She seemed like Ms. Charisma when we were fifteen."

"Yeah, but we were fifteen. And who wanted to look like that? We wanted to be Joan Baez, or Marianne Faithfull or something. And Ave's into drugs. In fact—I wonder if Burton knows that. Oh, he must. Well—listen. I haven't seen Ave alone in ages."

"Ella! Don't you say anything! Don't you dare."

"Of course not. It's just—I mean, I'd want to help if I could, no matter what. But you've been so great with all this Frank stuff. I mean I know I've been really obsessive and boring about it—"

"What *is* happening there?" This made her feel almost normal. In some kind of control.

Ella responded with animal noises. Cynthia had asked the right question. "You remember Stephen was away last week? So I had Frank over for lunch. I mean, we never get to do anything normal together, like eat. So I thought it would be like— Oh, I don't know what I thought. It was okay, sort of, but then he was really cold. He said—do you know what he said? It's really incredible. I can't get over this. He said he was extremely *fond* of me. Fond! Can you believe that? I mean, who *uses* that word? That's like, uh, 'fondly yours' or—it's like a word you might use about some kind of food you don't really like: 'I'm fond of apricots.' "

Cynthia didn't know what to say. We never do anything normal together, like eat. His awkwardness the second time they went for cappuccino. His not kissing her good night. His kissing her.

"I mean, if you had to choose between me and at least what he's told me about his wife, it would be no contest."

"But maybe that's not the point. And if he says he loves you—well, he probably feels like that would commit him to something."

"Well, exactly. Of course."

"Did you say it?"

"Urlgh, don't make me hate myself more than I already do. I didn't exactly say it. But I probably didn't exactly not say it. What a good thing I can't marry him. What a shit! What a disaster that would be."

"Maybe all men are shits."

"Stephen isn't."

"He can be a shit to you." Cynthia shifted over the soreness and stickiness inside her pants.

"All right. But I still think Burton isn't. I think you're perfect for each other."

15. Well, Burton

Burton didn't care. His heart sang within him. Had he ever not cared before? Wow!

Piously, he reminded himself of who had done this for him. He fixed her face before him, with its puffy, maybe disappointed cheeks, but his mental eye quickly slipped downward, memory imperceptibly slipping into fantasy, and he did not want to arrive home with a hard-on. He fixed the face before him again. Her characteristic look was downward. Was she sad? Of course she was sad. He would have to do something about it. Wasn't that at least part of why he'd been attracted to her in the first place? Was that why he was attracted to her? He *wanted* to do something about it. Didn't he?

Making his way down Hudson in the almost balmy dusk—it had a nip, but after winter it was exciting, enticing; but maybe he would feel that way no matter what—he almost walked by St. Luke's but stopped in his tracks. He looked up at the square tower as though he might worship the building itself. And he might, or anything else about the place. Yes, anything. Why not, they had met there. A triangle of yellow spilled from a doorway along the path. It was magic hour, the sky lavender but still sufficiently lighting the world, so that the electric-yellow windows in the buildings look surreal; the lit windows made the dimness dimmer and the brightness of the illuminated clouds above a surprise. He walked up the path; he shouldn't be dawdling, but it was so delicious to prolong the moment. (Yes, he should have prolonged it with her; next time, next time; he would make it possible one way or another.)

In the anteroom, where coats were flung on piled folding chairs—it had the jumbled, forgotten air of a hall where a household's oldest furniture and random boots and hats are dumped—nervous men set up for a meeting. One with a salt-and-pepper mustache and bony scalp walked in tight steps with a paper plate of packaged cookies. The unevenly lettered sign now read, AA TUES. SAT. Burton, as one who would never join this brotherhood, smiled. The head of the man with the cookies jerked up as though he'd heard a gunshot, and he fixed Burton with a ferocious look, reaching with his long arm toward the door, closing it, his face downshifting into wounded: "Can't even enjoy the weather . . ." The nasal voice trailed off as the door closed and Burton advanced up the path, past a statue of Mary looking like a nun modeled in Plasticine, and the windows of the school whose construction-paper bunnies and tulips made gray silhouettes within the reflections.

Why are scents stronger at night, Burton wondered. The winter garden smelled of sweet dried grass and the healthy decay of foliage into well-aerated mold. Burton sat on a bench under bare branches that would soon blend blackly with the sky. The hiss of traffic stopped on Hudson; then the traffic squealed forward. A cat slunk from under the bench and let its cool fur run between his hands. It felt scary and magical to be in the garden like that, privileged but also cut off. A woman in rimless glasses passed across the yellow panes of one of the vicarage houses, talking. The cat jumped into his lap, her tail much softer than his beard against his throat. She walked back and forth, claiming him but uninterested in settling. "Yes, I will have to do something, kitty," he said. "I definitely have to do something." The cat's look suggested that it was goofy to talk to cats, and she bounded onto the invisible grass, leaving his hands to rest on the bumpy velvet of his corduroys. If Cynthia were sitting next to him—he imagined her hands bundled into one of his jacket pockets, her head pressed into his shoulder, her fine electric hair tickling his ear, the bulkiness of bodies in thick cloth, the hug-muffling wool with its dank odor. But he couldn't imagine her happy. He couldn't imagine her happy. I'd be happy with her, he thought, but there's no reason she should be happy just to be with me.

But he recognized this for the false and self-serving thought it was.

Cinzia—Cheen-zia. The Italian version of her name kept springing up, and he played with the sounds, Cinzano, sin, the implied caress of the long *e*. He could just see the cat like a ghost over by the shed, rearing back on stiff legs from an imaginary enemy.

Was the best over or yet to come? "TK," they said where Ella worked, for *to come*, she had told him once. Amusing. Was the best over or yet TK; it was a question that would not have occurred to him if he hadn't remembered how depressed he had been at the beginning of winter. Just around the time Ave showed up. Was he so distracted by Ave that he'd forgotten to be depressed? It wasn't very much fun, if you were an earthling—and he was very much of the earth, bearlike, cave-dwelling, with that domestic, vegetal, hibernatory bent—to play with an intergalactic mermaid. But maybe she was some kind of magic for him. He didn't like her very much—no, he didn't—but maybe what happened with Cynthia, Cinzia, wouldn't be possible without Ave. Maybe if he could be with Cynthia they would both just be depressed together. What a depressing thought.

He supposed he didn't believe in true love anymore. If

you have fallen in love and then stopped loving a person, how can you possibly? Well, all right: you might tell yourself it hadn't been the right person. *The* true love. But then what was it all about, that magic and fairy dust, if it was the wrong person? Hmm? What was it for anyway?

Ave, of all people, believed in true love. She had told him. "Of course I do!" Indignant. He had been so afraid she would claim him as *it* that he hadn't pressed the point. Ave. He tried to read his watch. Well, it was black out.

From the gate of the churchyard he looked up at the bright squares of Ella and Stephen's windows. *There* was true love. In college he had once come by and found them sitting up in bed together. "Young love," he had said, and Ella had sounded as indignant, in a quiet way, as Ave: "No; *true* love." Maybe it only came to people gifted for it.

Maybe he was gifted for adultery.

Not that it was a gift that had shown itself so far.

Not that letting Ave camp in his bed was marriage.

He felt too tired suddenly to walk home. Besides, he was suspiciously late.

"Where've you been?" Ave glared at him with the full force of her personality. She was crouched among discarded clothes and magazines in the center of the bed. The cat in a wary huddle on one corner seemed to give Burton a look of both resentment and commiseration out of its yellow eyes. He smoothed her back on the way to administering the obligatory recidivist kiss. "You smell of sex," Ave hissed.

He turned from her smoothly, walking back out toward the kitchen and living room. "I didn't know it had a smell."

"Yeah, well, now you know."

He peered at her, astonished, but she was leafing through a magazine. Did this constitute knowledge, permission, indifference, or what? She had the phone on the bed and dialed, ignoring him, and in moments was laughing with whoever was at the other end (Jorge? Who was that?), as if to say anyone's company was preferable to Burton's. Well, fuck you too, thought Burton, feeling rebuffed but not displeased: such are the rewards of mutual agreement. She rose, in a satin robe trimmed with lace, hanging open, revealing striped bikini underpants and her perfect breasts, arousing despite the labors of his afternoon.

"I have to go out," she said with so level a look it seemed to be conveying some other, more important message. She threw off her robe, keeping her eyes on him like a challenge. He shrugged, turned away, and despised himself, feeling he'd yielded her the upper hand. In what? And if anything, he should be feeling bad for her or guilty and instead there was this panic, as though she were dangerous and offended and he had to find some way to mollify her.

"I just got in," he said, sounding pathetic in his own ears. "What about dinner?"

"Why do you think I'm going out, fuckface."

Perversely, the hint that she might want another man made him want her to stay. "Ave."

"Oh, you never know an endearment when you hear one." In her finicky slow-motion way she had stepped into a tiny skirt, not particularly in fashion but crudely suggestive, and pulled over her bare springy tits a sweater whose lower rim just met the skirt's waistband, so that her every movement invited with a glimpse of skin. She finished this off with the string of her grandmother's pearls.

"Just for groceries?" he said, leaning in the doorway.

"You know my standards," she said, applying the blush shame would never grant her.

"I'll get them," he said, thinking for some reason of her running out mornings with her bathrobe underneath his overcoat. She left, as though she hadn't heard.

He returned to the living room and put on a record. The sounds of Fischer-Dieskau claiming *Ich grolle nicht* rolled out. That brought Ave running, shuffling in the toes of her shoes.

"Turn that vile caterwauling off."

"I thought you were gone," said Burton.

"Not quite yet," she said, clutching her coat, a new one. Occasionally he wondered where her money came from. He didn't give her that much.

Ave ran out, not noticing the balminess of the air or its bracing edge. In this state nothing could touch her. Why did she always forget what it was like, having a new lover? What a drug it was, much more powerful than the cocaine they shared. Though the coke helped . . . She laughed in the sheer intoxication of being her. So alluring, so deeply sexy, so in every way desirable, no man could look at her and not feel the tug. Oh yes, she thought, holding up one (sexy, adorable, kissable) arm for a cab, I'm Queen of the Night, or—what was it Jorge had called her?—La Exigente, like the coffee ad, because of her fussiness about the quality of the drug, or rather her insistence on her own expertise in recognizing what it was cut with and by how much and her claim to be able to identify where it was from.

It was really true about Latin lovers. God, they knew how to make a woman feel like a woman. She couldn't believe she'd waited till thirty-three to discover this glory—nearly twenty years of wasted time.

The cab zipped over to eastern Chelsea in no time, or maybe that was just the drug. She got out of the cab— *alighted,* she felt, as though she were something weightless and lit that she bore glowing before her, and there was also that movie unreeling in her head for which the word *lumière* seemed to stand, in which she saw her silvery figure (in the film) *alighting,* infinitely glamorous and carefree. She paid the driver with what seemed to be prop money (*plenty* more where that came from) and pranced to the entrance of the club, where the doorman (who obviously wanted to fuck her) lifted a velvetized chain to let her in.

While she was looking around for Jorge, someone put hands over her eyes from behind, murmured "carita" in her ear, and nipped the lobe. She laughed her "ah-hah" and turned within the circle of his arms, meeting Jorge's full lips that always seemed ready formed into a kiss. With his lips still on hers, he took both her hands and made the moves of the merengue, which he had begun teaching her the other day, his eyes half-closed in a manner to suggest sexual ecstasy. Another man stroking Ave with his eyes said, "Nice going," to Jorge in Spanish. "The men, the men," said Jorge, "they are all jealous that I am with you, La Exigente."

Oh, Latin men. They were great.

Jorge's skinny body executed the steps without engaging his attention, which was all for her. Not wearing his counterman's white linens, he was almost handsome, despite a shiny navy shirt unbuttoned to display chest hair and a tangle of predictable chains and medals; despite what appeared to be greasy kid stuff in the flattened waves of his black hair; despite being only two inches taller and despite that cliché of a gold tooth. Or maybe not despite at all. Though, Ave thought, at least he's not Puerto Rican. He was Dominican. Oh, the cruelly deprived. She knew what that was like. Latin men, they were great. Except some of them were pigs.

They had been dancing in an entryway that led to the bar. When the number finished, Jorge held her waist and led her to the cavernous dance floor downstairs. Latin men were so masterful. They knew what they wanted and they took it, adoring you for it. Or at least acting that way, which was enough, after all. Lots of people said hello. Cousins. Friends in the band. A woman with dyed red hair who gave Ave an approving once-over. That woman had the last bullet bra in the country, over which was molded red satin. Next to these people I look like a WASP, Ave thought, a Quaker. She preened in her own amused and gratified self-approval. She danced. Even her mistakes were adorable. Really, she needn't have bothered with the coke. Jorge was nuzzling her hair, which she was allowing to go frizzy again, when someone cut in, a fabulously handsome black man who said Jorge couldn't keep her all to himself, then Jorge cut in again and said Let's visit the back room, or bathroom, she wasn't sure which, but bathroom must be what he meant, to do a line. But when they were in the stall he lifted her negligible skirt and just like that against the partition, this hadn't happened to her for years, passion, oh God, how fabulous, and he was telling her she was a goddess, the queen of his heart, his addiction, his fix, your witch eyes they put me in your power— et cetera, et cetera.

Actually, standing up, and with the sounds of flushing and the disinfectant smells and who-knew-what underfoot— well, never mind.

He grinned fiercely, huffed like a runner, ground a kiss, and looked exultant. He rested his head on her shoulder. "You make me weak, weetch." Several kisses to the neck and an excited bite.

"Hey, careful. My husband." That was how she referred to Burton. It was too difficult to explain.

"Enchantress. Sorceress." He fixed her with his eyes so that she had to hold back laughter.

They did a line. She found she wanted it. Several, in fact. Latin men. They could be rather—tiring.

Her underpants were on the damp grime of the floor. She stepped out of them with aplomb, leaving them.

Out on the dance floor, the bandstand, the fabulously handsome black man was singing. An angel. A black angel. Ave asked Jorge what the words meant.

"I love you I love you. I love you forever . . . My country I can never leave you . . . I am not in you, my island, but you are in the, in me. Never—never I can leave."

Ave had tears in her eyes. The singer had tears in his eyes. She clapped passionately.

"You like the salsa."

"I like the salsa." She almost choked on a nervous little laugh. He gripped her waist, to which she responded by taking a step away from him, her hands still clasped beneath her rapt face. The angel, as if reeled in by her gaze, stepped off the platform and stood before her. The band started up an instrumental number. She stepped into his arms and they moved off, vertical and formal. At the end of the dance, they let their arms drop. She did not find his attempt to compel with a look laughable. She was compelled.

His name was Dionisio. Dionisio Suelto. Quite famous, as it turned out, actually. In this world new to her. Dionisio. She swooned against him. Against the far wall in the dimness Jorge was watching her, a group forming itself, no, a formation, all with grim looks at her. The woman with the red satin bazongas came forward, her look never wavering, tossing back hair too stiff to follow the motion of her head. Ave stepped back from the angel, Dionisio, and his velvet regard. "Where is Jorge?" said Ave, touching her own sprouting frizz with studied nonchalance. "Hey, chuckles," she said, claiming Jorge with a hand to his shoulder. He looked grim until she touched him. Then he looked as if he were holding back tears. "I'm tired, tired." She laid her head against his quivering chest, checking out Dionisio beneath her lashes. The satin doll was ranting at him in Spanish. Dionisio's face was serene.

"Excuse my wife," he said.

"Your wife is charming," Ave said, the heroine of a war movie. "There's nothing to excuse." Oh, how noble!

Dionisio bowed slightly and returned to the bandstand, immediately setting off a fast number.

"Jorge. You're too much for me, Jorge. Jorge, I have to go home. Come get me a cab, Jorge."

She needn't have instructed him. Latin men were gentlemen. They always saw you home or got you a cab. As she climbed into the cab, more careful than she might have been because of nothing under her short skirt, she pressed a glass vial into Jorge's hand and patted the fist he made around it. Nothing so pitiful as a man who has to try to look stoic, she thought, flipping him a wave as the car started away. Jorge stood on the curb in his shiny shirt, lights catching at the medals.

On the way home she would stop and get takeout. Or she wouldn't. She had no idea if she had been away for hours, or fifteen minutes. She opened the toy pocketbook she carried and took a little snort. Oh, well, Burton. She wasn't going to start worrying about him. If he asked, she'd say she stopped off to see Ella. Ella would back her up. Ella was in no position not to.

16. Where there's smoke

She could smell the smoke, but she couldn't tell where it was coming from. In the pretty flowered nightgown she had made imagining that Frank would someday see her in it, she leaned forward to her knees, letting the covers fall from her. The light was out, of course, but it was always light in the bedroom, in New York, the sky its usual nighttime sickly pink sending in its sick pall through the windows above the thin inadequate curtains she had also stitched together, when she and Stephen moved in. She looked over the top of the curtain. There was the opposite sidewalk, six floors down, the row of buildings and orderly row of city trees lined up in their indifferent, indifferently persisting way under the intermittent penumbras cast by the artificial street-light moons. A vision of still, serene gray, a deserted set, automatically translated into paint by her painter's eye, a gritty De Chirico, a nighttime Hopper, a gray Magritte, an Utrillo—ugh; the kind of painting she was never drawn to do. Since moving in three years before to the rickety if charming tenement, the fear of fire had often haunted her nights—getting out, getting the cats into their carriers, would she try to rescue the pile of sketch pads dating back to the fourth grade that made a kind of record, a diary, of her life? Did the smell come from inside the building or outside?

She lowered her bare feet to the comforting fuzz of the oriental carpet that covered the mungy old boards. Maybe she was just nervous because Stephen wasn't back yet. How odd it was that after all she had returned before him. She should have gone to meet him, however late. But she had been afraid that showing up at that late hour would have damned her more than just going home, where in any case she had expected to find him. Nothing out the south window except the budding tree in the tiny garden of the adjoining house, and the fake gas lamp that flickered, suburban and ludicrous, at its door.

She crossed back to the north windows, to the one in Stephen's miniature study all but filled by the piano and his desk, opened it, and leaned out. Nothing except this newly balmy air that made her want to cry with its softness and her separateness, and all the events of the evening.

A siren sounded, drawing closer, and then others. Its glaring redness invaded the gray, one fire truck rocketed right below on the narrow bending street, sending its crazy beams like the sequined reflector of a dance hall as it fled, zipping around the corner. Well, it couldn't be the building, could it. She would have liked to go out, to find out for sure where the disaster was, but she didn't dare not be home for

Stephen at this point. A sudden chill swept her as she got back under the covers. She huddled into them, listening for Stephen's key in the lock. Still, the smell was awfully strong. She would just be cremated in her bed, she supposed, shutting her eyes but absurdly stiff and tense, like someone feigning sleep.

When the tumbler turned in the lock she had her feet on the floor before fully waking, the muscles of her back still tight. She flew toward the door. "Stephen!" The bristly stiffness of his wool jacket, the coolness of his face as she covered it in kisses; it was his befuddled smile that looked sleepy, his clumsy movements. She felt like a mother with her arms around him. Especially after Frank, he seemed so small. "You're drunk!" Her voice was unreproachful, but high with surprise. His smile got dopier, and in his heavy-lidded eyes she read the theatricality that marred almost all his behavior with exaggeration, turning life into a performance, a hammy one that elicited the inverse effect intended. It was a kind of behavioral hyperbole. She hadn't recognized it when he was acting, intensifying, his love for her in their first year—that, she had been willing to take at face value. But now guilt accomplished some of what hungry egotism had before. He was suffering, all right, but the melodrama made the noble martyrdom of it implausible—it wasn't noble if you went around thrusting your stigmata into people's faces. No matter how much he drank, Stephen never got drunk.

Slurring his words, and in a weak voice, he said, "I kept waiting—I kept ordering beer—you didn't come—hey, waiter—" He mimed gesturing a refill, smiling through sleepy uncoordination with the perfect calculation of a maudlin clown.

How could I have done this to him, Ella thought, as she was supposed to. "I'm sorry. The party went on much longer than I expected." Her stricken look must have been satisfying, and he saw his advantage.

"Must have been some party." He had gotten his jacket off, turned on the kitchen light, and took another beer from the refrigerator, with which he sat heavily at the table in the living room. She sat opposite. It had been some party, horrible. She shivered, got up to get a shawl, and sat again. All she had wanted was to get Frank away, alone, making love to her. He had left her with terrifying, accomplished, famous strangers. He didn't introduce her, however.

"How was Oliver?" She named the pianist Stephen had gone to hear, a well-known jazz musician Stephen had gotten to know over the years, from buying him drinks in one little boîte or another during the pianist's breaks. Ella had said she would meet Stephen there if she got away early enough.

"Oh, he was, he's great. A great guy. Oliver."

"Did he sit with you? During breaks, I mean," she asked, anxious that someone, at least, should have taken her place. "I'm sorry I didn't get there."

"He said, 'Stephen,' he said. 'Stephen, do you suffer from a secret sorrow?' "

She smiled without conviction. He shouldn't be making her play this scene. Yes he should.

"How about that, huh? 'Do you have some secret sorrow.' "

"I'm sorry. There were a bunch of people who wanted to go for drinks afterward—you know." She had frankly told him about the party, including that Frank would be there; but Stephen didn't know what that meant.

He smiled unfocusedly, head weaving.

This couldn't be her. This couldn't be her life. Only the thinnest membrane, growing transparent, separated them both from disaster.

"I waited. I waited and waited. I stayed through every set. I kept waiting for you to come through the door."

She saw the glass door, with its white lace curtain, opening, the sound of the little bell it made, as if it had been she who waited, though she had never been into this particular place, which was new (and would shortly close), though she had at times passed by and looked in. She thought of what she had been wearing, how carefully she had dressed for Frank, the beautiful slip underneath. There was nothing in the whole evening that wasn't tainted by shame. She had worn red shoes. She curled her bare feet around the rungs of the chair.

"I guess I've been home for a while. I thought you would have left. Oh—did you see fire trucks or anything? I can smell this—"

He looked alert and suddenly quite cheerful. "Oh, *yeah,*" he said, the smile now perfectly unfeigned, the voice inflated with the delightful awfulness of what he had to impart, his eyes big with drama. "It's the church."

"St. Luke's?"

"Mm-hmm. You didn't see it? Everyone in the neighborhood's out there. I've never seen so many fire trucks."

"It's not burning *down,*" she said.

"There won't be a stick left. Not a stick. Or brick, I should say." A joke. "The whole thing's gone. They were just trying to keep it from spreading to the other buildings."

"No!"

He laid it on, lit up by her reaction, repeating again how many people were there, how the flames shot up, the spectacle of the fire fighters, the water, the splintering and popping, the asphyxiating smoke, the priest on the sidewalk. "You should have seen it. People were crying."

"I don't blame them," she said, holding her heart. Between her cold hand and thin nightgown, her chest sweated. "I passed by there. On my way home. Everything was fine."

But, actually, it hadn't been.

When she had passed by, she and Frank had been at that stage of silent fury that every couple has where you speak

entirely in symbolic actions, the kind where the woman fee-
bly tries to exercise her power and can be humiliated by the
memory forever after. She had finally gotten him away from
the party, he who claimed to hate parties—had gone ahead
with his friends, the few who had taken her up, to the bar
where he was to meet them, and that was after she had lingered, attempting to look as though she had some reason to,
in the vicinity of the ladies' room of the arts club where the
party was being held, lingered a good half hour, forty minutes, lingered thinking she should go join Stephen, but the
lure of whatever the lure was kept her there, self-conscious
and anxious and irritated, but that wasn't why she was angry
or they were fighting. At the party he had been preoccupied,
been his most determinedly noncognizant of Ella's presence,
while talking to a woman in purple with the thrust-forward
bust of a bowsprit but the head, as if mistakenly attached to
the body, of a grade-school librarian, in harlequin glasses
and hair that could have been carved and painted. Resolutely Frank had not introduced her. His friend in the bar, a
blasé woman who fished in her pocketbook for cigarettes,
said the bowsprit had been a model for Vargas—and so then
Ella knew that this was the woman Frank had thrown over
for her, Ella. Frank had bragged about her, about having a
Vargas model, a calendar pinup; he had been her Thursday
boyfriend: as *Playboy* had a Playmate for each month, she
apparently had a little playmate for each day of the week.
Ella had never been enchanted by the idea of Miss February,
but for the first time some of the repugnance rubbed off on
Frank.

But still that wasn't why they were fighting, though everything went into the stew. As Ella waited in the bar she thought
of Stephen at his bar, or restaurant, waiting for her. It was
ridiculous. It wasn't as if she didn't know it was ridiculous.
But she talked to Frank's friend, or professional acquaintance,
a woman ten or twenty years her senior, naturally, and it

passed through her mind how little she knew Frank, really, how little he knew her, really.

And yet she felt so close to him. She did.

And then Frank appeared and the five of them chatted and the time passed and it got later and she didn't want to drink anyway and the friends weren't particularly alluring though they were nice, and in any case she would never see them again, probably. (The blasé woman had asked if Ella worked at a fashion magazine—"You certainly could," she said, looking at the red shoes. Ella had been absurdly flattered.) She'd never see them, except at professional parties of this kind, occasions only peripherally allied to her profession, insofar as she could be said to have one.

At last they left. "Shall we go to your studio?" Ella smiled up at Frank, leaning in to him. He began his quick step (he walks in chains), head twitching, not answering.

"Now, look," he said in his exasperated way.

"What?" What kind of idiot, fool was she for not knowing something apparently perfectly obvious?

What kind of shit was he for assuming she should know whatever it was that made her question exasperating?

But he was powerful, he had secrets, if she understood them she too would know how to be—oh, whatever it was that she was supposed to be, that she so clearly wasn't. Able to—to be in the world.

He didn't want to go to his studio. Somehow this struck her as funny, the evil seducer of the virtuous housewife, semi-housewife, and yet it was she who couldn't get him to bed. "I promise my intentions are strictly honorable," she teased.

He was not amused. He had disengaged his arm. "We're in a public place," he said.

She threw up both her arms. "Why did you take me to a party where it was perfectly clear you were with me?" He had come in with her, it had been obvious enough she was

the bimbo, not to put too fine a point on it, despite his ne-
glect of her; he liked people to know. Obviously, he liked for
people to know. In fact, at that moment it seemed as if he
liked that better than just being with her.

"Now, don't be a baby," he said. "You're so smart, so brilliant, don't be stupider than you are."

They were walking toward his studio. They walked. "So—
where are we going?"

"I'm taking you home."

She wondered why then they were walking west, but
she—hopefully—said nothing, about that. Then he veered
south, to her very street. Of course really if she were going
home this early, she wouldn't go home, she would go meet
Stephen, several blocks north. They came to a doorway
where Frank had once stopped, pulled her in, pushed her
against the wall, and kissed and kissed her. It was an arched
entryway, lit up yellow in the dark street whose grayness she
would later that night look down at as though it belonged to
another life, as it did. When he had kissed her there she had
been scandalized—right on her street, that was really asking
for it, he wanted to be discovered, and she was thrilled. And
they hadn't been discovered. It was no less rash for her to
kiss him there this night. Stephen might be coming along at
any moment, would pass that way. She pulled at Frank's
coat. Limply he let himself be placed in the hall, where he
had pressed her up against the tiles the other time. This time
he hunched inward. "What?" he said. She reached up to kiss
him. He let her, his thin lips slack. Now she said, "What?"

"You're the one who wanted to kiss."

She stared at him a moment, then walked straight out of
that hallway and down the street. That was when she had
passed the church. She walked up to it and stopped. Frank,
walking behind her, stopped. Not coming too close, as
though she were flammable, would go off like a Chinese
rocket. She had turned southward again, without a glance at

him, her heels noisy on the pavement, practically sending up sparks. She could hear him behind her. She heard him clear his asthmatic throat. She could have recognized him by that telltale sound in a roomful of people. She knew him.

She kept walking.

And he kept walking, ten steps behind. Like a slave, she thought. Only it was clear who the slave was, to her.

Down around Houston he cleared his throat again: "Do you want to go home?" But she kept on walking. In her red shoes, refusing to answer. It was only many months later that she would learn how effective an aphrodisiac her silence and her anger were; but they would be no use to her anyway, even then.

At a certain point in her walking she almost forgot about him, forgot about why she was there or how she came to be: she loved walking. "We're going to get mugged," he said from his ten steps behind. If she had been speaking she might have let him know what contempt she had for his fear, she might have said that these empty streets were empty, there wasn't anyone there to get mugged by. He had been horrified once when she told him she walked there alone at night, coming from her studio, thought nothing of it. She had, actually, felt contempt for him then. Mr. Streetwise! Mr. Dangerous Travel! Mr. I Go Anywhere, I am a Big Brave Man. Big brave pussy, she thought. And it seemed to her she'd never met a man in her life. She hadn't. So with each step she felt stronger and more invincible. And with strength, more ridiculous. She should stop and speak reasonably. She believed in reasonable speech. But she didn't stop. She walked him to her studio. "What's this?" he said, when she stopped at the door and took out her key, but of course she wouldn't answer, and he followed her in, babbling now, angrily, about her unreasonableness; perfectly reasonably, relatively speaking.

Her studio was a rathole, a stinkhole, worse than Frank's

Anna Shapiro

in its way, but in different ways. It was white, well lit, huge, in a secure, not entirely ill-maintained old warehouse, on Laight Street. (Pronounced "light," which Ella liked, a street no one had ever heard of, which was also nice. Except police people: the police stables were there. You heard the horses' hooves on the cobbles.) But this was a studio shared with six people, in unequal shares: Ella had the tiniest, the windowless, the cheapest corner. Like Cinderella, she was not immune to thinking. Her studio in college had been a basement, and her "secret room" in her childhood home, the only place of privacy, had been the earth-floored old coalhole. Her fate was to cook and clean and do her work secretly, in a hole. Her fate was to paint, and show no one her paintings. She had erected screens around her little space, for secrecy, and kept a cloth over whatever canvas was in progress. When she had painted at home, in the bedroom, hers and Stephen's, it was impossible, her pictures had gotten tinier and tinier, useless pathetic things that made her want to kill herself, though the wastefulness of a studio, for her, was painful too.

She switched on the fluorescent lights, which buzzed with a hideous glare, and walked straight back to her corner, noisy heels echoing on the spattered cellophane-covered floor. They passed paintings she half-admired or envied, but mostly she tried not to be too aware of what the others were doing. She swept the tarpaulin from the picture she was working on, which was nearly done. She hadn't known she was going to do this. (But when did she know what she was going to do?) Then she wanted to hide, but it was too late.

Frank collapsed into the only chair, a wobbly piece of metal and leather office furniture found between lumps of snow on the street, which farted on contact. He looked old and gray, or old and green. Ella had experimented with the lights in her corner, trying bulbs advertised as having the light frequency of daylight, but they didn't, and she tried pink bulbs and yellow ones but came back to the glaring white that made everything ghastly but, she thought, honest. If her paintings could survive it, they could survive any scrutiny. Not that there was any to survive. She hadn't let anyone see her work since college, when she had been forced to. Not even Ave, who had always loved it, and kept any scrap of a drawing Ella had ever let her have since she was eleven. She didn't let Cynthia see the work, Cynthia who never judged anyone. She made Ella too tense. Ella would have shown the work to Stephen when it was done. But Stephen didn't want to see it: it made him too tense. In any case, her own scrutiny was the worst.

Frank thrust his fingers under his glasses and rubbed his eyes, so that his glasses stared emptily. Then he pushed them into his face and goggled, mouth open. Then he hummed between his teeth. Ella crunched against the wall in her elegant black coat, very black against the white. She buried her hands inside her elbows. She admired the red of her shoes against the colorful spatters of the floor. She thought the floor was the best painting in the whole room. Frank shot a look at her, as if for guidance, then back at the painting. She would only look at him when he looked at the painting. He didn't look angry at all. He looked—absorbed. Some heavy object shifted treacherously under her diaphragm. She grasped her ribs, through her coat, with all ten fingers.

He said to her averted face, "You only paint sky?"

"You know I've been painting the sky."

"Why?"

She looked up as though she might find it there, on the embossed metal ceiling. "It's always there. Going down a street, when it seems as if there's nothing left of nature— when I can smell a season but there's nothing of it around me except what clothes I should wear—I can look up. I mean, obviously, even the sky in New York—sometimes it's this tiny square, or some horrible weird color from the lights, but—I don't have to explain this to you." Of all people. For the first time she met his look.

"That's right," he said. He looked back at the painting. "Do you want to show me the others?"

She shook her head no. But then while he continued studying the clouds at dusk that she had tried to make as big and palpable as real ones—the canvas stretched all twelve feet of her corridor-like space; when the studio was empty at night she removed the screens and got distance; she was always fighting myopia—she brought out another, all solid cloud, gray, from the kind of overcast day that is like being inside a whale's mouth. Frank smiled, almost laughed, as though recognizing the endearing quirk of a childhood friend. Ella came over and put a hand on his shoulder. She would have liked for him to touch her hand. But his face smoothed out—his "Chinese" look, she had called it when they were first together; happiness, he had said. She bent and kissed the trackless tundra with its few silver strands.

The fluorescents hummed. The cellophane below rattled with every movement. When they left, the paintings of the other six looked like children frozen in mid-tantrum, put under a spell of silence while crying for attention.

She didn't object when Frank went toward the street with the heaviest traffic to raise his hand for a cab. In the backseat he held her tightly around the shoulder. He gave her a quick kiss as the car stopped to let her off at prudent St. Luke's, still not burning. "You're not talented," Frank said, "but you know how to work." Punctuated by the door slamming and the whine of the accelerating motor.

Ella stood in front of the church while the traffic stopped; started; stopped.

And now, as safe, importuning Stephen gloated over the drama of his news, "Do they know how it started?" she asked.

He shrugged. "Something in the wiring or something. Who knows?"

In the bedroom, as Stephen pulled off his shirt, he said, "Are you having an affair?"

Ella, tenting the covers as she backed under them, saw his goofy smile, the kind kids have when they announce an accident or death. The membrane grew transparent. It almost snapped.

"Why do you ask that?" she said, the same stupid smile on her own face.

He shook his head, then disappeared inside the tee shirt he would wear to bed.

As usual, she lay in the crook of his arm until he turned on his side to settle into serious sleep. Kissing good-night first, as they always did; as if they left each other when they dreamed.

Part II

· · · · ·

Such men as these, such selfish cruel men
Hurting what most they love what most loves them,
Never make a mistake when it comes to choosing a woman
To cherish them and be neglected and not think it inhuman.

—Stevie Smith
"Major Macroo"

17. The road grew narrower

The road grew narrower. If Ella had been alone, she would have worried about having taken a wrong turn. What they were on was no more than a double track worn by car wheels. Maple leaves, by this time a full June green, damply thwacked the windshield like green hands as branches swept aside, scratching and wheedling against the metal doors. Ella watched Frank letting a tune through his teeth and squinting, in profile. He shot his clever, prideful face her way, turned back toward the rutted track, reached an arm to pull her toward him on the seat of his old car, and made a throaty animal sound of gratification as she nestled into his harshly grooved neck. But then she had to sit straighter, to see.

The close maple and birch wood gave way to open field on each side, and at once they drew up to a farm barely set back from the road and fronted by two trees with the thickly swollen trunks and beam-like branches of great age. Ella drew in her breath and grabbed her heart. "It's different from what I expected."

Frank took her bags in the courtly manner of a generation that assumed this to be his role, and Ella, in the manner of one accustomed to the ruder treatment of her generation, appreciated it.

"You don't lock the door."

Frank laughed. "Anyone who wants to just breaks in anyway. Then they see there's nothing to take."

But this wasn't true. Ella let her handbag down onto the round oak table, surrounded by its four matching chairs, straight-backed, with decorative scrolls. The walls were covered in a pale green pattern with a border near the ceiling. Still holding her chest and her breath, Ella followed into the next room, where Frank thumped her suitcase next to a double bed whose square oak headboard rose nearly to the wallpaper border. Ella walked over and touched it. "The auctioneer in the town we used to visit when I was a little girl, he once offered some of these as 'good attic pieces.' He started the bidding at a quarter and then said, 'Sold!' as soon as someone raised their hand."

It got the same delighted laugh from Frank that Forrest Lowell had raised from the old auction crowd.

"Let me show you the upstairs." He was already darting forward in his electric, elusive way.

Off a narrow landing, three slope-roofed bedrooms: one, tiny but with a generous dormer window. "Finch's?" Ella asked, her heart hurting.

"Umm-hm."

An instant stab of jealousy caught her off guard. Her heart hurt not because the room was Finch's, or because Finch did not belong to Ella, but because the room didn't.

Beyond the bedrooms was the largest room, a semifinished attic, full of light, containing nothing but a chair, and an easel. It was an antique easel, such as Ella had seen in paintings called "The Artist's Studio"; carved. She turned to Frank almost accusingly.

"My first wife liked to paint." He winced as he spoke, as though remembering the happiness of his first wife were too painful, yet he glowed at the same time: Ella's scrutiny, which could itself be painful to anyone under it, fairly electrified the place. So intensely did she experience these objects that it seemed possible that the physical world could by the eye be possessed.

Which is what an artist does. She looked up, to catch him seeing this in her. He nodded his head as though they had spoken. She went into his arms. "I'm glad you could come," he said as though he had just made up his mind.

"Mmm." She pressed her nose into his shirt. It smelled of soap; underneath, he smelled like a horse. "You smell like a horse."

"Maybe I need to take a bath." He spoke in a low, intimate voice, as though of love. "I haven't been washing as much as I should." He spoke into her hair. She felt each breath, with the whiffs of horse.

"Really, even for me you didn't take a bath?" Her voice was teasing and affectionate, but even so, she felt the risk that he might push her away.

"You think I should fix myself up for you?"

She made a noise into his shirt.

"Hmm? Hmm?" He applied his lips to her hair, hovering and touching down and touching down again. "I didn't think I had to. I feel comfortable with you. I feel comfortable with you." He spoke as though it were a secret. Well, it was, wasn't it. Had to be.

She shook her head into his shirt. Then she said, "But if you want, I'll wash you."

He sucked air between his teeth, and his fingers tightened on the flesh of her hips. Then she felt him shift from an erotic into some other mode. "You're so thin! You were always skinny, but now"—he rubbed his thumbs along her sides—"it's like all the topsoil has washed away."

She laughed to hear the analogy. "Think nothing'll grow?"

"Have you been eating?" he asked in his seductive murmur. "You miss me so much you can't eat, is that it?"

She laughed and rubbed her cheek against his shoulder. "It's true." She hadn't been able to eat for the past few weeks. Since she'd told Stephen. Frank left and she told. The awful feeling, coupled with the look on Stephen's face, that prevented her from being able to eat, came back for the first time since Frank's call summoning her. She clenched the cloth of Frank's shirt in her hands, waiting for it to pass.

"You cold?"

"No. Yes . . ." Ella had splurged on clothes, and everything she had on was new. Culottes had just come back in; skirts were long that year, but somehow, with that dividing panel, it was all right to wear these black, slinky, not-quite-shorts at mid-thigh. A pair of backless sandals made the legs look longer, barer. The top was a negligible garment knitted of string. Her vertebrae showed. It had been hotter in New York, by this time divided from her by more than four hundred miles. But nothing could divide her enough from the mixed images that dwelt in her. That day that she came home with these clothes, in the unaccustomed freshness of their heavy plastic bags looped with coiled pulls and rustling with tissue, she had to try on everything again, pulling the cool, thin cloth over her skin as though it were Frank's gaze. Stephen came home just then. He stood in the bedroom doorway watching her in the mirror, where their eyes met. Stephen's face crumpled. "What?" she had asked, though she knew what. "You look beautiful," he said. He had never said such a thing before. "Other men are going to see you." He had been unable to get the final sounds out. He was unable to speak, and he wasn't exaggerating.

Back downstairs, Frank dropped a wool shirt, heavy as a blanket, around her shoulders. It covered her, the pretty new clothes. She wanted to be covered. "I didn't even realize I was cold."

She leaned in the doorway of the preserved, antique house. "Your mountain. I didn't understand that it was right here." It filled the view horizon to horizon.

"I told you." For a moment he leaned his chin sharply against the top of her head, his weight in his hands on her shoulders. He was so male. Maybe that smell wasn't horse but man. "We'll climb it tomorrow. If you like, we'll climb it tomorrow."

In bed that night, after lovemaking that she could not have admitted was uninspired—he seemed pleased enough, in a tame way—it was she, and not her famous insomniac, who couldn't sleep. It was darker than it gets in the city unless there is a blackout. Afraid of waking Frank by moving, she lay looking into the undefined medium that was the same as the inside of her eyelids. The noises he made with his lips, his nostrils: again he reminded her of a horse. He whiffled and snorted. Ella had to pee.

To get to the chamber pot, she would have to climb over Frank. She would bump into things in the unfamiliar night, and she could imagine the sound of her water hitting—and then, which would be the greater risk: the splashing or, in the morning, the possibility of his being greeted by the stale yellow bowl?

They had never spent any time together. They had never spent more than three hours together. Was this what life with him would be?

If she went outside, there was the grass. Just thinking this brought back to her the long-unconsidered sensation of dew on the bottoms of her feet.

Slowly, as though hoping to escape the notice of a predator, she rolled the cover off her inch by inch. Whiffling erupted by her side; Frank's hand fell heavily upon her. The night seemed to have gotten brighter, or her eyes had adjusted: she could see his face darkly, the turned-down mouth of a child sleeping hard. She resumed. If, once she got her feet free, she slithered directly down to the footboard, she could crawl off the foot of the bed without making much of a disturbance.

She hit a creaky board and stopped. Her skilled fingers found the fuzzy object that was the shirt he had draped over her, which she needed; the night was by this time truly cold and she was, of course, naked. She made her way through the back kitchen, over nasty granules on its sheet of curling linoleum, across the dry mud and hay of an attached shed, and out into the barnyard itself, indistinguishable from the hayfield beyond it after its years of disuse. She made her way toward the small ash tree that nominally separated the two, between a hen coop and splendid barn that in daylight were the unpainted silver of such buildings, and squatted. Small tickling tendrils and cool dew brushed her thighs and buttocks, and the other parts so recently used: it felt sexual. She heard her own spurt of water and felt heat rise. She ripped a knot of stalks with which to clean herself. They made the sound cows and sheep make eating when they tore, which strangely pleased her. Just in front of her the black leaves of the ash flashed to silver, as though a light had gone on. She turned, letting the tails of the wool shirt fall to cover her down to the knee. Behind the humped black mountain a crescent of moon pushed itself up, so white it made the night look clean. I'm happy, she thought; I'm happy!

Pulling the shirt up so it wouldn't get wet, and then pulling it off and bundling it against her middle, she lay in the soft, scratchy bath of chilly dew to greet the moon as though it knew her.

"Are you out there?" Frank's voice called softly.

"The moon, Frank, the moon!"

He stepped out into the night and spoke on two rising notes: "Oh, yeah." She had stood, and he surrounded her shivering shoulders. He tapped her buttock. "Get back into bed," he whispered.

She scampered like a bunny, leaping into the bedclothes, and called his name. For answer she heard his pee hitting the grass, and this pleased her too.

He snuggled with her in the bed, rubbing her back. She became so tight with desire it hurt, but he was not going to come through for her, so she pretended that affection was enough, not opening her lips too much to his soft, thin, un-questing ones.

He had told her that he always got up early because of not being able to sleep, but he no more woke up early than he didn't sleep. She was the one who'd been restless, with lust. "Sleep well?" he asked, nuzzling and tasting here and there.

"Mmm."

"I slept the sleep of the blest. The sleep of the blest." He paused in his kissing. "Want to go to church?"

"*Church?*"

"I thought you liked to sing. Singing the hymns, it's great."

She was thinking of what he'd said in the past when refusing the possibility of her visit, about the neighbors seeing her, about people laughing at his wife. She remembered her rain-dampened plaid stockings and the sweat under her arms as she talked on the phone at work. When he had called the week before, from the pay phone at the little post office, it was in a kind of desperate loneliness that came upon him only in the country, that he had once or twice told her about—so desperate it had a kind of romance, in the telling. Of course she had offered to alleviate it. The miracle was that he had accepted. The miracle was that she was there. She remembered waiting in St. Luke's garden hearing singing from inside. "Sure. I'd love to go." It would be like Blithedale.

He had pancake batter that came ready-made in a wax carton. "I love this," she said as she ate: "real maple syrup from the guy down the road, and—"

He finished, laughing, "I know, they're not even real eggs in here, prob'ly. Pure chemicals. Pure delicious chemicals, yum. S'just a launching pad for syrup and butter anyway." He showed his happy teeth.

It was impossible not to enjoy his pleasure and enthusiasm, like a young boy's. He slurred words together in his rush to get them in before being cheated by asthma.

They would have gone to the church he'd grown up in, the Episcopal, but there were so few congregants that there was scant possibility of choral song. Instead they chose the robust congregation where the plumber and a carpenter who'd worked on the house greeted Frank and explained to their wives who he was—swaggering men with abashed church manners, one wife hawk-eyed and huge in a mint-colored pants suit, the other too busy with a young child to worry who Ella was. Frank introduced her as a former student.

"Oh, a student," said the mint wife. "I didn't know you was a teacher." She grinned. Frank said he sometimes taught, which he—sometimes—did.

Her husband marshaled her into a pew. Frank, hardly bothering to be surreptitious, pressed Ella's hand to the side of his thigh. They gave each other little looks as they sang. "You've got a pretty voice," Frank whispered in Ella's ear, and wore a secret smile throughout the service, lips tightened inward. Also a greenish suit jacket that looked too warm. (There was no mention of her voice being *froglike* as he'd called it on the phone, so that her voice became ugly to her.) Ella wore a full denim skirt that reached past midcalf, and felt conspicuous. There were other women in denim, other men in suit jackets over chinos; but Ella's skirt came from France; even without clothes at all, you could have told from the length and style of their hair that she and Frank were of another class. You could have told from the expressions on their faces, or just from their faces, fed on the healthiest food, their eyesight perfected by the best lenses, their teeth preventively scraped and scrubbed, straight and in place, but above all from their alert, disengaged, well-informed eyes. She was not ashamed to be seen with a married man, but she was ashamed of their unfair advantages.

She even managed to be shamed by her singing voice, trained by Blithedale's choral master ("*from* the diaphragm"), with its rolled *r*'s and extended vowels. She could hear the same training, from his prep school, in Frank's voice. But how impossible not to give in to song—they sank into the music together as if it were sex for tenor and soprano.

> *God works in a mysterious way*
> *His wonders to perform*

The extremes of spirituality and romantic love share the same transcendent nature. It is a transcendence also to be found on mountaintops. They climbed Frank's mountain in the afternoon, after eating sandwiches Frank made with a fish he'd caught, on soft sliced bread, gushing mayonnaise.

Ella said, "You have to let me cook."

"You don't like my sandwiches?"

To her it seemed like an error in taste to use spongy bread and spoonfuls of mayo from the jar. But piggishly delicious. She was eating! She'd been so starved. "I love it," she said, licking mayonnaise from the corner of her lips. She thought of him catching the fish, alone, before she got there. "Are we going to swim in your pond?"

"Um-hmm," he said with that pursed smile that suggested delicious secrets, whose nature she perfectly well knew.

He handed her the big hairy shirt for the hike, saying it would be cold on top of the mountain. By this time wearing shorts and sneakers, she tied it around her waist, wishing he still found her pretty, so that, as he had in the beginning, he exclaimed over it. She supposed her looks had declined, that her surprising rise in looks status was over. Still, hopefully, she had outlined her eyes, pinned her hair up carefully in the afternoon heat.

"Mmmm." Frank made one of his moving and endearing sounds, regarding her with great seriousness. "You're so beautiful. So beautiful." There was always a touch of regret in his voice when he said this, as though he were looking at her through a barrier and she represented something unattainable. As indeed he must think she was. She opened her mouth.

"What?" he murmured.

She held out her foot. "Do you think these shoes'll be all right? I should have brought my hiking boots." On his feet were high-tops whose white parts had turned brown and whose black parts were a different faded dirt color, whose frayed laces were repaired by knots, and which were so worn that even the rubber parts showed rips, like the yellowed underwear he refused to be embarrassed by. "I guess it doesn't matter," she said. She was anxious about the hike, whether any part of it might be too difficult for her limited strength and skills, and whether it would reveal her as, if physically inadequate, then inadequate to be his wife. Though she knew his present wife would no more have climbed the mountain than have gone to church. But his present wife had gotten herself pregnant to marry him. And he hated her.

Sure enough, Ella's loose sneakers were sucked off in the marshy mud in the field leading to the path. Frank, speeding ahead, did not notice. Ella felt saved from shame, slipping her feet back into them and taking quick, skipping steps to catch up—in time for a twig he'd held, to make way for her, to snap instead in her face. As they reached higher but still level ground, the carpet of pine needles made each step require backpedaling on their slippery surface. They wound through a knee-high surf of fern. Frank said how much he loved this part of the path.

Ella thought of a woods she used to know, where she and a friend had a "secret" place of birch and feather fern. Here, peeling cedar made a dark tent over the standard triumvirate fern of the woods, with its brown-spotted intaglioed fingers. The woods looked the same in every direction as far as could be seen, pleasant and monotonous. "It's amazing there are no mosquitoes."

LIFE & LOVE
such as they are

They got to a rockier place where the path started to climb. He was smiling and humming under his breath. She was able to keep up, her feet seeking each rock or packed outcropping his feet left, until they reached an imposing granite face. He scrambled up like a sticky-footed fly and turned to face her below.

"I don't know if I can do this."

"Too scary?" he said in the knowing, loving, murmurous way that so often contradicted the substance of his words.

It did look as if you would have to fall off the mountain if you attempted to cling to the smooth surface.

Frank took a step or two down, holding out a hand.

Ella was studying the rock, a diagonal crease that might offer a foothold where she could, at the same time, grasp the roots of an adjacent scrub pine with her fingers. She held up her palms to indicate that she needed to think and to be left alone.

She did not take Frank's offered hand; the trees were more secure. But her feet slid even as she rose; with pinched silent lips she cursed her smooth-worn rubber soles. There was more smooth rock ahead. She let Frank go on, then handed up the cursed shoes. In her bare feet, like a monkey, she could cling with her toes, and made it to the end of the slabs, where she finally dared to turn and be truly scared by the drop she had negotiated.

She would never be able to get down.

Frank took her hand and sought her distracted mouth. Vigilant about a fall that seemed to her a mere matter of losing her balance, she lost the kiss, the experience swallowed by fear.

"Like spring water," he said.

The countryside spread out far below their feet. "See my house?" Just a corner of roof showed behind the intervening trees.

"It's beautiful," Ella said, conventionally.

"This is nothing. This is just the first view. Wait'll we get to the top."

"This isn't the top?"

The rest of the climb, though steeply uphill, was easy, a matter of twisting packed-earth trail and walking along exposed ridgeline. In a grotto just short of the peak's tip a wooden box was nailed to a tree. Frank opened its door and removed a pad and pencil. They emerged from the trees onto a platter of stone overlooking two lakes and a pond, several other famous peaks across the water, and the intensely green fields of a farm with a red barn, and a red tractor vibrating against the green, several thousand feet below their dangling shoes.

Frank looked to Ella expectantly. "Isn't that something?" he said.

Ella had seen more thrilling views. In particular one with Stephen, at the peak of their love, in the peak of autumn color. "Are you going to take a picture?"

At once his lips curled grimly inward in condemnation.

"It's just that it's so—"

"You know I don't take pictures of, pretty pictures, now, do I?" and he turned upon her a grin of pure yellow-toothed hostility.

Her heart, the freshwater snail, shriveled in the corrosive salt of his displeasure. She looked at her fingers. He didn't even have his camera with him. The famous view floated bluely just past their faces. At any moment a single movement could carry her thousands of feet down to that green field, the red tractor. A wind sprang up. It was still warm. She looked at the view; a gust ripped into her, of homesickness. But the home she was sick for no longer existed.

Frank put his arm around her bare shoulders. "You're oversensitive. You're too sensitive." He said it with concern, as though the hurt came from an impersonal source with which he had nothing to do. She turned her face into the hollow between his shoulder and chest, seeking comfort from the source of her pain.

He began reading from the notebook he had taken from the ranger's box, comments from other hikers, making fun of their bad spelling and prosaic attempts at poetic description. She had never known him to be cruel or critical of ordinary people. She looked sidewise at him, not wanting him to know her thoughts. He was everything out of sympathy with her, and she was out of sympathy with all that he was.

It was revolting, but it was liberating, exhilarating as the mountain peak should have been.

"Do you want to go back the way we came," he asked, "or the other way?"

"Oh, a new way."

"You're scared of those rocks."

"Why repeat what we've already done?"

"I like that way better."

"I'd like to see the other way."

By the time they reached the foot of the mountain, she had resumed her slavery. She granted him the right to judge anyone, and especially to judge her.

As soon as they got to the house he threw skinny pork chops from the supermarket into a skillet. "I never thought of cooking them that way," she said, meaning bare of everything, even seasoning. He practically crowed, expounding on how the cheap cuts were the best. "I cook pork all the time," was all she said, thinking of the thick chops she dredged in flour and slow-cooked with onions and apple, or tomato and garlic.

This unadornedness, which could look so attractive in its austerity, was also unforgiving, cold and ungenerous. Absolute. She felt corrected, as though her desire for sensual gratification were greed. She was reminded of camping trips at Blithedale, often in rain or snow, and the cheery obliviousness of the leaders who were baffled by her shivering (and, as it seemed to her, Jewish) reluctance in the face of what was exulted in as invigorating challenge. She was bad, she was wrong, she was unfit, she knew this. But she would have liked to offer Frank, who was like the spirit of her puritanical boarding school incarnated, the sensual riches she also knew. She didn't accept what was cruel and harsh as a given. Hers was a remedial view.

Outside, plunging her hands in the pans of rainwater in which floated cut-off heads of lettuces, again her perspective shifted. She stooped to pull off the tender leaves, rinsing them and shaking them out. One fat lettuce took the water like a rose. Another, with leaves like arrows, resembled a chrysanthemum, while the third had rabbit-ear petals that looked dipped in blood. The exquisite, jewel-like gorgeousness could be felt on the tongue the way the softness of the water was apparent to her fingers. She was squatting in grass. Birds called around her, their last calls as they settled, and the insect chorus that grew louder at dusk had begun to sound. She knelt by the stone foundations where rainwater collected from the roof. Bits of earth floated harmlessly and sank to the bottom of the pans. Once more she thought of Blithedale, but this time of how much she had wanted to go there, how much she had wanted to fit in, and of how she had believed that it would be like this: that she would leave home for her true home, her spiritual home, where she could burrow into nature like the inoffensive inchworm she removed from the wet leaves.

She bore the filled earthenware bowl back inside, where Frank was pushing the furled gray chops onto paper plates. "I've always wanted to live like this!" she cried, tears standing in her eyes.

Frank was stilled and serious. "My first wife hated this place. Maxine won't even come here." He looked at her. "You're the first—You're the only one—C'mon, eat your food."

There was nothing to put on the beautiful lettuce except dressing that squirted from a bottle as glutinous orange sauce, indeed just like what they'd had at boarding school.

By the end of the week Frank had gone so far as to take a picture in Ella's presence—she'd been allowed to share in the great man's work. It did not occur to her to do so much as sketch. Everything was so mixed!

They left the door open when they ate in the evening, to watch the granite faces of the mountain turn pink in the reflected glow of sunset, sometime after the sun disappeared behind the mountains. As all color faded into the blueing sky, the sound of crickets grew, and a cool smell invaded. Frank shut the door against the chill. Ella lit a kerosene lamp and carried it into the living room to light the other lamps. Without meaning to she noticed a photograph on a table in the living room and turned resolutely away.

"See my picture?" Frank asked coming in. She knew he meant of, not by, him. She turned as though it would never occur to her to snoop on anything in his life, when in fact the very way she listened to him amounted to snooping. He handed her the shot. The low hairline of his youth gave him a rude, Neanderthal look. The lips were pompously pursed, the jaw cocked upward, as though he were daring whoever was looking at him to say he wasn't the best they ever saw. But it wasn't a cocky challenge, it was the surliness of a scared one. He wore the stiff nervous suit of the insecure.

"I hate the person in that picture." She handed it away from her.

"Oh yeah?" He was fascinated, delighted to be so surprised, waiting for the golden insight. She felt raised to a position of unaccustomed authority. He looked at the image on the bending sheet in his hands. "I thought I was handsomer then."

"No! You look—belligerent and supercilious."

He laughed, looking hurt. "You're right. You're right! I was. You're so smart!"

Too pleased by this praise, she said, "I ought to be able to read a picture."

"Smart about human psy-chol-o-gy."

The crickets were muffled by the closed doors and windows, but their dim, rhythmic whir came through as the two people stopped talking and settled onto the pleasantly scratchy striped camp blanket of the studio couch. Ella leaned against Frank, but found she was so aware of him that she couldn't read, and worse, worried that he could tell. This was the eternal other side of being raised up by him, the oppression of having to live up to it. She moved to the brown wing chair, trailing a plaid blanket that unfolded over her legs as she sat. Frank looked up, smiled as though reassured without really seeing, and went back to his book— Benvenuto Cellini. The crickets screeched.

She knew she would have to tell him sometime—she wanted to. She felt like a liar, having kept it back. But here, he had listened to her criticism of him—belligerent and supercilious!—and laughed. She would in any case be giving him a new address, a new phone number, the temporary one care of Cynthia, her own apartment when she found one. He would have to know sometime. And she needed to tell him. She ignored how her need to tell conflicted with her sheer need of him. She battled down her fears. To distrust his reaction was to be disloyal to him.

"I told Stephen," she said to his soft smile and unfocused eyes.

A complex change came over his face. The smile was the same, the eyes the same—that was what was the matter: they had set. "What did you tell your friend?" he said in his whispery, smiling voice.

As if there could be anything but the one thing. It was clear that he didn't want it to be that, however. Panic rose in

Ella's chest. She felt the prick of tears that accompanied revealing herself. "I've been looking for an apartment." The tightness of an inappropriate smile was stuck on her face, but she could do nothing about it. Her leg muscles ached from holding still.

"Are you sure that's the right thing? Are you sure you're doing the right thing?" His voice was soft and murmurous.

The violence of her yes was in proportion to the confusion and terror she felt. For the first time since she'd arrived, the pain that had been held at bay tugged at her internal organs. "I've never lived alone," she said as though this reasonable consideration had governed her decision. As if it were a decision. And how did Frank think she'd been able to spend a week with him? "It's about time I tried it," she said instead of saying that as soon as Stephen knew, she had dreaded to be in the same room with him, and that the sight of him was hateful to her. She did not admit these things to herself.

Frank slumped back against the pillow of bare ticking. Creases appeared in his cheeks as his mouth went grim. "I'm not getting a divorce. I told you in the first place and I'm telling you now." He cut the air with his hand. He spoke very fast, as though there might not be time to get the words out.

"Who's asking you to—?" She wasn't asking, but she had never stopped hoping.

But he already had his back to her as he left the room. She heard the click of a door, and the screaming insects as though someone had turned the volume up before the door clicked again.

The tugging turned to yanking. Gasping wails escaped her as she pawed half-blindly over the tables for Kleenex. It will be fine, she told herself, I'm doing the right thing. I never believed he loved me anyway. That doesn't mean it's not right to leave Stephen: I don't love him anymore, she told herself, meaning Stephen. This more than anything seemed crucial to assert. It had been crucial to say it to him; he wouldn't leave her alone until she said it. I don't love him, I *want* to be alone. And indeed the word "alone" conjured an image of calm and serenity. For a long time she had not known what it was to feel calm. And at this point it was worse than ever, with that tugging inside her, tightening.

The word "alone" also brought on the tears. But after all, it's not as if I love him, she thought, and this time "him" meant Frank. The sobs subsided. She must not let him think that she loved him, that she wanted anything from him. She didn't, she told herself. It would be enough to be— But she didn't dare think the word "alone" again.

In the bathroom she held cold water cupped over her eyes. On a water-stained raw wooden shelf she found a vial labeled *violet essence,* with a violet pictured on it, and dabbed some on each side of her neck. By the time Frank got back, her real feelings were concealed. His manner was angry; she behaved as though she did not notice. "I'm going to bed," she sang out. When he got in beside her, turning away, she pretended not to notice that either. She reached out a hand, touched the softly loose skin, and quickly pulled back.

He was pretending she wasn't there.

In the morning she had a painful red streak on each side of her neck as though she'd been burned. She kept touching the spots. "It was just one of those natural essences." She spoke into silence.

Frank drank without sitting. "Finish your coffee. Hurry up," he said. He rubbed his eyes, revealing the cruel red groove his glasses left on the side of his nose.

At the bus station—a drugstore and the space in front of it, on the short main street—she turned to kiss him goodbye as the bus with NEW YORK showing under its visor farted and lumbered into place, spewing fumes; but Frank, looking thoughtful and preoccupied, growled, "We're in public," and refused his face to her.

18. Cake

The first thing he had done when he'd gotten his latest gig, a Broadway musical, at the beginning of the summer, was hire Cynthia for the pit. Because Burton couldn't have anyone accusing him of nepotism, he warned her that at the theater they could be no more than professional colleagues. As music director he was always up to his ears anyway and would hardly have had time for her. But it only made the looks she gave him—while he was conducting!—all the more awful: secret little half-hopeful smiles. Which he had to pretend not to see. When the show finally opened the week before, after more than a month of previews, he'd half hoped himself: for bad reviews. He'd be out of a job, but he'd be out of at least *that* awful awkwardness. However, it was looking like the show would run. Burton wanted to make things straight with Cynthia, but everything seemed to conspire to make everything more circuitous. Nothing was straight.

Getting to the top of his stairs after the matinee performance he all but staggered into the apartment, which was dim with the shutters closed against the heating sun, and still. Where was Ave? To his surprise, he recognized disappointment in not finding her. Maybe it had begun to seem like a natural appendage, to have some woman or other hanging on to him. He had tried to imagine what it would be like to come home to Cynthia, but received only a blank. He didn't have the kind of imagination that supplied such things, he guessed. Another, uncalled-for picture did appear, however, of Ave's devout face around an anonymous penis. He fell onto the couch as though the image were evidence that a private eye was showing him. She's not leaving *me,* he found himself thinking.

This too was a surprise. All this time—it was January when she had stormed in on him, and here it was July—he had been looking for a way to dump her without destroying her. It should be nothing but a relief if he could catch her playing around. Yet he felt so diminished at the thought that it was inadmissible. He barely had it before it coalesced into another picture, strangely, of him pleading to Cynthia. Yes, he'd be too diminished to take Cynthia on. Because Cynthia needed a strong man. She was going to need shoring up. All his fault, but there it was: she was drinking. She and Francine Weymouth, what an unlikely combination. He'd heard Francine, the show's star, telling a giddy Cynthia in her southern accent that she thought the conductor would be well hung; had Cynthia tried checking it out? Cynthia's answering giggle echoed down a corridor in his mind. Hysterical.

He was glad to be home.

He turned to his old brown pudding of a cat and had a friendly wrestle with her, five fingers against four legs and her eager but careful mouth: when she had him in her grip she looked up, as though checking to make sure he understood whose power he was in, and how, in her queenly way, she was refraining from exercising it.

"O Queenie," he said, "you're a good girl. You're a fine fine fine." And he buried his face in the double fur-and-fat softness of her belly.

Music didn't give him enough. Or women either, he thought; maybe he should work in a zoo, or on one of those game farms. He would happily wake up next to a lion instead of a woman. Or not wake up. There were worse ways to die.

He hadn't realized he was so depressed. He didn't *feel* depressed, but obviously it was there, underneath everything, waiting to swallow him; like Queenie's mouth, just holding back but capable and ready.

If he were with Cynthia at least he could make *her* happy.

For some reason the image this evoked, however, was of her filmiest, laciest underpants. He couldn't make her happy if she made him feel like a bad person. But of course he'd be less likely to feel that way if he were *with* her.

One thing about two-timing is that you inevitably feel less respect—feel contempt, in fact—for your lover for letting herself be used, even though she doesn't know it; for letting herself be duped. For accepting so little. It showed such a lack of self-respect, of healthy selfishness. Sometimes he wanted to say something to her just to restore her in his own eyes. But in a way that was almost eerie, it was as if she prevented him, always sidetracking him at *exactly* the right moment.

The river through the partly opened shutters twinkled with its lubricious winks, its complicitous, serene sparkle; silver, impersonal.

There was the view that these women were taking whatever they could get, however little that was.

Or maybe that was all they wanted of him.

Certainly Ave always looked out for number one. He knew he only knew of her what she wanted him to know.

All at once Queenie passed her point of tolerance for teasing and bit him in earnest.

"Yow!" She looked at him, unmoved. As far as she was concerned, he should have been paying attention and he would have known to stop. She curled her tail to her nose with an annoyed look and humped herself together, shutting the big yellow eyes against him. He would have liked to hit her, but of course he would never. He went to wash off his hand, which was bleeding. You probably couldn't die of a puncture from an animal that never left your apartment. What possible diseases could she carry? She hadn't been outside these two rooms for years, except to go to the vet. Still, holding a tissue to stop the bleeding, Burton went to his *Merck Manual* to see if it would tell him anything useful.

Then, using his bloody hand, he jerked off, thinking of
Cynthia. He could have called her, which might have
cheered her up, but he preferred to fantasize. It was easier.
He was imagining . . . He came with the drooling spurt jerking off invariably yielded, unsatisfying and too soon, and
with the unpleasant gluey aftermath that reminded you of
what you tended to forget in the process, which was that
you were in fact alone with your hand and a sticky Kleenex.
A wounded hand. He noted that he was injured precisely
where Cynthia had a small pink shiny scar, as though she
had transferred some small part of the injury to him.

He turned back to the apartment which was, as usual, a
sty. If he threw down the Kleenex and left it, it would fit
right in. How had he gotten used to this? But maybe it was
good for him, to be a slob. Ave relished calling him anal re-
tentive. He began gathering things from the floor: pairing
shoes; carrying them into the bedroom; folding garments, or
tossing them into the overflowing woven laundry basket in
the corner of the bedroom, whose lid now sat like a hat on
top of the protruding wad. Carrying dirty cups to the sink,
and dumping wobbly aluminum-and-plastic takeout containers, with their pleated corners and bits of lettuce that had
turned transparent and dark, or brittle like seaweed stranded
by the tide. He closed thick fashion magazines and piled
them, stuck bits of paper between pages of books lying face-
down on the rug and stacked them on the magazines; threw
cushions back into order against the wall; until all was looking reasonably dull brown neat and orderly. He didn't look
at the pieces of paper, which bore phone messages, tele-
phone numbers, names of bars and restaurants, and some of
which were receipts, with a scribble of blue ink or numbers
stamped in lavender. Ave, who always carried one of those
automatic cameras with her, must also always ask people to
snap her, he assumed, because there were many pictures of
her, baring a shoulder or vamping, with her lips stuck out

and her cheeks sucked in. Many had a peculiar finish: the cat liked to lick them. Despite the automatic focus, they were fuzzy, or just made surreal by the glare of a flash. Scenes from the loony bin, he thought. He knew she'd gotten into Latin music. It was another thing that made him feel sorry for her. She had no profession; his was music; she had found the one kind of music where she would have no competition from him, since it interested him not at all. But why did she have to compete with him in the first place? For all her talk, he'd never met anyone less musical. Why couldn't she find her own thing? Why did she have to horn in?

For a moment the sun came out of the glaring haze and dazzled the neat, dusty room, hot against his shoulder and across his chest. Then it withdrew.

Downstairs he heard the creak and slam of the outside door, shaking the house. Footsteps up the uneven stairs. Ave burst in, or had the effect of bursting. At least he wasn't slouched on the couch with his pants open. She cast a hooded look around and said, tonelessly, "You've cleaned up. How nice," and dumped a box on the floor. "Look. This fucking coat." She was wearing a metallic raincoat against a thunderstorm that hadn't materialized, and held out a sleeve with a hanging button.

"It can be sewn back on," he said.

She let the coat fall to the floor. "You do it. You're good at that." She stalked to the toilet.

He got the shoe box from the closet in which he kept stray buttons and spools of black, white, and brown thread with a needle stuck through one of them. As he bent to pick up the raincoat, he heard scratching from inside the box, the one Ave had dumped. A grocery carton that said Tropicana. "Ave?"

"Wait a sec."

The scratching was frenzied. Something squeaked. He put his hand on the side of the box. Things knocked around. "Is this a giant Mexican jumping bean?" he said when she emerged, pulling her blouse down under her skirt. She was wearing navy underpants. She revealed herself as unconcernedly as if he were a woman.

"Ha-ha," she said at her most deadpan, the skirt falling into place. She sniffed. She made the kind of sound you make when you have a drink after an ordeal. She made it again, delicately pressing one nostril with her pinkie held out.

Still squatting, he put his hand back to the side of the box, much as someone might feel a pregnant woman's belly. "What is this?"

"Don't touch that. Go sit over there. There. Wait a second. It's—I got a present for us." He thought of the Venus flytrap. He did not feel the cheerful anticipation the word "present" is intended to provoke.

She went to the sink and ran water into a glass, dumped it, filled it again, dumped it, filled it, and drank, leaning against the counter. He knew that if he tried to rush her, or even paid attention, she would slow down further. He rummaged in the shoe box and threaded the needle with brown thread. He began to sew. "You have to promise not to get mad."

"How can I promise that?" He already sounded mad. No, petulant.

She struggled with the flaps of the carton. Four pointed ears immediately surfaced like sharks' fins, and there were piteous cries from two tiny pink mouths.

"Ave."

"Aren't they fabulous? They're pure Angora."

"What are you—?" The two kittens, like spiky puffs of smoke, were scrabbling at the sides of the box. He lifted one onto his hand and up to his face. It dove under his beard, whence a fortissimo purr resounded. The minuscule paws got to work kneading his sweater. "Ave, these kittens aren't old enough to be weaned."

"That's why I took them," she said as though explaining

something to a person impossibly dense. The second kitten was still struggling to leave the box, over which Queenie had quickly come to loom with a horrified, cautious angle to her ears and tail. Then she reared back with a dragon hiss. The kitten subsided, submissive, terrorized. Burton gathered the second kitten to his chest and used his free hand to calm his cat, but she wasn't having any. She moved out of reach and sat looking, lashing her tail.

"Ave."

"Some guy had them in a box on Fourteenth Street. He was torturing them. I had to take them."

Burton considered whether this story might be true.

"I can't have three cats."

"It isn't you, it's us. It's our six-month anniversary present. Anyway, we can give one away. You can find someone in the orchestra, at work."

He wanted to be angry, he found, but unfortunately the suggestion appealed to him, to give Cynthia something so warm and generous that she could not help but love it. It would keep her company. Since he couldn't. He wouldn't have admitted it to Ave, but already he was reluctant to part with either kitten. On the other hand, Queenie looked as if she might swallow them both up like so much dandelion fluff.

"Do you know when they've last eaten?"

"The guy said they could drink from a bowl."

Evidently as practiced a liar as Ave—if what she was reporting was true.

It was perfectly evident that the tiny creatures could not drink from a bowl, which was appropriated in any case by the big cat, who growled. An attempt with a second saucer yielded snortles and chokes and the infinitesimal explosions that pass for sneezes in the cat world.

Burton packed the nurslings into Queenie's carrying case and went to the vet, returning some time later with formula and bottles that looked like the kind that came with Betsy Wetsy, only the nipples were soft. Ave, wearing his brown terrycloth robe, was cross-legged on the bed reading, looking improbably pundit-like in glasses over *The New Republic*. She riffled some pages, saying "What shit," but went on reading.

"I'm leaving the cat with you. Don't let her out." He had to hold Queenie back with his foot, shutting the bedroom door.

The kittens, out of the case, flopped along the floor, their high mews piercing with fear and hunger. He felt it acutely. He cursed every second it took him to mix the formula, heat water, and while waiting for the full bottles to warm. He turned from the utility alcove to stoop to the floor. "Just a second. Just a second, little one." With a terrible squeal, as if he'd squashed it, one of them was lifted to his knee, where it clung. It purred then. It pressed its nose to his shirt, looking for a nipple. "In a minute. Really. *Poverina, poverina*," he sang softly to the notes of an opera. It set the tiny thing crying again, as though song were a cry to answer. At last the bottles were warm enough. He tested the milk on the inside of his arm the way he'd seen women do, his sleeve pushed up on the brawn. "Hey. Hey. C'mere. Yes." He gathered the little balls of fluff, anxiously bony under their fur. "Hey. Yes." It took a moment for them to understand what the bottles were. Then their attack was frantic, scarily muscular and desperate, as though they could not get the substance into their bodies quickly enough. "Hey, whoa." Their sucks were a breathlessly quick clicking. After a minute or so they settled to a slower rhythm. Their paws worked his shirt, pushing, pulling back, pressing systematically, in a way that, on a breast, might help squeeze the milk out. They finished the bottles.

"More? Do you want more?" He did not feel in the least self-conscious talking baby talk, much less to kittens. One of them snorted, sneezed that risible "nff," licked a paw, and—

he was sure this was not his imagination—smiled, a dopey, sated, sleepy look. The double purr rose like a car motor. And then they were asleep in his lap. He stroked them behind the ears with the ends of his fingers. He wondered if he would make a good father. But no human child could be as beautiful as this quiescent wildness. They were gray, but he noted tracings of darker color along the tips of the ears, while the paws were paler, milky, with such small pads they were like pink pearls set in a pattern, exquisite, like a miniature that pierces the heart for its workmanship, its refinement on the apparently cruder original.

Queenie scratched at the door. The kittens slept. He would not move from the couch while they slept. He would have to, quick, get a cab uptown for the evening show. In the meantime, he slept. If he could have, no doubt he would have purred.

19. Eating it

Ave noted the dark tracings of Dionisio's tan lines, the startling whiteness of his nicely but not too fussily cared-for nails, and the pearly luster of his wine penis, now sweetly curled as if in exhausted sleep. In happy satiation herself, she wriggled her hips deeper into a mattress of forgiving softness and easiness, lushness—a refutation of Anglo-Saxon rigidity and limitation. Burton would never have a mattress like that. He would think it was bad for his back; even rest and relaxation had to be good for you, like raw vegetables. The very mattresses of Dionisio's life said *feel good, enjoy*— never mind that it was the hotel's mattress. Who else could have found a hotel like this, with red satin curtains and a painting on the wall that—she had to laugh. The painting showed a woman with dark willing eyes and a big cross set between truly startling garbanzos, like goiters. The bed, it might be added, was in the shape of a heart. Only the best for l'Ave mía, he had said, or words to that effect. She did laugh, for the sheer pleasure of it. Oh, to be treated like a woman! None of the rest mattered. She felt like a soft pillow herself, to be plunged into, wallowed in, for pleasure.

Of course, there could be too much of a good thing. These guys always had to prove it, manhood. But that was all right. At least they could.

At the moment she liked everything about him, especially asleep. The fuzzy little clumps of hair dotting his chest like the boluses of wool that collect along the sides of sweaters, and a second plantation of the same around that discreetly vivid wang.

She flipped to her tum and pulled at a prickle in the pillow. It expanded under her fingers as a white puff of down, so soft it almost couldn't be felt. She looked down at her breasts, pointed and perfect, and thought, Thank you, God. She brushed the puff of down across the tip of Dionisio's unpointed and perfect nose. He snorted and pawed at it as at an insect, without waking. She let it drift into the pubic plantation, white and soft among the firm clumps of black. She lifted his penis in her palm. It was warm; it had weight. But almost immediately it became lighter, losing gravity as it gained volume, until it waved, straight up, like an alert animal looking for its burrow. Such a friendly creature. She ran one finger from the base to the tip of the nether side, and this time there was a convulsion, all of Dionisio awoke at once and without even fully opening his eyes he was on top of and inside her. This struck her as almost rude, in a comic way, and she said, "Hi, I'm glad to see you too." But he grabbed both her breasts and went right on. He was kind of a terrible lover, by conventional standards, but it didn't seem to matter, she was so turned on by him and came, even several times, sometimes just at his entering. The fact that he came very very quickly seemed a proof of her magnetic power. He just couldn't help himself. Really, for a man to control himself is a kind of insult, a refusal to give himself over, indifference, even. Though the worst was the kind of man who went on and on and on, like punishment.

They came together. "Tú es demasiado," he said, falling on her, rolling her on top of him, and yelping as he sometimes did in certain songs, making them *filthy* when the words themselves might have been innocent. She spoke a phrase from one of his songs that had taken on special meaning for her, partly because he had looked directly into her eyes as he had sung it. Feeling his long fingers along her back she imagined their blackness against her extreme whiteness, and liked to think they could leave a mark, like charcoal. Of course, when she was apart from him, there was nothing of him left with her, nothing that could be, and this was a sadness. She respected his wife. She understood the code here: men were expected to cheat, but if the wife caught the other woman, the betrayed wife would bloody your eyes, defile you in public, exert her considerable strength. Rosalía had about a hundred pounds on Ave, Ave figured. Ave was very respectful. As is usual in such cases, she felt, because she was the one who knew about the wife but the wife couldn't know about her, that she was the one who was really loved. She would have said, however, that she was under no such illusion: Ave always knew the score, she didn't kid herself, she was too smart to be hurt; that it was the wife who was truly loved because she had the official position, and because the wife was the one who would last.

But a woman fucking a married man never believes that the wife is the one who is going to last. And she is always—almost always—wrong.

Dionisio was between sets. They had to go back to the club separately, or at least enter it that way. Ave took her time getting dressed. Dionisio wanted to send a car for her. He insisted. She exulted in the people who knew she was with him, and in having the secret, and in all the ironies in between. The man at the desk, for instance, knew; he would have to. And there was no point in Dionisio's using a false name, he was too well known, he was famous; in certain circles. The man greeted her with great correctness; she might be a bimbo, but the bimbo of a star was, at the least, a star bimbo, was she not. Touched by greatness. At the club—it was only a few blocks away, it was ridiculous, using a car, although maybe not; she might not have survived the walk, in those shoes, in that outfit, at that hour—the members of the band were in the know, were active collaborators. One of them, Virgilio, was the official pretend boyfriend. "Avelita," he greeted her, "querida."

"Mm mm mmm." She pursed her lips to the maximum and made ostentatious kissy noises on his cheek.

"Buenas, Señora Suelto." Ave all but curtsied to Rosalía, who presided at a forward table, in yellow satin, wearing a glittering brooch that seemed to anchor the dangerous rockets of her breasts. She didn't always come to the club, she could no doubt do without seeing her husband's performances, in every sense—but then again, she liked to hang out, she was touched by greatness (was she not a star wife?), and there was the question of keeping an eye on her gorgeous husband, much good though it did her. So she could look. That was about it. Well. Not quite.

"Buenas noches, señorita," said the self-possessed wife, flexing the rockets. The tightness of the satin on her superabundant flesh had the effect not of padding but armor. She made the word "señorita" sound so diminutive as to be degrading. Ave could only hope that her own polite "señora" had made Rosalía feel fifty. She certainly looked it. No, no, she was above such pettiness. Rosalía was entitled to whatever she needed. Ave, after all, had so much more going for her. Beauty, intelligence, charm, talent, youth . . . All that cunt had was a secure marriage to someone rich, famous, and fabulous and three adorable children—nothing but a *housewife.*

Rosalía, if she hung out at all, often brought the children, or the baby, who was three. Ave strongly disapproved. Children shouldn't stay up so late. So what if it was part of Latin culture, how were they supposed to get up for school in the morning? And she didn't think a bar was a salubrious environment for a three-year-old. Little Dolores, Lola, was sitting on top of the bar attended by rowdy musicians and hangers-on, pouring sugar from a dispenser onto the counter and making patterns in it.

Ave said that Rosalía had a beautiful daughter, in Spanish. Rosalía responded with a skeptically hooded look. But it was followed by a fond look at the child. "Lolita," she said in a carrying voice. Lola held up her arms to be lifted down and ran on wobbly legs to bury her forehead in her mother's tight lap, Rosalía's hand possessively on her shoulder. The child said something in incomprehensible Spanish. It might have been incomprehensible English, for all Ave knew. "El gatito? El minino?" said Señora Suelto. The little girl strenuously nodded her head.

All the while Ave could feel Dionisio's presence like something hot, like sun, like a spotlight, all down that side of her that faced the stage, even though he wasn't yet on it, the little raised disk with a microphone and trap set. He would be in the area; the heat was the heat of his gaze. He must be looking at her.

"Kittens?" said Ave. "You have kittens at home?" Ave could say some things in Spanish; rarely could she understand what was being spoken.

The little girl smiled and smacked her palm to her lips.

"No," she said protestingly, correctively, "aquí."

Ave smirked; her golden dress sparkled along her undulating lines as she turned: wasn't the child cute. Wasn't she wonderful with the brat. She turned back. "Dónde estan?"

Lola pointed toward the bar. Rosalía, by this time showing a grudging pride in her brilliant offspring, indicated that Ave should follow the child to the bar. The barman brought the carton up from behind the bar, and there were the kittens, pure Angora, as everybody kept saying. Where was the kittens' mother, Ave asked, la gata, la madre, but she only raised laughs, and someone made a remark in which she caught words that might have been "with the rest of the loot"—or maybe they were only Spanish words that sounded, to an ear eager for English, for sense, like that. Lola made to lift one of the kittens. "No!" Ave said in a sharp voice that startled everyone and brought tears to the little child's eyes. "They're much too young to handle." Lola went wailing back to her mother, whose face settled in the folds of a lizard that has just caught a fly at the end of its tongue.

The band started up. Ave was given another forward table, by herself. If Dionisio's imagined stare had felt like sun, his wife's felt like double bullets to her exposed shoulder blades. She sipped self-consciously at wine she didn't want; she never drank. The first number was loud and fast. She would have liked to dance. Dionisio prefaced the second with an announcement that caught her off guard: "We would like to dedicate this song to a beautiful young woman honoring us tonight with her presence—Mees Ave O'Shownessy." And he bowed slightly formally; the official pretend boyfriend, a trumpeter, shook his shoulders at her, pursed his lips, and blew her an ostentatious kiss.

Ave was not used, ever, to feeling embarrassed or self-conscious. What she felt above all was exposed.

A waiter came over to her table with a note scribbled on the back of a bar check: "Join us." Ave turned to wonder who could possibly be asking. Rosalía gestured to her with the peremptoriness of a fortune-teller in a store window. Ave took her glass over to the crowded table, where she was introduced to the women—girlfriends, sisters, aunts, who knew?—and an indifferent man with a white mustache and striped paunch, who leaned his wrists in front of him on a cane. Lola was limp in an aunt's lap. "How does she sleep through this?" said Ave, too ready to be friendly. Rosalía's smile could have kept a meat locker in business, it was so cold. She shrugged elaborately, arms spread, her eyelids as colorful as butterfly wings.

During the break Ave could escape to the official pretend boyfriend; while he threw his arm around her unnecessarily and so on and so on, she nibbled with her eyes on her god. The o.p.b. had little English. But it seemed to emerge that he was the custodian of the kittens. Once again Ave tried to find out why they weren't with their mother—they could barely be four weeks old, and she had grown up with cats, she assured him, she was an expert at these things, *autoridad*— but when her words were translated, once again they were met with laughs. Someone said Virgilio would sell her the animals if she was so interested; he was supposed to be selling them for a pal of his. This was not satisfactory, but the break was ending, and Ave was compelled to rejoin her nemesis. She was escorted by the o.p.b., as though a woman could not get from one table to another without assistance; she forgot that she would have liked this if it had been Dionisio. Virgilio seemed to have quite a lot to say to Rosalía, who seemed pleased to hear it. It only struck Ave at this moment what a lowlife he was, and how unlikely that he would consort with La Reina—much less with herself. How awful if they were all thinking that this was *appropriate*. Virgilio looked like someone who would have a pal for whom he sold things, if he didn't steal them himself.

Not that she had anything against stealing. And Virgilio

was a customer. He needed money for blow.

Ave decided she had to leave. There had been a chance that she might be able to see Dionisio for a very short time after the gig, but she would pass it up. This wasn't worth it. She would say she wasn't feeling well. She wasn't.

"But if you are feeling bad, you must not leave," said Rosalía, taking charge, demanding symptoms, offering cures like putting a raw egg under the bed.

"No no no, really, I—" Ave felt as if she would really throw up, or pass out. The loudness of the music was suddenly not so much exciting as it was like the thrum of a ship's engines, in her stomach.

"I must give you something." Rosalía's English was excellent, with musical alien intonations. "Los gatitos! You like those kittens." She listened to Ave's protests over this no more than over anything else. She would not take no for an answer. She was not going to get hurt. She knew the score. "From our own darling mother cat in our home for a beautiful young lady who is an *autoridad.*" In fact, Rosalía and Ave were roughly of an age. "My Lolita would want you to be the one to have these little ones." Rosalía's eyes glittered.

The best Ave could manage was not to have to take them home right then. How could she have explained that? No doubt she would have managed. Maybe the wretched things would die by morning and she wouldn't have them to deal with.

It happened that Jorge was there. The little counterman was not so friendly anymore. He had to be prevailed upon with bribes to have the animals at the diner in the morning for Ave to retrieve. Everyone had to promise and swear in front of La Señora to get the animals where she intended them to go. As Ave bartered with a Jorge very much on his dignity, every other word sarcastic, despite an entire free gram, she saw Rosalía hand Virgilio something. Possibly money. For those darling gatitos from her happy home, her gift of the heart. Those hideous little creatures in the box, shitting and mewing and climbing on each other and toppling; that fat hideous creature like a big happy frog. The whole episode was sordid and bestial in the extreme. Sordid and bestial.

Maybe the wretched things would die by morning. But of course they didn't, allowing Ave to bring them home to Burton like a social disease.

20. Orgasms never saved anybody's life

Cynthia wasn't sure if the kitten woke her, or if she only became aware of its tickling whiskers and the soft hot quiver of its mass against her cheek as a result of waking. She stayed still, so that the kitten wouldn't be disturbed, but it seemed to sense her attention and turned its tiny head and oversize ears to rivet blue eyes on hers. She had to laugh. The kitten cried, then purred almost inside the cry. Cynthia found that if she voiced nonsense syllables in a very high voice, the kitten cried in answer each time, but only purred louder, getting agitated and butting its head against her chin.

She was completely charmed. She hadn't meant to have a cat, but now that she'd given in to it, she couldn't help falling in love.

The kitten, too early deprived of its mother, and despite Burton's efforts with the nursing bottle, still needed some form of breast or nip and took the ribbon of Cynthia's nightgown into its mouth, kneading its paws against her chest. Burton had waited till the kitten was a good two months, by all indicators, but it was still small enough so that Cynthia could support it with one hand as she sat up. It was smaller than her breasts. Distracted by the movement, it began to play with the ribbon as though the ribbon were prey. Its little needles easily pierced the cloth of the gown, but it was hard to mind. This must be how mothers felt, Cynthia thought; you just don't mind whatever. Shit smells, drool, being stepped on like a log or mattress: it all turns into love. Though somehow Cynthia couldn't imagine her own starchy mother not minding. Her mother would have expected one to behave *well*.

Burton said that for a while the kitten had used his bed for a toilet, so that he had had to keep the bed covered with plastic, finding little pools and poops when he came in. She would have minded that. But maybe not.

What she minded was the thought of his bed at all. Not that she *minded;* what she minded was not being in it, ever. Ella had told her recently that Ave was off in the Dominican Republic for some reason (Cynthia remembered an awful family vacation there; but they had all been awful). Comments about Ave were not infrequent in Ella's conversations, but she seldom mentioned Burton, whether out of tact or simply because he was more Stephen's friend, Cynthia did not know. But Cynthia felt saved from contact with a reality she tried never to remember. She had never threatened the complacent surface of her dubious romance with Burton by so much as suggesting that they go to his place, about which he had embarrassedly once volunteered, apropos of absolutely nothing, that it was really crummy and she would never want to see him again if she knew how he lived. Which ought to have been true, considering that how he lived was with Ave.

Knowing his address, Cynthia had once wandered by to feel the tug of its romantic isolation and dilapidation—the lone house that was still standing on that stretch of the river, with a willow in a tangled side yard, out of time, out of place, so special and eccentric it couldn't have been more poetically tailored for its inhabitant, one of them at least; and for herself, who would never get to live there, probably; or even, at this rate, see it from the inside.

But—she had felt such a rush of hope, hearing that that bitch was off somewhere without him; surely . . . It seemed to Cynthia that surely it was the beginning of the end of Ave's reign, or maybe it was the end? Ave couldn't love him. They were all wrong for each other. Though Ave probably had orgasms by the truckload. Maybe men didn't really care about that, one way or the other, for all that some of them practically tried to force you to come. Well, orgasms never saved anybody's life.

The kitten was climbing into her nightgown. Cynthia tried to pull her out but she clung, and this time Cynthia did mind. The kitten got its way, though: Cynthia let go, and the little creature pressed on, toward her armpit for some reason, where it chose to lick with its ratchety tongue. Cynthia's yelps at being so tickled accomplished what pulling had not. The kitten made its way down the length of Cynthia's body to get lost under the bedclothes, where it gave a pitiful mew.

It had been awfully bold of Burton to present her with a cat. It wasn't like giving someone clothes or records or even a plant. It was appropriative. She liked that. She liked that he felt he had a right to her, could be just a little high-handed, because if such a basically good and unassuming person felt that, then he must feel her almost a part of himself; and giving her something living like this, well, it wasn't like having a baby with someone, but it wasn't entirely unlike having a baby with someone. That is, it was like some part of him living with her, a part he could detach. And certainly a loving and dependent part: the kitten kneaded and purred, rubbed its head against her skin, had to be in contact with her, responded to her movements and sounds, if with the generic limitations of its species. But anything it wanted of her, she could easily give, in which it had an advantage over lovers.

Cynthia looked over at the jug on her night table. There was still some wine in it. It seemed too far to reach, but her head, she knew, would feel better if she drank it. Her head felt oddly swollen, as if the skull were too small for what had to fit into it. She was getting used to waking up this way, and a quick drink took care of it pretty well. And it was so much easier than the drill of making breakfast. She thought back on that with the contempt-edged indulgence with which one regards one's younger, more ignorant self. All that unnecessary business with measuring out coffee, heating water, messing around with bread or cereal or fruit, or even if you went out, having to get dressed when you were barely awake, not feeling ready for the day.

Though when did she, really, feel ready.

During Ella's intermittent residence as a peripatetic apartment seeker, Ella made the coffee. Ella was into granola and grinding your own beans. And Ella *said* she could barely function in the morning. Though actually—Cynthia's brain was in better working order than it had been lately; maybe having this little beast around focused it—Cynthia had never been sluggish or bad tempered or in general found it difficult to rise out of sleep until she had started drinking to get to sleep, or at least started falling asleep drinking. Not that there hadn't been that period when she couldn't get out of bed at all, but she was just a baby then, that had nothing to do with now. Or with drinking, of course.

It even made practicing easier. She rather liked reeling around the living room with her violin under her chin.

She reached for the bottle and settled back with a grunt, snuggling into the sheets and taking a slug. Oh, what a relief! In a funny way, she never really realized how much she wanted it until she had it—how dry her mouth was, for one thing, which seemed really funny when you thought about it, since what made her dry was *drinking*.

At the same time, the taste, the fumes first thing, were sour, sharp, pushed one away, were something to be overcome. But were overcome. After a slug or two, it began to taste good, and with enough of them, she might feel inclined to get out of bed. Or if not, it wouldn't matter. It would feel as if it didn't matter; and maybe it didn't. What mattered was not to feel so terrible. Whatever you did.

Though the most terrible moments of the day were before those first slugs, when you remembered what you had been doing, when you thought, well, today I won't have to do that. But she had to. And today there had been this wonderful kitten to distract her; she hadn't had to feel too bad about the night before.

Though actually she'd had a *fine* time the night before, perfectly okay, fun. Francine, bitchy star though she was, had spotted the big jug Cynthia was lugging, well, swigging from in the stage-door alley and invited her to her dressing room, of all things, to share it, "Not that I can't get my own, honey, but one isn't always so blessedly foresighted." It was rumored backstage that there was nothing Francine wouldn't put inside her body, one way and another. So look at that, Cynthia had thought; obviously it didn't hurt to do what she was doing. You could do this and be a star. You could do this and not have anyone notice. Burton, who stopped a whole orchestra when one unfortunate flutist was off by a halftone or a tympanist wrong by one sixty-fourth of a beat, Burton didn't notice anything off with Cynthia lately. (Too busy getting off.) Oh, he had been so wonderful, coming over yesterday with the kitty.

She had come to recognize his step on the stairs. Not that she hadn't known he was coming over, he called first, and she had just buzzed him in. But it was kind of a thrill, a thrill of fear when she heard that sound, as distinct to her evidently as the precise rhythms Burton ruled over as a conductor. She couldn't tell why she recognized it, but she never mistook her male neighbor's tramping feet for Burton's, even when it happened that the neighbor came home just when Burton was expected. It was so personal to know someone's sound that way. And there had been something slightly different about it yesterday, and she had seen at once that it was because of what he was carrying, which he had not warned her about.

They had kissed with big smiles. "What's in the box?" she had asked, afraid to be quite sure that it was for her, but feeling it was, feeling rich because she had a lover who brought her a present. And inside the box, funnily enough, was a carrying case—"I wanted to surprise you," he said—and peering out from the mesh front, the extraordinarily beautiful toylike face of this small wild animal, marked as if by an artist, an ancient Chinese painter, for decoration, for the purely frivolous delight of the human eye. And the little animal appeared to be about delight. It played with the torn strips of newspaper with which Burton had considerately and prudently lined the case; it ran and sniffed and plopped into one's lap with perfect trust, as if its own pleasure could not be distinct from yours. "Does it have a name?" she asked.

"Oh no," said Burton. "I wouldn't do that. That's up to you." He had his warm hand around her shoulder. She loved the soft warm feel of his flesh through his shirt too, where she had her own fingers circling what are famously and she thought quite correctly called love handles. She looked from the puff of incarnate smoke, whose sleeping belly like a small round bellows expanded and sank in her lap, and up to Burton looming next to her, his neck pulsing between beard and collar. She pushed the top of her head into his neck like a cat. As if she were a cat, he rubbed his big warm fingers behind her ears.

"This is perfect, Burton. I won't get lonely in bed." This was just the kind of remark he hated, she could see it, and she always pulled back immediately, watching his fear and relief. It was the fear and relief that made her feel malicious, so that, sooner or later, she prodded the sore spot once more.

She held a hand protectively over the kitten, wanting to pet it, afraid to wake it up. It made an adjustment in its position, curling its paws more tightly to its nose.

"I was afraid you wouldn't want it. I would have taken it back if you hadn't. I mean, I wouldn't want you to feel like you had—"

"This is the best present anyone ever gave me. Alive! I always wanted a pet. I'd sort of forgotten I wanted one. I completely forgot. It was something I'd promised myself when I grew up."

"Oh, no wonder," he said, and their faces both pulled into wry suppressed smiles in recognition of being supposed to have grown up.

"Or maybe it's that when you grow up—" she began. "You're so disloyal to your childhood wishes when you grow up. Not just sort of silly ones like this—you know what I mean—but sort of important things. Did you make those kind of promises when you were little, like never to say something mean about someone behind their back, or that you would never ever hit a kid, or that—you just believed that you could always do exactly what you set out to do, that you *could*, that people who didn't were somehow letting down the side."

Cynthia thought about a certain exalted moment when, very young, she had stood on a hillside commanding houses dotted along thin white roads and huge sky. She had felt intensely, just then, what it was to be her, precisely, specifically, and how that blended in with the hill and the sky. "That you would just be faithful to a certain feeling that was maybe very hard for you to recapture but that you felt it was really important to remember . . ."

"It's uncanny. I mean, I shouldn't say it's uncanny, I should be used to this with you, but—yes. I've thought exactly those things and exactly that about being disloyal to them. It's like adult life—instead of becoming more who you are, growing up means being unfaithful to yourself, renouncing the most real things. Do you think other people are just better at forgetting?"

Cynthia couldn't help a sharp look, to see if the other people he was thinking of were Ave. "It doesn't seem fair to say so."

"Yeah, but being fair is one of those things. You know, that kids see the importance of but truly adult types throw up their hands over. You know, 'Nobody said it was meant to be fair.'"

"I guess loyalty is one of those things itself." Cynthia didn't quite intend it pointedly. "Well," she said, directing their attention back to the sleeping gift, "she'll never have to know about any of it, will she."

"Oh." Burton got up. It turned out there was more to his present. From the box he brought out several gift-wrapped packages. "I wanted to put a ribbon on the kitten, but they really hate that."

The first package, in paper with pastel bunnies and lavender ribbon, sounded like a maraca when shaken, and proved to contain a box of dry cat food for kittens. The second, heavier, held two earthenware bowls painted blue inside. "These I don't have to open," said Cynthia of the two cylindrical packages, "unless the flavors are *really* strange." Poultry Platter and Prime Entree.

"Fish isn't supposed to be good for cats," Burton told her. "Did you know?"

"No."

A violet envelope held the vet's paper certifying that Kitten Shumlin had had its shots.

"It was really sweet of you to wrap all this stuff this way," she said, unwinding the last of the tissue paper from a rabbit's foot, a packet of foam balls, and a catnip mouse. The kitten was playing, manic, with the wrappings. Even as Cynthia unwrapped the mouse she had the most absurd hope that the tissue would contain, oh, anything for her. What was I expecting, she thought, pearls from Tiffany's? But she would have been very happy with a Woolworth's diamond. "And, all this stuff, on top of the kitten. It's, uh, overwhelming." She had been happy about the kitten. Why was more less?

"I should have gotten something just for you," he said, taking her hand.

"No you shouldn't." She kept her eyes to the floor.

He held her hand with both of his, kissed the meaty pad of her thumb. "Yes. Yes."

"But it's tons of stuff for me."

"The kitten is for you, but—"

"The other stuff, it's incredibly considerate. Maybe there are favors in the Friskies. You know, like the ones in Wheaties?"

They kissed on the floor, on the rug, while the kitten thrashed through the colorful detritus or cried when it got itself into a spot it didn't see how to get out of. They smiled at the noises, in between kisses. Burton began to move down, to kiss her breasts, his hands exploring into the tight waist of her pants, giving up and clutching at flesh through denim. It was always like this, as though the sex were accidental, and then just something he had to have.

"Wait. Stop. Wait."

"Are you all right?" he asked, his hand inside her shirt on her bare midriff.

"Um-hmm. I think so." Her upside-down eyes were nevertheless still cast down, as so often, with so many people. "Could we—would you still come and see me if we didn't have sex?"

"Of course I would, I'm nuts about you, isn't that obvious?" he said so quickly that in the flutter of panic and dizziness that followed, it was hard to tell if it wasn't those things that had made him say the words in the first place.

He fell to his back as though all the air had gone out of him, fist to forehead. "I can't believe I said that."

"You didn't mean it," said Cynthia's resigned little voice.

"Oh God"—he was hovering over her again—"of *course* I meant it, are you kidding, you just don't, I'd like to—Cynthia—"

Their similarly grayish-blue eyes traded secrets, mysteries, with inarticulate urgency. "What?" He was about to say it, to admit it . . .

"It's just that—it's not as if anything can change. I'd like—"

Panic and an almost equally terrifying euphoria fought in her chest. "Don't say anything," she said. "Don't say anything." He lay on the floor like someone who'd been shot, his arms up, in a position of surrender. She parted the frontward tails of his blue shirt and pressed her mouth wetly to his fleshy furred belly button. Unbuttoning, she worked her way upward to his throat, kissing the bristling forest as she went, and then working back, letting each pale, negligible nipple harden between her lips—male nipples, useless things, men didn't even like you to touch them, but who could resist, or keep from hoping?—down to the cruel belt, which she undid, all the hardware below which men conceal themselves, all the metal of heavy zipper, metal button, buckle, the slight dampness of the overheated area where she engorged engorgèd him. She was practiced at blowjobs. Women who can't come, like impotent men, are frequently expert in the strategies that call on their potential strengths and call nothing into question. Oh, she was very good at this. And had little occasion to practice on overeager Burton.

"Oh. Oh," he said, or sounds vaguely approximating that, one hand spasmodically clutching and releasing her head, her back.

His penis was a beautiful even pink that matched his balls, under this treatment firmly tightened in their pouches and roiling under the skin, ginger blond hairs moving like spider's legs. Cynthia ran her tongue along the underside of the shaft from base to tip. Some men loved this, some didn't. She teased his balls with her fingertips. She moved her mouth up and down on him and she held it still, moving her tongue and sucking. She tasted salt. He seemed to like everything.

But unlike many men (and there had been an awful lot), he didn't forget her in selfish ecstasy. He reached down and spun her big nipples in his fingers. Of all things, it was Cynthia's nipples—that and kissing—that turned her on. Unlike anything at all done to her far-away crotch, which always made her feel manipulated and alien and objectlike, absent. But this was—this was—awfully— She began to feel weak, and the urgency between her legs, in her very center, hotwired to those nipples, was absolute, so that for once she actually wanted the wet sticky firm thing there. And put it there. Burton let out a terrific groan. But after a second she realized it was all right, it wasn't a complaint.

Men had tried putting her on top—plenty of times—but then they always moved her hips with their hands as they would a doll. But Burton left her free, still busy with her breasts. She pressed down, following the elusive liquid heat, which to her surprise increased when Burton moved inside her, and now she groaned, feeling too weak to go on in that way. But she had to. She moved back against him as he moved up into her. My God, no wonder people wanted to do this all the time! Why do I ever do anything else, she wondered. Something black and hot filled her head, her whole consciousness, what was left of it. And then—plink— the enormous sensation ended. She pressed against him some more and felt it ebb back slightly. But it was over.

Was that coming? Was that all it was? But then again—she felt quite . . . quite *amazing*.

"Oh. Oh." She found she was laughing, and he was laughing with her. He kissed her ferociously. He knew. And knew enough not to ruin it by saying anything. Almost. "You?—" was the only word, and "Yes," she said amid her laughter, and he hugged her very hard. And stayed inside her which, oddly enough, she always wanted men to do—their penises were so friendly then—but which men so seldom, incomprehensibly enough, wanted to do, after all that incredible eagerness to get in there, all that striving. They were not content to rest inside her, as though, having gotten what they needed, they didn't like being in there at all.

Then Burton made a terrible face. He looked as though he were in intense pain. He reached around behind him and produced—the kitten. "Little shtunky," he said. It stared at him gravely with *its* gray-blue eyes. "Now it will really look as though I've been making passionate love." He caught himself. "Not that there's anyone to care."

"I care," said Cynthia, soothingly. "And we have been, haven't we."

He kissed her. He called her darling. And then they did disengage, still touching. Cynthia propped herself on an elbow, looked at his face, full of riches, and shyly away. "Do you think—could I spend the night at your house? I promise not to look at stuff. Or you could come here." Ave was, after all, away. She knew he *could* do it.

But it seemed he didn't want to.

Maybe he was worried about phone calls he would get, or phone calls he would not be there to receive.

But so what? And wasn't that what answering machines were for? Or rather, in his case, his service. He used a phone service; which certainly made her messages safer, perfectly empty and dull. Anyway, he was nuts about her. What did he care what *Ave*—? But this was like the presents all over again, *more* weirdly turning into *less*, or at least something more painful than nothing at all.

He was nice to her at the show—God knew, it was awkward enough, being a pit musician in a show where your boyfriend was the conductor, and on top of that, wasn't publicly your boyfriend. There was one fuzzily bearded clandestine kiss. But he had left in his usual crisp fashion, instantly after the show, without so much as offering to share a cab. It wasn't as if it were compromising to share a cab; people who didn't even like each other shared cabs. But Cynthia knew, or thought she knew, despite herself, that it was his guilt alone that sent him off into the night, as though he could minimize the damage by keeping a distance; by not making even an implicit promise. If only she could *not* sympathize with him, and push her own interests. But she was who she was. It was enough of a struggle just to be that.

So Cynthia had shared the jug, with the flamboyant Francine.

And now the kitten was crying in a most annoying and persistent manner. It would not be satisfied with the distilled or fermented liquids of forgotten fruit, however nutritious or invigorating. It wanted the veal Gerber's, or lamb—baby mush from the jar. Which it was a good thing Burton had brought, since Cynthia rarely got to a grocery store these days.

21. Flight

It was definitely the best way. A note.

Ave hadn't expected to feel so nervous. Until this moment, what she had felt was happy, ecstatic. This was what you took drugs for, but no drug was this good, no drug was as good as love. Oh, the real thing, it was unmistakable. She always knew Claude would call, she knew he would find her, she knew he would want her in the end. He had to. And thank God she would be through with this disgusting city, the humid August heat, the cold, and back in California. Away from this old gravy brown crap.

She looked at the captain's-bed couch with its plaid blanket, the shelves to the ceiling with their alphabetically ordered musical scores, the oriental rug with its threadbare patches, the hundred talismans of Burton's life, and her very skin recoiled as from the worn or soiled possessions of strangers. "Nature" colors, the colors of the Northeast—the maple-pine "climax community," Burton had called it. Imagine saying that with a straight face! Well, he had smiled . . . The things in Claude's house were streamlined, glass, beige, white, black, sand—sand. The beautiful beach.

She'd tried to call Dionisio, to tell him she was leaving, but he hadn't responded to messages left with Virgilio, the fuck. Well, that never had any future.

In the bedroom, her bag was packed. Well, not strictly her bag, there was Burton's dumb old plaid suitcase, the annoying kind of heavy, hard-sided luggage right out of the fifties but never mind, it was big, she had just squeezed in her pink suede shoes, he'd never miss it, the big dope never went anywhere, he hated to travel. On the bottom of the suitcase she had put the photographs she had taken in the West Indies. She had been startled at how well they came out, and had exclaimed to a musician she was traveling with, "I'm a brilliant photographer." The conviction had begun to grow in her that she was an artist.

Ave got off the bed, where she had settled on her stomach with a pad, sucking a pencil, and paced from window to window. The remaining kitten, who had reached the gangly adolescent stage, got underfoot, got stepped on, and let out a sound that could have come from a hen. Ave stooped to pick him up, but he ran off to lick his hurt paw. "Be that way," Ave said, turning back to the view. It couldn't be denied that the Hudson was okay. Sort of: the sky was like white ash, the river pewter. Everyone talked about the pollution, a "temperature inversion." What did east coasters know about pollution. In California, even the pollution was spectacular. Did she imagine it, or was there something mocking in the way the river winked at her? If it was a message, surely it was for someone else. Nature didn't send her messages.

The suitcase rocked as she dropped onto the bed with the notepad, sucking the satisfyingly sharp point of the pencil. The kitten too leapt up, purring with that gratifying instantaneousness of kittens as it curled against her. "All right, kitten. Enough now. Mommy has to work." What the hell was she going to write?

"Darling—"

Oh, that was ridiculous. She scribbled it out. Then she doodled over the scribble in spirals that were like a penmanship exercise. Then she made the winding herringbone of quilling. Then loops. She folded over to a new page. I'm turning over a new leaf, she thought. It made her feel fresh and clean, this thought. I'm becoming a *virgin* again, she thought, and laughed at the joke. In fact she always felt like a virgin with each new man, or each new try, as in this case; as though there had never been anyone else. But she never remembered that.

"Dear Burton," she began.

It was obvious that nothing was going to be right. "Shit." The kitten looked up, moon-eyed. "You think of something. Earn your keep." It closed its eyes with a cat smile, purring again for a second before it dropped off. Ave sprang off the bed, jiggling kitten and case. The big cat had curled up among her folded clothing. "And don't think I'm taking you."

She wandered over to the Venus flytrap, which was thriving horribly, and teased it with the eraser end of the pencil. It wasn't having any. It knew shit from Shinola.

She picked up her clear plastic pocketbook and counted
the bills inside. She had cleaned up on her last shipment: it
had been clear profit. She found she had little interest anymore in using the stuff. Maybe she could just leave Burton a
wad of bills and a simple note—nothing but "Thank you."
That would be elegant, that would be classy. But the hell
with it, she needed the money. She had earned it, after all.
And maybe he would be insulted. Maybe he would feel like
a prostitute.

At the word "prostitute" she saw a picture of him in drag,
with big gold earrings, a bouffant skirt—and his beard, that
obnoxious beard! And the hurt, bewildered look he would
have on his face as he picked up the money, trying to figure
it out. The calf.

She was so amused at this picture that she felt a real tug of
temptation. But the tug of the money was stronger. It would
make her strong—she would arrive glamorous, beautiful,
and with wads and fistfuls of bills: what could be more attractive.

She hated any image of herself that suggested the waif.
Ella could be a waif. People like that Cynthia person could
be waifs. Pathetic. Pitiable. Though not to be pitied by her.
Compassion was nothing but self-pity turned on its head.
Ave would not be pitied even by her own supreme self. If
she ever reached that condition she would just as soon be
taken out and shot. Or something.

The plane was in three hours. She would be out before
Burton could be back from that recording session. She'd
been so proud to arrange it, but could hardly remember at
this moment why. Did she look all right? The bathroom mirror, the only one in the apartment, was wholly inadequate—
you could just see patches of yourself, and had to stand on
the toilet to do that. The new dress was, well, virginal—horizontal stripes of pale and paler blue, woven into the fabric
with a kind of silvery effect. Long, full princess-like skirt and

a real Barbie bodice, cinched, and then bare shouldered except for the squared-off straps: perfect. Gazing into the silver mirror, Ave saw herself approaching: became Claude, in order to fall in love with her vision of herself. Approaching, walking languidly, but with a certain lovable spring, across the pavement, across the runway apron, the wind lifting the full skirt to mold it momentarily against the dreamy hips . . . She was so turned on she wanted to fuck herself. In the mirror she narrowed her eyes and, as if waking, examined her makeup critically, smoothing a barely visible line of powder caught in the almost invisible fur of her cheek. Why was it that eye shadow always insisted on leaving the upper part of the eyelid for the lower? So that you left home a vamp and arrived an amphetamine queen. She pursed her lips, gleaming under a coat of something called Bronze Age. Really, you couldn't help but look fabulously sexy when you had lips like mattresses. Irresistible. Ave opened her eyes nearsightedly on her eyes. They were the same pale colors as the dress. Her slightly hooked nose dipped as she pressed her lips to distribute Bronze Age that much more evenly. She had to go, she had to go; it was hard to tear herself from the mirror. If only she could just shut her eyes and be there. She would buy Italian and British *Vogue* for the plane. She would read E. F. Benson. She would read Edith Wharton. She would smile graciously, and they would all wonder where they had seen her before.

If only she had a better bag. If there were time to run uptown. It spoiled the image. Would she look dowdy, pathetic? But she wouldn't be carrying it, it would be on the carousel, Claude would pick it up, and then she would pass it off as a joke, the last vestige of New York clinging to her, that would be all right. Or—she could just see it—he would lightly swing it upward, saying, "Vintage. Cool." He would be wearing a sport jacket and shades.

She fell back on the bed, the silvery dress spreading

around her in an even semicircle, a hundred and eighty degrees from hip to hip, and shut her eyes. She could feel Claude's grateful bony weight sink upon her, the energy of him grinding toward her, and nearly groaned, weak with desire. Nine hours, ten hours before this fantasy was to become fact. How could she wait, how could she survive the interval? She spread her legs a bit, pressing her palms to her crotch. She never masturbated. What, her? Forget it. Like all those plebeian things she disdained to know the practical use of her hands for. She held up her hands for admiration. But they were not an admirable part of her body, betraying her with that thickness of all her farthest joints and limbs, and she slid them under the slick fabric of the dress, the heavy warmth of her behind, for comfort. There was nothing you could do about hands. Old ladies wore gloves to hide the wrinkles. You could have a face-lift (she would not hesitate when the time came), but you couldn't do anything about hands. Liver spots! But that would never happen to her. She wouldn't let it. You had to draw a line.

She hadn't yet been thirty when she was first with Claude (and she had felt like a teenager, racing down Santa Monica Boulevard in his car with the top down); and now, inconceivably, the number thirty-three presumed to have application to her.

Luckily, everybody else kept getting older too.

But she seemed to be feeling that terrible way you feel when you wake up and remember it's your birthday, alone under the covers, alone even if not, alone with your great age, the inconceivable years, that can't possibly be fleeing so quickly, so—deprivingly. Taking something away each year while pretending to add. Where had she been these last four years? It couldn't be four years. She felt the way you do when you are sitting in the taxi and realize you've forgotten your keys. No wonder they gave you things on your birthday. It is a day when everything becomes something missing.

Those years fleeing so publicly. Everyone could look at

you and judge you. Judge what you had to show for the time.

If she stayed in this apartment another minute she would be committing suicide. It was an apartment to slit your wrists in. To jump out onto the highway from. To be drawn into the murky river.

The phone rang. She let it. To think that a few hours ago it had been Claude, transforming her life.

Quickly she scribbled on the pad and, with a kind of inspiration, stuck the bent page into the mouth of the flytrap before fleeing with the bulky suitcase bumping one side and the clear plastic bag bumping the other artfully draped hip. Completing the last swivel of the lock on the dented metal downstairs door, she slipped the keys through the mail slot and listened to their faint clink as to a bell of freedom.

22. Hypocrisy

Burton found he was at his stop. Without awareness he had taken in ads for hemorrhoid creams, Kool cigarettes, an abortion service, and the reflective windows of the subway train. A man was picking his nose, which Burton tried not to watch. In another corner, a heavy young woman in a frilly blouse unconcernedly chewed a hot dog whose pungent scent pervaded the car. Burton never took the subway if he had time to walk, and cabs only very late at night or for transporting more than he could carry. A flood of incoming passengers nearly prevented him from making it off the train before the doors slammed their rubbery edges. A newspaper caught in an updraft flung itself against his leg like an importunate dog.

How wonderful to be that man who picked his nose, or

that girl who chewed her hot dog. To be so complacent and at ease. Clearly they wouldn't take shit from anybody.

For the first time in years he felt the urge to eat meat. A frankfurter.

Lost in the flurry of more faces and images than could be registered, and which attention, bent on purpose and practicality, screened out, the traces of these scents and images drifted off like the pesky paper. The recording session Burton was presiding over was in a big building on Broadway; he missed the arching sinister entryway, attended by a sleepy guard with a sign-in sheet, and had to turn back. Annoyance at Ave bit at him. This was not his gig. She had begged him to do it for her club friends. She said it would be a big deal for them, an uptown musician like him. He hated studio work anyway, and avoided it about as successfully as he avoided the subway. When he did it, it was for the money, and in this case he wasn't getting any. It was shit all around. All he did was take shit from Ave. Surely he could manage to stand up to the creature for once! For this gig, for the gig of his life.

The only light on in the windowless room was behind the glass panel of the recording booth, where the engineer fiddled with equipment, as engineers love to do, while keeping a cigarette going in the empty cylinder of a tape canister. Burton ostentatiously let his backpack drop so that it echoed in the empty room, and switched on the harsh overhead lights. "Where the fuck are they?"

The engineer responded by activating the switch that let him communicate with the room, and by pulling loose one side of his headphones. "¿Cómo?"

"Where is everyone? *I'm* ten minutes late."

The engineer shrugged. The air-conditioning was fierce, and he wore a flannel shirt. Though he had answered in Spanish, he wasn't; he had a dun brown ponytail and wire-rim glasses sliding down a complicated bony nose. He bounced to whatever it was he was listening to. Burton went into the booth. He had worked with this guy before, on "uptown" music. Brant? Grant? Brad? Skip. "Hey, amigo," said Skip. He broke out a reefer. "These guys are always, uniformly, without exception, reliably late, man. Relax." Burton couldn't believe it. Recording time cost a fortune. They could waste that money, and he wasn't even being paid. He was damned if he was going to relax. There was nothing to do but go over the scores again of this music he abominated. He made notes viciously, like incisions. Skip shook his head. "You ain't gone live long," he predicted.

The talent, as they say, arrived more or less in a bunch, passing a bottle of Bacardi amongst themselves, joking, giggling, high but with a certain serious swagger that suggested the underlying earnestness of their endeavor. They bore the usual hangers-on, including one formidable woman with scary breasts like torpedoes. They referred to Burton as El Marido.

To Burton they were like old jazzers, the real guys. Already he felt shame at his anger, but was no less angry.

One of the last hangers-on to arrive was Cynthia.

She was dragged in, literally, by a skinny guy with straight black hair that fell over his face. He kept pulling at her and saying, "Come on, guapita, you a good-time girl, you like music." She laughed giddily, tripping over feet, hiding her face and saying "No no no." She was dressed in high Fourteenth Street, a shiny purple top that was generous with cleavage, and glitter-gold Lycra pants with what a friend of Burton's called full labial definition. Seeing Burton, she pointed, covered her mouth, and laughed helplessly.

"You know El Marido?"

"El Marido?" She choked, laughing so hard she couldn't get her breath. "El Marido de Ave?" she asked in improvised Spanish.

"You know Ave?" The official pretend boyfriend was

amazed. Some jabbering and exclaiming went on. Dionisio shrugged. Cynthia looked up from the excited cluster and soberly met Burton's eyes, her cheeks pouching as her mouth settled into rosebud solemnity. She shifted out of the crowd, inching toward her lover.

"What the hell are you doing here?" he hissed as she came within range.

"I don't know." Her eyes looked lost, terrified, as if she'd awoken in an unknown place. Her tentative hand folded on Burton's sleeve.

"Well, what happened?"

"I was—I'm drunk."

"I can see that."

"You hate me."

"Cynthia. Cynthia." He put an arm around her crumpling shoulders. "Cinzia." He placed the syllables tenderly in one shell-like ear. She smelled awful.

She clutched his shirt with both hands. "I don't know what's happening to me. Really. I don't know how I got here."

"Did he pick you up? Were you in a bar?"

"I don't even know who this guy is. He kept saying come with me. He was making a record, he kept telling me, like, you know, very big deal. He thought I didn't believe him. We were in that park, you know, Clement Clarke Moore Park, near me. He—we shared a bottle. I think. I—I was feeling really bad. I didn't know, I didn't know he had anything to do with, you know. *Her.*" She said this harshly, the word unloosing fury. Her voice could barely be heard as she added, "Your girlfriend."

He had his hands on her shoulders. He tightened them. "You mean you knew?" He was the one who'd been duped! Protected.

She shook her shoulders to get free, not looking up, as though she were the guilty party.

"How long have you known? Have you been talking to Ella about this?"

"Ella?" He knew her high-bred discretion. Now he had doubly betrayed her by questioning it. She would have prevented any such talk, of course.

The guys in the band were nudging each other. They got a kick out of seeing a fellow fellow, and a stuffed shirt at that, blatantly fondle a sexy woman who was not his wife. But they had not anticipated a bad turn. "Hey, you be sweet to her," someone called. Burton's head shot up. The whites of his eyes were red. Virgilio, who felt he had rights to the woman, squared off in front of Burton, but Burton didn't wait for him to speak. "Enough!" Burton said. He was used to being in charge. "Places." The men did as they were told. In the distraction of conducting, Burton failed to notice his darling's outrage. "Speak fucking English!" he had called to the men, and at this final outrage to his own self-love, such as it was, he lost track of Cynthia entirely, only letting himself know that she had slipped away well after she was gone.

23. Facing down the undead

Ella always felt she should atone on Yom Kippur. The trouble was, you had to believe in the utility of these procedures for them to work. She had fasted once, as you were supposed to, but hadn't felt purified, just deprived and annoyed with herself. In any case she had been fasting most of the summer. She recommended heartbreak, if that was what it was, to anyone who wanted to lose weight. Or didn't recommend it: it was too horrible a way to go about it. You didn't feel virtuous for not eating, or in triumph over your appetite, which gives a certain thrill to dieting. You just felt baffled at the betrayal of having so reliable a pleasure turn on you, so that you were trapped in a world where the agony of the soul could not receive the solace of the senses.

Ella had wandered into the seminary garden near Cynthia's after looking at another futile apartment. The irony of being in a church garden on the highest of the Jewish High Holy Days was hardly lost on her, but it seemed only a proper reflection on the manifold ironies of her life. She came to the garden often to get away from Cynthia, who seemed to cling to her like a lover. Ella felt in no condition to help. She felt guiltily annoyed that she couldn't get Cynthia to let Burton take her off Ella's hands, as he'd been begging Cynthia to do since Ave's convenient departure.

Ella sat on a cement bench and looked at the sky. It seemed she hadn't looked up for a long time. It was a high blue, promising autumn, accentuated by the frame of false-Gothic arches and decorations on the black buildings that made a quadrangle around the tall trees and weak grass. It felt, that autumn sky, like the hint of a new beginning for her, as autumn always did. I must be truly Jewish after all, she mocked at herself, since the Jewish New Year also came then. But she knew her feeling came from the lifting of summer torpor, and the conditioning of years of starting school in the fall. How fitting, she thought: the Jewish year is the academic year; and really, I'm a pagan. Druish, Stephen used to say, when he wasn't storming about her infidelity to Judaism like some crabby Old Testament prophet.

Bells rang. She looked at her watch. Evensong, vespers? She felt the sting of pain before she could fend off what provoked it, and managed to push it back before letting herself fully recall standing in the church with Frank. It was the pain that came when she thought the word "alone," or if she thought of Stephen's knuckles red and wet with tears, the pain that tugged when she brought food to her mouth. Defiantly, as though to say "Let it do its worst," she stepped up to the seminary's little chapel.

LIFE & LOVE
such as they are

The arched doors yielded as though weightless, opening on a stage where the show was already in progress. A man in a golden dress stood on a round, fenced platform far in front. Rows of faces on each side turned toward Ella; there was no chance of leaving. A young man, who had the plump, early-balding kindliness of one who believes his every gesture to be the Lord's work, half stood, motioning her to the space on the wooden pew beside him. Ella saw that they were all holding black looseleaf notebooks and took one from the wooden pocket in the seatback that faced her. A female seminarian reached from the seat behind to show her the page, striking smartly against the hand of another eager seminarian bent on the same errand of mercy. Everyone stood. The plump young man looked at Ella benevolently, so that she had to stand too.

The sweat of panic at her fraudulence and wrongness wet her ribs.

The good men and women who properly belonged were intoning a psalm from the notebook, about you did evil, you did wrong, you lost all and were fallen but yet you had the Lord's strong right arm to lean upon. Ella shielded her eyes. They would all see that she was weeping and beam upon her, repentant sinner that she was. A kindly hand pointed out the next psalm, and once again, as soon as she got her mouth around the words, up spouted the hot tears, pouring from her nostrils, splitting her welling heart like a softened pit. Sensation flooded back with such force it might have been a heart attack, an orgasm, a vicious splinter in the sole of the foot.

She looked down when they crossed themselves. They did this incessantly, at every mention of Jesus or God or Our Father and even "heaven." As she quieted, less panicky if no less of an imposter, the dim gleams of dark wood at the end of the vaulted room coalesced into the familiar loin-clothed, sad-faced hippie. Worshiping idols! she thought: God forgive

me. She looked down as a woman near her made the ostentatiously pious demonstration of crossing her forehead,
nose, and cheekbones with her thumb and then spreading
her arms wide.

> *. . . for that which I have done*
> *. . . for that which I have left undone*
> *. . . lead us not into temptation*

They did the words in plainsong. She had left her record
of Gregorian chant with Stephen, who hated it. She kept
knowing which notes should come next. Stephen would say
that this was because the church dealt in musical cliché. She
pushed this away, not liking to think of Stephen teaching her,
of his expertise, of the way she had once worshiped him.

Each time she started to voice the words, she had to use
her handkerchief, so wet it chafed the raw places.

A silence was announced for prayer. To Ella this seemed
the first opportunity for something genuinely spiritual. She
closed her eyes and tried to find the transcendent feeling of
melding that to her was spirituality. Instead she got the jum-
ble of ugly, expensive, and unacceptable apartments she had
looked at. Giving in to it, to her own lowness, she thought,
Let me find an apartment. Let me hear from Frank, she
thought, but she was so sick of this wish, haunting her every
hour, that she felt embarrassed, as though the judging Jewish
God had read her selfish thoughts. I want my life back, she
prayed.

The brief service ended with an organ recessional so nutty
it was like a scene from a horror movie, *Night of the Living
Dead,* Ella thought, though she had never seen it. The music
was all mysterioso whanging decoration and dissonant high
tones. It sounded as if a madman sat at the instrument,
working his will. With what seemed amazingly straight-faced
solemnity, the priest and his acolytes filed out, carrying phal-
lic candles as thick as their arms, swinging censers and wav-

ing crosses around to the crazy music, as if leading the foolish natives to face down the undead.

Climbing the steps to Cynthia's alcoved room, Ella remembered the apartment search with Stephen that had led to them, and her and Stephen's life in this, their long-ago first place together. She thought of this each time, but for the first time she let the superstitious fear that had been troubling her come to the surface: that she wasn't finding an apartment because she was meant to go back to Stephen; that she did not hear from Frank because she was not meant to be with him. The word *meant* in this context had to do with love, which Ella secretly believed to be the way whatever *God* was made itself known. She had no doubt anymore that she must be very evil, though at the same time she felt she could not have helped anything that had happened.

The stain above the heat vents on the whorehouse wallpaper of the hall had not grown visibly blacker since Ella had lived there years earlier. The same neighbor still had the apartment across the hall at the top of the marble steps. Ella dreaded running into him. An ambitious pianist and cabaret singer, he had tried to befriend them when they had lived there, and whenever he saw Ella he was full of questions about Stephen. Sure enough, as though waiting to ambush her, the young man, whose long bangs he continually tossed out of his eyes, greeted her gladly and asked how *Otella* (the play's finally determined name, at last) was going. Ella had remembered in the past not to mention Stephen's genius, but she slipped this time. "Oh, *wow*. Do you think I could meet him? Whoa, whoa, sorry, I know I'm being really pushy, but—wow, that's really great." Ella inserted herself into Cynthia's apartment as the litany faded.

Cynthia was sitting at the table, half facing the door, one hand crunched at an awkward angle between her crossed legs. "Scott?" she said, saying the neighbor's name. Ella put her finger to her lips and nodded so that Cynthia would ask nothing else; from the hall you could hear what went on in each apartment whether you wanted to or not. Cynthia put her finger to *her* lips in response, pretending to repress laughter that wasn't there. "Stephen called," she told Ella. Ella nodded fatalistically. He was always calling, waiting for her to give up and come back.

In the bathroom Ella pulled off her sweaty clothes—fresh that morning when put on to impress a landlord with her respectability—and pulled on a pair of shorts and a tank top. It was still summer in the skylit apartment. "Don't you want the air conditioner?" Ella asked coming out. Cynthia shook her head like someone too addled to speak. Ella switched the machine on: "Do you mind?" When Ella went to close the window, she saw that a pane was broken. "When did this happen?" Cynthia shrugged. Ella came and stood over her. Cynthia was cradling a teacup. What was in it did not resemble tea. Cynthia had told Ella that she thought she was becoming an alcoholic, but it sounded wishful to Ella—willed, in fact. Ella thought Cynthia's problems were worse than alcohol. Retrospectively, she recognized them from as far back as Blithedale. Ella sank into the other chair. "There any for me?" She flipped a hand at the cup.

"In the fridge." Cynthia's eyes were glassy and unfocused in a way that did not look drunk but deeply distracted, as though there was something she was looking at that Ella couldn't see.

The buzzer sounded. "Burton," Ella said, and got up to buzz him in.

Burton came by every day.

Cynthia smiled in that unfocused way, her eyes looking somewhere past Ella, so that Ella felt tempted to turn around. "He feels sorry for me."

"Is that why you won't—?"

But Ella knew that humiliation had everything to do with Cynthia's refusing Burton. Ella had stayed in the apartment for a few days here, a few days there, all through awful July and August, alternating with other friends' temporarily empty flats. She had heard Cynthia's half of phone calls, and then, inadvertently, a careless phone message from Burton that gave the show away. Cynthia's response had been mortification. "You should be angry at him," Ella had objected. But Cynthia hadn't been angry until that recording session, when she felt so exposed. She didn't want her friends knowing how she had let herself be used. She hated Burton's knowing. It was almost the same, Ella could see, as hating him, to hate what he now knew. Ella could see also that this upheaval of opposing feelings was bringing back an old Cynthia, a bad old Cynthia that Ella had hoped never to see again.

They heard his deep sigh as he knocked, a sigh that might have been from climbing the five flights.

Ella wished she were wearing something more attractive than shorts that looked like balloons. Her eyes were pink, her eye makeup all worn off. Why should I care, she thought, angry at herself for wanting to appeal to a man in love with someone who needed that love—for being so competitive and acquisitive. Ella looked at Cynthia, to see if her wickedness had registered. Cynthia looked good. She always did. She never had a pimple to cover up, she had that peaches-and-cream skin, that straight blond baby hair, blue-gray eyes but dark lashes, height: unfair. The blue-gray eyes were still strangely glassy.

Yet as Burton came in, kissing Cynthia but not Ella, even though he always used to kiss Ella on the cheek, Ella felt slighted, rejected, as though she had lost her allure and been insulted by having this loss made the object of attention. She thought of something she had seen, through the burnt church door of St. Luke's after the fire, when she was drawn irresistibly to look at the ruins again and again until they were boarded over. A beam had fallen at an angle onto the charred pews and blackened remains of the roof and floor. It bore a legend in gold whose Gothic lettering was still legible if you twisted your head: AND I IF I BE LIFTED UP SHALL DRAW ALL MEN UNTO ME. Ella's smile twisted sideways, and she pointed to her cheek for Burton to kiss. Was she sensing nervousness in him because she too was now single? Was he attracted to her? She found she couldn't help hoping so. She looked into his kind, earnest eyes. He looked away.

She held up the bottle sweating from the refrigerator. "I was just going to have some. You want?" She found that when she talked to Burton she often fell into Stephen's jocular, exaggeratedly colloquial mode, which was really their shared college mode.

"Don't mind if I do." Burton responded to the cue with matching irony—raised brows, slightly scornful smile, knowing eyes; the mode mandated that all ready-made phrases were in themselves jokes. At the same time she could see he felt that neither of them should encourage Cynthia by drinking, and that it wasn't a subject for jokes. Probably, Ella thought, because his mother is an alcoholic. She raised her glass. "Cin-cin."

"Ella. I may have a place for you." And he told her about an apartment on Hudson Street a friend of his had told him about. The tenant had died and the place was apparently a mess, but Burton's friend thought Ella could get it cheap if she fixed it up herself.

Ella took the friend's name and number, which Burton had already written out for her. At once she was afraid that someone else would already have taken the place. "Do you mind if I call?" She moved to the couch, where the phone was.

"Of course not," said Cynthia and Burton together. Burton was holding the hand Cynthia had been using to support her teacup, as though this would stop her from drinking, and Cynthia's eyes belied her words by pleading with Ella not to call, not to leave her, and above all not to leave her alone with the man who loved her. As Ella dialed, her eyes wandered around Cynthia's alcove where the glass was broken. She was wondering if she would be able to find a piece of cardboard to put over it, and if there was tape in the house. The violin case was pulled out from under the bed, with fingermarks in the dust. This meant Cynthia had been using her good violin, not the one she took to the show, which meant she was practicing. Ella turned to point to it and signal her pleasure—Cynthia had been saying over and over that she couldn't play anymore—but Burton, still standing, was leaning over and kissing Cynthia, who still kept one hand awkwardly crunched by her thighs. Ella turned away to regard her own uselessly skinny knees with despair. Because of course it wasn't Burton's kisses she wanted anyway.

The friend answered and gave her the building manager's number. Amazingly, he was in. He was amenable to the idea, or to getting his unit fixed up at only the slight expense of slightly lower rent, and gave her the number of the superintendent. Her luck held: the super was in too, and said she could come by the next day, though he would not set a time. He assured her he would be around. "You don't want this place," he also assured her.

She was about to report to Cynthia and Burton, who must have followed some of the transaction, when she was distracted by sounds from the skylight. "It's raining!" So much for the autumnal blue of the sky. Thunder rumbled, and the darkened room was momentarily lit by lightning.

"No, not there," cried Cynthia as Ella set down the phone. Cynthia had become weirdly particular about exactly how various objects must be placed, in a way that had nothing to do with practical or aesthetic considerations, and grew panicky if Ella didn't comply. Ella tried to place the phone as Cynthia wished. "No, the dial should face the other way." But Ella didn't do it exactly right. Cynthia began to stand, the hand that had been hidden between her thighs lifted toward the phone, which started to ring. Thunder rumbled again as this hand of Cynthia's was shown to be caked in blood, with a fresh geyser of it escaping from a place in the palm that flapped open like a book.

By the time Ella screeched Burton had already taken hold of the damaged hand as though it were an animal he could pacify. Cynthia met Ella's eyes with a shy smile: "The dust on the violin—it was so long since I practiced. I put my hand through the window." She spoke as though under these circumstances, this was the only logical course of action, and anyone would have followed it. She turned toward Burton with a kind of voluptuous ecstasy: "I won't be able to play in the show."

They could hear Stephen's voice coming through the answering machine. "Ella, hi, are you there? Call me if you get the chance. Just want to say hello." All these things happened all at once.

"I'm calling nine-one-one," said Ella, intending to get an ambulance.

"A cab'll be quicker." Burton was hustling Cynthia into a pair of shoes, trying to keep his handkerchief around the hand.

"This is so stupid. I'm fine," said Cynthia with her social giggle. It was clear that the injury, once she did not have to hide it, was no more to her than an inconvenience, as if she did not feel it.

Ella grabbed a shawl and slipped into her sandals. It was suddenly chilly. Broken glass lay scattered where the kitten might be hurt by it. Ella shut her into the bathroom with her food dishes.

All the way to the hospital, Cynthia giggled and said, as if they were being very, very silly, "You should be taking me to *Bellevue*," and she bugged her eyes out and whirled a finger around her ear to signal insanity.

Ella's speech had the medicinal effect of a slap: "You don't have to work so hard to make things worse." Cynthia's face pouched in its sad way. With her good hand she took Ella's. Ella thought of how often in high school they had talked about suicide, and knew that Cynthia would know that this was what she would think of, because the idea of suicide was what Cynthia, in her blocked but willful way, intended to convey.

Burton caught Ella's eyes for a moment and they both looked away. The streets had the beautiful shine of patent leather, mirroring the white lights of cars and the green and red ones of traffic signals. At the same time the city looked softened and countrified in the light-shot mist.

> *. . . for that which I have done*
> *. . . for that which I have left undone*

Ella was sorry the words came back to her and shifted in her seat. Cynthia thought she was trying to get away and abruptly let go of Ella's hand. Ella reached for Cynthia's hand and took it again, between her palms.

In her awkwardness in helping Cynthia get out of the cab while Burton took care of the fare, Ella let Cynthia's head crack against the frame of the door.

Ella touched her own head. Cynthia did not appear to be aware that she had been hurt.

While the injured hand was being taken care of, Ella and Burton, in a corner of the grim waiting room of the emergency ward, argued.

"You can't just take her home to nurse back to health like a stray cat," said Ella. "She needs professional help."

"She needs love," said Burton.

Ella threw up her hands. "Who doesn't?" It hasn't worked so far, she wanted to point out. But besides not being able to, she saw something: that what Burton had to offer wasn't love in the first place. He wanted it to be, because if he were truly good, he would love Cynthia; but he didn't really love Cynthia. But, she thought, he doesn't know this is what he feels. He can't tell the difference between his intentions and what is. Oh, he might be in love, Ella thought, with some poetic notion of Cynthia, but he hadn't known her reality, and he wasn't in love with that. He still didn't accept it. He was in love with the idea of his own goodness.

"Oh, Burton. Leave her alone. Leave her in peace." It was torture to have love beckon, this Ella knew.

The hospital took care of Cynthia's hand but nothing else, doping her up with something so that when Burton took her home to his place, she didn't protest.

The next day Ella looked at the apartment on Hudson Street. It had gaping holes in the walls, rusted plumbing, a rippling floor—it was the apartment version of Frank's sordid studio. Ella didn't have to take it. She had Cynthia's to herself. But she believed she would not be comfortable until she had her own things around her, arranged to strict aesthetic demands. She believed that once she had made some place her own she would sit in a patch of sunlight, she would paint, and dream of Frank, and feel like herself again.

She picked up Cynthia's red phone and set it down again at the less crazy angle that felt right to her. She found a torn, twice-mailed buff envelope and taped it over Cynthia's window, using Band-Aids. As she thought of the apartment she had looked at, it seemed fitting to her *for that which she had done* and *for that which she had left undone* to begin her new life in surroundings that would form a shroud of damage and grime.

24. Lead

A man dressed as a woman crossed the stage. "Tush," said the actor, in enormous high platform shoes and a long red dress with sequins on the bust. "Do you realize there's a

Shakespeare play beginning with the word 'tush'?"

The audience, eager to be amused, laughed.

"Hey, you were the one who pointed that out," said Ave, in a subdued voice, to Ella looking glum and unamused beside her. Ella rocked forward once in a way that might have been bitter or resigned or grimly ironic. Holding up the playbill, which it was bright enough to read in seats so near the stage, Ella put her thumb over the first two letters of the play's title, so that "Otella" became her own name. "Got it," said Ave. The play went on.

Ave was more interested in dramas closer to hand. She had caught a glimpse of Burton as they filed in from the lobby, Burton with his new sweetie, whom he had found with such wounding speed—with such speed that, if he hadn't been dumb inept Burton, she would have suspected the liaison predated her own departure. Which, when she had said this to Ella, made Ella so peculiar that, if it had not been Burton they were talking about, she would have feared was confirmed. But Burton hadn't liked sex enough to possibly have wanted *more* of it. It was horrible enough to be rejected by Claude, that shit, again, but to come back and find herself superseded and unmissed by someone she *disdained*—it was a nightmare come true. Burton didn't have the grace even to pretend to be hurt. When he caught a glimpse of her with Ella, he had just nodded and shepherded his big girlfriend as though she needed protection from Ave's evil eye.

Ave had a sense of where they were sitting, and had to fight the urge to get a better look at Cynthia. Uncomfortably aware of the girth of her own thighs and of gray she might have failed to pluck out of her undyed hair, she sharply felt her own inadequacy. Cynthia was a thin blond with this fucking talent everybody raved about. Ave found she had to briefly study the program in her lap as though it were more interesting than the play.

Anna Shapiro

· · · · ·

OTELLA by CAMERON DRISCOLL
Original music composed by Stephen Heller

"Where's Stephen?" Ave whispered.
Ella shrugged. "Probably with the techies."
The theater was small, run-down, and as camp as what
was onstage, decorated with cardboard vases with flowers
painted in them and other props from old plays. The only
live instruments were the tape recorder and the voices of the
actors, none of whom were trained singers—which only
seemed to increase the enthusiasm of the partisan crowd. In
any case, Driscoll invariably got big reviews. Ella had
pointed out the critic from the *Voice,* who as always had to
take an aisle seat to accommodate his bulk. If nothing else,
Ave could feel that she was at an important event, and was
important, as the special guest of the composer, herself. She
wondered if there would be an opening-night party, and if
so, whether Burton and that slut would go there or give way,
as was only right, to her.
Ave had been staying, since she'd gotten back, on
Stephen's couch in the old apartment, which was stripped
down and bereft, dingy, like a cottage rented furnished, full
of the miscellaneous leavings of indifferent tenants and barren of comfort. Just looking at the apartment made her feel
sorry for Stephen. He obsessively talked about Ella, cried for
Ella, ran, Ave thought, like a dog to Ella. Ave supported him
in his insupportable grief, assuring him that he was better
off. His dependence on her, almost like being a girlfriend,
made up, to a degree, for the dreary repetitiveness of these
sympathy sessions. But they were paying off in an annoying
way: he was starting to see this woman, with the improbably
apt name of Melody, seriously.
Noticing Melody in the intermission standing near the cur-
tained corridor that led backstage, Ave pointed her out to
Ella. You could say Melody looked like a model, or you
could say she looked like a boy. "Oh yeah," said Ella, "I

know." She snorted, and Ave couldn't help for a moment appreciating Ella's perspective, which was that Stephen really liked boys better. But Ella would say nothing bad about Stephen these days. Neither of them made a move to leave her seat and mingle.

"I thought Melody looked like you. I mean, she's much more of a star beauty—you know what I mean, Ella-Bella."

"Gee—thanks." Ella looked unmoved. "She's nothing like me. It's just an advertisement for your insecurity when you go out with a woman like that. And he wants so hard for me to be jealous that there's no reason for me to be, know what I mean?"

As if to confirm Ella's hypotheses, Stephen, in his classically distracted manner—eyes darting, rumpling his shaggy hair, twittery as a bird—appeared in the backstage entry, a hand touching Melody's beautiful waist, but his eyes on Ella. He tilted his hair back toward Melody, to tell Ella not to signal to him and that he couldn't signal back. The jealousy that had to be placated was Melody's.

"Well, I'd be jealous of her clothes at least, if I were you," Ave sniggered.

"Mmm."

Melody wore an actual designer outfit, a narrow coatlike thing of a length so eccentric it was recognizable as having to be the next coming thing.

Ave wanted to get up and walk around, but dreaded to run into Burton. She wished she had come with a handsome man, though she could not offhand think of any available. An evening like this with Dionisio could never have been possible. Ella dug her in the ribs, to warn her that Cynthia was coming over. "Are you okay for—?"

"What do you mean okay?" Ave snapped. "You think I ca—"

"Ella!" Cynthia addressed Ella, but her nervous upside-down eyes were on Ave. Ella had warned her about who she'd be with. Cynthia was holding out an envelope. "This was there when I went to check my mail." Cynthia hunched her shoulders as if to make herself smaller, bandaged hand held close to her ribs, as though Ave might hate her less if there were less of her. It made Ave feel like a witch. She kept her expression neutral, watching people in the theater. That man looks like he feels like a jerk, she told herself about a plump balding business type who had probably never seen drag theater before. A woman in the row ahead tugged her partner familiarly into the seat next to her.

Ella inspected the envelope, turned it over, and looked up at Cynthia, who hovered in as absent a way as possible. She's the kind of person who makes you want to hit her, Ave thought. "No return address," said Ella.

"It's got a Maine postmark. I hope you don't mind that I noticed."

"No! Thank you."

"I wanted you to have it right away."

Ave noted the breathless childishness of Cynthia's voice, and what was almost a lisp hidden inside the nob intonations and grand party manner—a kittenishness that came from an unsullied ingenuousness. As soon as she left, Ave said, "Where does she get off with that baby act?"

"Whatever it is Cynthia does," said Ella, "it isn't acting."

"If it isn't acting, then she's a total retard." Ave was glad the lights were dimming on her extra ten pounds. Ella held her letter. Ave looked away, so that Ella would open it and she, Ave, could read it. With a frown, Ella slid the envelope into her purse.

Desdemona, in this play, was turning out to be the bad guy, though she was also turning out to be a guy. Desmond. There was a terrible pun about *Desmond moaning,* and an appreciative groan, with scattered claps from the crowd. Driscoll's boyfriend, given this star part, stood in his male underwear trying to believe he could pass as beefcake. Before the end of the play, he would be relieved of this strain, when the briefs were removed to reveal prosthetic female parts added both above and below.

Ella's comment on this was, "Oh, perfect—it takes a man to be a woman. That's what Stephen thinks. Once, when I was worried that my period was late, he said, 'If *I* were a woman my period would come every twenty-eight days without fail, on schedule.'"

Ave showed her gums. "They should put that in. It's funnier than the play."

But she was thinking: *that* was the thing about Stephen. He was girlish. She felt comforted that he had not reacted to the sight of her naked. She began to feel that she had done better than Ella in getting Burton.

As the audience filed out, Ave saw Burton with Cynthia, the way he touched her elbow solicitously, proprietarily, and how straight and tall Cynthia stood, as though she knew it was her due. Ave's dress felt like a sausage casing. The boa that had looked so flattering in Stephen's mirror stuck to her skin. As they stood, she lifted the soft marabou, fanning herself. She headed for the stage.

"I don't want to go backstage."

"Oo-oh. You want to read your letter."

Something shut down in Ella's eyes. Ave felt a prick of triumph, combined with panic: she couldn't afford to lose Ella.

"Never mind. I can congratulate Stephen later."

"No," said Ella. "I probably should."

Their pretty heels scraped against the cement floor. Stephen was shaking hands with someone, bobbing like a mandarin, with a look of pleased self-mockery. Melody stood languidly to one side, smoking a long, slim cigarette. Stephen introduced them.

"If looks could kill," said Ave in Ella's ear as Melody, having touched their fingers, turned immediately away. Ella, blinking, told Stephen, "She's beautiful. She could be a model."

A spiteful look came over Stephen's face, as though he'd

been insulted. "She could," said Stephen. "And it's all natural, too. She doesn't have to try." He said this in the pleasantest possible way, as he did almost everything.

Ella's expression was indescribable. As though Melody understood her ascendance, a laugh came from where she allowed herself to be teased by the hugely tall actor in the red dress.

"Ella!" came Cameron's carrying cry. Ella followed his voice through the backstage warren of dressing rooms to where he was surrounded by a full court.

"Well, Cam—you've done it again." She said the words with a mischievous emphasis mysterious to Ave and a full recovery of poise.

"Wicked girl." Ella was teasing him with an expression he had taught her for what to say after a play you haven't liked.

"No, really. I didn't think it would work, but it's, you *have* done it. You know Ave, right?"

He lifted Ave's hand and brought it to his lips with veiled eyes and a brooding, Valentino-ish fume. "Oh, New York!" he said. The company had just come back from San Francisco. "A city where even women wear boas." He laid his head against her like a dog.

"I knew you were a genius from your plays," said Ave, "but now I know you are a total genius."

"Oh, bouquets, bouquets," said the genius. Amid the hubbub, he concentrated his gaze, with a will to compel, on Ella. "So how's life alone in the big city?"

"Oh, you know Ella," Ave answered for her. Ave loved meeting famous people. "Miss Cottage Industries. When she isn't building bookcases, she's sewing curtains or painting the Sistine Chapel."

Cameron waited for Ella's answer.

"It's strange. It feels really strange." Her eyes glistened, and her voice wobbled.

"I'll tell you something," he said. "With Stephen? I never saw that you got anything out of the deal."

The mental picture of Stephen's barren apartment presented itself to Ave. But Ella's place looked worse, Ave
thought with an unaccountable satisfaction that nevertheless
had the cold lead of fear at the bottom of it.

Ave was telling Cameron about her trip to the Dominican
Republic, calling herself a photographer. Ella wandered
away. Ave didn't know it, but Ave had chosen up sides.

25. Group sex

Burton felt like a less horrible person once he had Cynthia
firmly under his wing. He changed the dressing on her hand
every day, bathing the stitched lacerations with Zephiran. He
took care of her as he took care of the cats, which had come
to include Pinky, of course; he cooked healthful meals, he
stored up anecdotes from work (Cynthia was not going to be
able to play for a while, if ever) and from the newspaper,
since she never read it. He even chose what records to play
when he was home, with an ear toward what would please
her, or make her least sad. He was able to feel like a better
person doing these things because he was sure he was doing
them for a better person. But each day he felt he knew this
better person less well than when they had sat opposite
each other over cappuccino and discovered how similar
they were. He wondered if anything she had said then had
been true, or just been said to make him think she thought
like him, and if any woman ever told the truth, at least to
him.

As he had bathed her hand two days before, she letting
him with such passivity that her lips hung slack, she had
looked up with sudden attention at the window.

"What?" he had asked, turning, but seeing only the metallic late-afternoon glare over the water.

"The days are getting shorter," she had said, and her lips had curled into a Mona Lisa-ish smile. She hadn't said anything more. He bandaged her hand with cruel tightness. Later her fingers started to swell, and he did it over, apologizing the whole time and kissing the tip of each finger, each square, pale pink fingernail, still so angry that his own mental state became the trapdoor he did not dare open. It seemed to him that her recent compliancy was even more of a lie than what went before. He felt as if he were acting for two people, moving her very limbs, carrying her in his arms without being allowed to set her down, because if he tried, she would fall rather than walk.

He missed the giddy high spirits of her imaginary alcoholism. Naturally, he kept her from drinking, but it wasn't difficult.

The day before, she had taken, it seemed to him, a turn for the better. She had looked at him quite fondly and said she wanted to go to the country, and voluntarily put her arms around his waist, letting her face fall against his belly. His access of emotion was as disproportionate as it might be when a cat, usually reserved, licks you or places its soft paw on your cheek—gestures, it might be added, that mean nothing to the cat. He had said they would go, they would go, naturally, the minute he could arrange it. He duly made the arrangements, but he felt something like fear in his chest when he thought of their departure, to take place the following day. He was stopping by Ella's first, as though he were going away forever and might not have another chance.

Burton tripped on the uneven sidewalk, staring at a garishly naked spread-eagled woman on the cover of a magazine in a store window on Hudson Street, apparently inviting him personally to stick it in.

It reminded him of Cynthia, before. "God *damn* it to hell!"

His ankle, twisted, throbbed. He locked eyes with the Pakistani news vendor lounging in the doorway in an apron whose pockets bulged with change. "You should get that fucking sidewalk fixed. It's a menace." The vendor closed his eyes and nodded with knowing imperturbability. By the time Burton noticed that he had passed the number of Ella's building, he had forgotten his ankle. "Better now," singsonged the news vendor on Burton's return pass. Burton avoided seeing the magazine display, whose colors he could feel calling to him.

The hallway and stairs to the apartment were gravyish and smelled of decay. The apartment was worse. Ella, having buzzed him in and left her door open, was sloshing a bucket of steaming water toward the front room, the only room of any size and the only one whose windows, despite a veil of brown filth, promised the admittance of light. "I've finally reached the point where I can think about the front room," she greeted him. "Looks awful, huh? This is nothing compared to how it was." She spoke with satisfaction and a kind of bravado. He asked questions about the place, and she showed him around.

"See, once I get this linoleum up," she said in the kitchen, the second-biggest room and the room of entry, "I can have the floors scraped." She lifted a corner of the cracked, buckled, deeply stained and gritty flooring to show the dried-up, age-darkened boards beneath. The battered cabinets, an ancient agate-patterned gas stove, a refrigerator with rounded corners, all were scrupulously scrubbed so that they looked like camp reproductions, but the walls were scrofulous.

"Does this actually work?" he asked, going to the rusty sink, where the faucet had corroded.

"I have to get a plumber. But, yeah—you can get water." She indicated the steaming bucket. "But I'm drinking bottled. Paying for water!" She shook her head.

The two back rooms, narrow and tiny, had been chastened to a brisk white. Oriental carpets covered what tiny floor space was left by the double mattress in the backmost room and Ella's well-remembered Victorian chest of drawers in the other. Each cubicle had a large window facing a grim brick wall, the airshaft, but Ella had already covered each of these with a sheet of bordered lace. It was clear that the apartment, by bohemian New York standards, was a deal, and would have the bohemian charm of his own. He felt his hands itch to carry on with her work. Already the two little rooms looked homier than, for instance, Stephen's did anymore, cozy in Ella's trademark style, with the also well-remembered patchwork quilt—remembered from her college room—and even pictures he could recall from that far back, including a life study from an art class he had posed for, unexpectedly upgraded by matting and an elegant frame.

"I should really give it to you. Or Cynthia."

"I'm really flattered. Wow. It actually looks like me, doesn't it." His *penis* was in this picture, right in the room where, presumably, she got dressed.

"Well," she said, leading him back toward the substantial square of the front room—he looked at her ass in the tight jeans as if it weren't—"I won't have the luxury of being neurotic about my work anymore, unless I never invite anyone home. This is going to be my studio."

"Great!" There were two rocking chairs that he remembered, and one he didn't, a mountain of packed boxes, paint cans and hoarded newspaper, rolled canvases piled and leaning, a drop-leaf end table he had happened to help her carry through Chelsea home to Stephen one day in the rain, in several pieces that she had later glued back together. "Did I ever show you?" she said, seeing him looking, and tipped the table on its side to expose, painted by some careless janitorial hand on the underside, the name of one of their college dormitories. "Isn't that amazing?"

"Do you ever think of giving it back?"

"Are you kidding? Anyway, I don't think they'd want it now that it's, uh, antiqued."

What was amazing was how nothing was just itself but always its own history and a hundred other things besides. Nothing.

He let this wash over him as she started in on the brown that filmed the inside of the windows. "Let me," he said.

"Burton. I didn't let you come here so you could work. *I* shouldn't even be doing this while you're here. I feel incredibly rude. We should go to Maurizio or something."

He might have winced at the suggestion. His heart winced. She began the complicated maneuvering by which New Yorkers reach the outside of their windows, and let him help to lower the balky upper casement as he told her he and Cynthia were thinking of going to the country.

"The country? I couldn't lure Cynthia up *here*. What happened?" But then Ella looked at the square of clean brightness where Burton had pulled the window down. "Oh, God. Oh, Burton." Her hand spread on her chest.

"What?"

She pointed to the square. He stood behind her, feeling her body heat. She stepped away. "What?" he said again.

"You don't see it? How can you not see it? How did *I* not see it?" She stood on top of the radiator and leaned out. "Look, Burton, it's right there. See where those windows are reflecting?" Indeed, they looked on fire, indicating a florid color to the west. "Right next to that. Where the bricks are painted black?"

"Oh yeah. Oh my God. Jesus, Ella." It was her old apartment, Stephen's apartment, all but staring down at her—albeit over the roofs of smaller buildings from a few blocks away.

They watched as Melody's narrow form came into the frame. Evidently she was enjoying the view.

"I don't think they'll be able to see you," said Burton.

"That's my life. Over there."

Being Ella, she went on with the task, her face clenched and ugly. This was what he would have done. He wondered what it would be like to be with a woman who might help him instead of the other way around. For some reason he thought of the kittens when Ave had first brought them home, their shark-fin ears coming over the edge of the box.

Ella drew her head back inside. "Maybe I should go away too."

When he heard this, Burton understood that this was why he had come, in the hope that she would join them. He didn't say anything, afraid of deterring her. Taking advantage of her stillness, he picked up the squeegee. She grabbed it back, and they had a brief tug-of-war. "Oh, all right, Alfonse," she said.

Impatient with the elaborate adjusting of casements needed to reach the outside of the window from the inside, Burton sat backwards on the sill, leaning back and holding on to the window frame with one hand.

"Burton, come inside. You're going to kill yourself. Only we're not even high enough. You'll just have some deforming injury."

He went on scraping off the mortal layers, enjoying the task as though he could wash filth in swaths from his soul.

From the outside, the dingy apartment had a far more attractive aspect. Maybe that was how Ella now saw her old life. She looked comical to him, slumped in there because he was doing this, as though she'd inflicted it on him when in fact he enjoyed it.

The piece of molding he was grasping came loose in his hand. He tipped back. Just in time, he caught the gritty top of the window with the other hand, painfully gnarled around the squeegee.

Though fear had, with its elevator effect, moved his stomach up through his thorax and he came in right away, he laughed as though Ella's fear were funny. She was furious at him, and this was funny too, delightful. He put his hands on her thin shoulders, so birdlike compared to Cynthia's. He felt competent and immensely potent, and in that mode it was not as difficult as it might have been to convince Ella to come with them. He simply ignored her complaints and reservations, as he had ignored her objections to submitting Cynthia to his sole care, and as he ignored Cynthia's incapacity. He had subs for him and Cynthia at the show which, mercifully, was closing. He even had someone to care for all their various cats.

The three of them together in a car again might have reminded them of the trip to the emergency room, but didn't. The day was autumn at its brightest, the kind of weather that can make the city feel like a punishing confinement, and they were escaping—when everyone else had to stay, apparently, since there was no traffic.

"We're going to do this in record time, we're going to *ace* this. Pe-dal to the me-tal," Burton crowed. The two women suppressed smiles. Burton, exulting in his power, felt indulgent. He played with the radio. "Hey—let Cynthia do that," said Ella from the backseat.

"Nah—for driving you gotta have rock." Again the women found common cause, in laughter, and Burton joined in, throwing in a "yow!" for a bit of electric guitar.

At Croton Reservoir, Ella burst out with *Ja, das Meer ist blau, so blau,* and for a while the radio was abandoned as they tried to sing, in bad German and misremembered lyrics, Brecht-Weill songs. Ella and Cynthia segued into Marlene Dietrich. Burton pretended to object to their accents, and they pretended that these songs could not be sung unless you did the accent, their voices mysteriously deepening as though that were part of the accent too. They seemed to go quite mad on the chorus, "Hot voodoo makes me wild, oh

heaven, save this child, I want to be crazy, I want to be bad,"
collapsing in little-girlish giggles.

The Taconic, a pretty road in any weather, seemed to have
been set up to glorify the autumn, with the trees more orange, more yellow, more keenly bright against a bright sky at
each move north. They all felt they should know each bend
and turn before they came to it, since it was the road to Burton and Ella's college, and to Blithedale, for that matter, but
something always showed up that they forgot—a steep sec-
tion through blasted rocks, or the names of the roads, so poetic you would think them unforgettable: Hardscrabble Road,
Nine Brothers Road—who were the nine brothers? "You
know," said Ella, "I have never once turned off this road."

"We've gone to that little restaurant in Chatham," Cynthia
contributed.

"That's like going to the school cafeteria," Ella said.

"Or like those official shortcuts off Twenty-two," said Burton, wherewith, at a black-topped road that lacked any sign
at all, he turned off into the rolling farmland.

"Aren't we near Sterling-Pine?" Cynthia asked. It was a famous private mental institution.

"The graduate school," said Burton. It was what they'd
called it in college, since a number of students had left the
one institution for the other. But Cynthia didn't get the joke,
since she'd been at her conservatory at the time, flipping out.

On the back roads they passed through suburban en-
claves, and farms with fat barns of reassuring prosperous-
ness next to cows that the three of them rolled down their
windows to moo to. The cows raised perplexed, unworried
heads and thickly fuzzed ears, then bent again to their task
of converting green growing things into milk and fertilizer
for green growing things.

When the car came to some horses in a dazzling meadow,
the women insisted on stopping, grabbing lumpy apples
from a tree just beyond reach of the animals inside their

barbed-wire fence, and scrambled underneath. The horses, clearly used to being greeted with treats, trotted over as though to friends, accepting the apples greedily, leaving the palms of the women wet and spotted with grass. The horses tossed their heads when stroked, indicating that they preferred fruit to petting, and the women smiled in their pleasure at understanding these silent communications.

They came to a knoll with a tree on it, past granite outcroppings surrounded by the even-grazed green. The horses followed. Shadows of clouds passed across the green like ships. From the small eminence of the knoll the countryside spread around them, smoke here and there trapped in upward spirals that deliquesced into empty sky. They knew this view. There was a lookout place on the highway for it. They leaned back onto elbows or with arms slung over knees, eyes half-closed.

"We should have lunch."

"Mmm."

They all half dozed. One of the horses nuzzled their faces and necks.

Ella, opening her eyes, said, "If I lived here, I'd want to paint all the time."

"If I lived here, I'd—be happy," said Burton.

"If I lived—" said Cynthia. Though she was lying down, she spread her hands, shaking them, the way you do when you can't remember a word. Burton took the hand closest to him, the wounded one. Cynthia threw her other hand into Ella's. "Funny you two never got together," she said.

They stood, brushing off their jeans. The borrowed Volvo, its dull metal heating and cooling with the sun and breeze, gave off clicks.

When they got to a main road, it was the state thruway. Trucks loomed up, sinking them into canyons of exhaust with a roar. The blandly landscaped roadside contained no farmhouses, no anything. The cars went fast. Somehow they

were as exhilarated as though they had been allowed off
campus for the first time in weeks. They bounced in their
seats and sang along to rock oldies on the radio. Cynthia
drove this stretch. She had a suave canniness that was astounding the way her violin playing was astounding, so that
you couldn't stand that someone who could do something
so well didn't feel as good about it as she sounded or was.
Without asking for a map check, without asking for confir-
mation of what the sign they'd whizzed past had said, and
having gone the longest of any of them since last traveling
this route, she made the correct turn off the main road for
the winding shuttle through Troy that would take them to
Vermont. "Troy!" they cheered as though the battered row
houses and gutted downtown represented everything they
had ever loved. It seemed to them the America they were
denied. Luncheonettes, bus stops marked by a bent metal
sign; someone's living room on a steep corner that overhung
a twist in the road, which had been turned into Lucie's Beau-
tyette, with a woman's pink profile painted onto the glass.
Burton and Ella speculated on the prices of the row houses
with spooled newel-posts and decorative turrets, knowing
that in Manhattan they'd be a million dollars.

"Romeo's Treasure Chest!" Ella shouted as they passed the
discount store they used to hear advertise low-price engagement rings on the pop station.

"We've gotta go in," said Burton. "C'mon, Cynth, stop the
car. This is *necessary*." Cynthia pulled into a space against
the ersatz brick wall. Ella was laughing.

Inside, it was as they might have dreamed, had they been
inclined to dream about Romeo's Treasure Chest. Cupids and
hearts hovered, ready for Valentine's Day at any moment.
Exclamatory signs marked competing bargains, all guaran-
teed "real" or "genuine," including Genuine Diamond-cut
Glass. A salesman—wearing, just as he ought, chains visible
inside the very open neck of his too-brightly patterned shirt,
with wavy, unwilling bangs combed to his forehead—at-

tempted to show them his best, with a good-natured, in-on-it look. He was undoubtedly used to crazy teenagers and liked them, liked their hope and high spirits. But he had to desert the trio for a very overweight couple who pointed out a ring as though it were a penance.

"Oh, this, this is the one," said Burton. They lined up in front of the Deluxe Special.

"Nah, that's too pretty."

"Yeah. It lacks a certain—tastelessness," said Cynthia.

"It had better. You're the one who's going to wear it." The salesman returned just in time to see Cynthia's stricken face.

"You're not with both these ladies? I couldn't decide should I be jealous of what a lucky guy or should I take and be glad I just got the one wife I got to pay for."

"No," said Cynthia in a furious whisper. Her tender skin was maroon.

"I want to get an engagement ring," said Burton.

"No." This time she sounded helpless and listless. She held her hands behind her back, where Burton couldn't easily get at them.

"Are you engaged?" said Ella, making a joke, as people often cover anger with jokes. She was unready to see Cynthia shanghaied.

But Burton had a more high-handed idea of romance. Maybe this was what he'd learned from Ave. "Give me your hand. Come on, so you can try it on." He tugged at Cynthia's arm. She whipped out the other hand, puffy, scarred, a gruesome sight even when you were prepared for it.

The salesman stood back from the counter, rocking on his heels.

"Here." She looked at the salesman with glittering eyes and a smile that she forgot, moment to moment, to maintain.

"Had a little accident, did you." He slipped on the diamond and garnet confection. Real diamond, and no reason for the garnets not to be.

"How clever of you, Burton. It matches." Cynthia held her

hand in his face, some of the skin so new it was white, some a raw-looking garnet.

Burton's hatred, so well suppressed he hadn't known of it, flared. "Check okay?" he said to the salesman.

By this time likewise reduced to silence, the salesman nodded his head. "With driver's license and picture i.d." Burton didn't have any picture i.d. Cynthia had a credit card, but he didn't dare ask. They left the ring.

By the car, Ella asked if she could drive, speaking in an undertone. Cynthia held her wounded hand as though it ached. She got into the backseat. Burton did likewise, on the other side.

By the time they drove over the border, she was letting him chew the rim of her ear, and she butted her head into his chest.

Once again they greeted familiar sights with shouts. "Look—that barn finally fell down"—a gray building that had been keeling a little more each year lay in a heap, a horse feeding around the ruins. Burton looked appraisingly at a pillared yellow cottage he had subliminally had his eye on for years, which was sporting an agent's for-sale sign. His arm tightened around Cynthia's slack shoulders.

At their old favorite hippie diner they felt glamorously older than the students who still flocked there. Waiting for their orders, Ella picked up a copy of *New England*, a glossy throwaway for tourists. She put her hand to her forehead and sank into it. "What?" asked Burton, trying to imagine the awful headline that had elicited this absorption. "It's an interview with Frank," she said without looking up. "It says he has a dog," she added after a minute. "He didn't have a dog when I was there. He doesn't have a dog."

Their food came. Burton was getting to hear quite a lot of detail about Ella's recent love life. He looked up to see by Cynthia's expression how much of this she knew and what she thought of it, but Cynthia had no expression. She wore the look of a new baby stunned at where it finds itself. For a moment she fastened on him with recognition. He saw that her paper mat was moving, that she was pulling it as if she intended to do a magic trick. A knife capsized and went over. "Cynthia," he said, grabbing at the place mat.

When she answered, her eyes addressed the wrong spot, like a blind person's. "I'm di—" She hesitated a long time, so long it seemed that was it. "—ssociating."

Glasses chinking as they were set down, the green, depthless froth of the Formica, the gleam and stripes of its metal edging, the scalloped paper place mat, the bulge-shape of the drinking glass, the bent tine of a fork, a waitress's receding back, the angle of light, all at that moment declared the absolute dead end of denial.

It was unanticipated, yet no surprise, when on the immediate way back to New York, Cynthia raised her hand commandingly at the turnoff for Sterling-Pine. They spent most of the night checking her in.

The next day, as Burton and Ella drove the rest of the way back to the city, Ella said that this must have been why Cynthia wanted to go away, to get to Sterling. "That's not true!" Burton shouted with the kind of angry energy we reserve for defending ourselves against the truths we don't wish to know. The anger he felt toward Ella for saying this damned her, in his mind, as though she were the cause of it all.

26. Reunion

Frank was bouncing on the balls of his feet, brown and handsomer even than Ella had remembered. But as he inspected her new apartment, his wariness was evident in the tilt of his body and the way he pushed up his glasses, looking not quite at her eyes but over her shoulder when he talked to her. Each gesture was a warning that at any moment he might cut and run.

She had been so hurt by his long summer's incommunicativeness that he had reason to be wary: he had given her so much cause to try to hurt him back. He broadcast the danger he felt himself to be in, knowing it is courting trouble to be around those you have hurt. So she knew she must go on not showing what she felt, not letting on the secret they both knew about his hurting her, so as not to scare him away. You could not scare away someone who loved you. Though it was also true that if he loved her, he probably would not have hurt her. She smiled in a cool noncommittal way. She stood an undemanding distance apart from him. She answered his speaking incommunicativeness by communicating the reserve he hoped for.

Still, she had to ask. "When did you get back?"

"Monday."

"You've been back a week?"

"That's six days. Now, don't start. I'm a middle-aged man. I have my heart to worry about." She curved her sandpapery fingers around each other in the effort of not responding. "I'm not going to push myself into a heart attack for you." He squinted at the pictures on the walls of the little dressing room, at an oriental woodblock print. "This is nice, when'd you get this?"

"It was up in my other apartment."

"I never saw it."

Actually, he had once remarked on it. She wondered if he remembered her.

She asked if he would like a cup of coffee.

"If you need to make it, if it will make you comfortable."

He was outrageous.

After he had paced the apartment several times and

squinted out the windows unobservantly—and she did nothing to aid his observation—he plopped into a chair.

"Do you mind that I live so close to you?" She had moved a few blocks toward his studio and apartment.

"No! It's convenient." He shot forth a lewd toothy grin. She pretended to laugh with him. She felt a buzz of rebellious fire in her chest, but felt at the same time that there was sufficient welcome for her to place herself on his lap. She sat apart from his body, on the bone of his knee, hands in front of her. Still, she could feel his damp radiance, like earth after rain on a hot day. He pulled her to him, her back to his chest, and began planting little kisses along her shoulder and neck.

Unable to stop herself, she asked, "Were you seeing someone else?"

"Hm?"

"Up there. Did you have another—?"

He had stopped kissing. "Umhmm."

She felt as if she had discovered she was sitting on hardened turds. She would have liked to leap off his knees.

In a peeved voice he whined, "I've been seeing her every summer since I started going up there, I couldn't very well, it's a comfortable arrangement, she doesn't want any more than that, what did you expect, that everything would change because you left your friend?"

She thought: I gave up everything for this.

"That I would go three months without sex?" he prodded.

"Would you rather have been sleeping with me?" she finally asked.

"Now, I've told you as much as I'm going to." He stood, tipping her off as you might let a napkin fall. "The world doesn't revolve around you!" he said, making for the door. As he let himself out he added in his devastating murmur, "If this is how you want things," and twisted himself past the door so that it clapped shut on his words.

• • •

In church they recited the Lord's Prayer, the Nicene Creed, a kyrie. The words didn't change. In that was their power to reassure. Everyone knew what to do, the moves were choreographed, the script written: this also was reassurance. But for Ella the words and the ritual were still so new that they had that other power, to open her up as helplessly as a fillet, to make her look through the eye of God instead of her own temporizing one and see her own wretchedness. The part of the service that was hardest was the peace, when she had to turn to her neighbors after they heard "Peace be with you," embrace them, and say, "And also with you." Each week she expected to be revealed as a pariah, that despite the mandates of charity, no one would turn to her.

Yet she was embraced. First by a plump, ostentatiously pious man she recognized as a former Jew, and hoped that wasn't why. Next, limply, by a slender woman with straight hair who represented to Ella what a woman was supposed to be, not straining after approbation but taking it as her due. The extremely handsome man to her other side took her hand and pulled her toward him with the free one, so that her cheek touched the gold stud in his ear.

She dragged her wet handkerchief across her cheeks and blew. People crossed themselves, even though they were in a gym and where the cross should have been was a basketball hoop. We worship hoops, she thought, liking it: she didn't have to feel so guilty for being there, in a school gym, even if her passions were responsible for the church's burning.

Her hands shook as she lit a cigarette in the church garden, looking at the buckled windows. The handsome young man with the gold stud said kindly, "You shouldn't smoke. You have a pretty voice." People really were kinder after they recited those words, for a little while. While thinking this, she could also see that he was the type of gay man who liked to cultivate especially feminine women. She was overdressed, and too sexily dressed, in very high heels and a dress whose deep neck she had camouflaged with a scarf.

She noticed her shaking hand. It reminded her of Cynthia's pointing to the loony bin. Sisters under the skin, she thought, and not very far under. That's why I always knew what she was thinking, she thought. But Ella knew about Frank too, she believed: his guilt, his desire, his irritable impatience, no way to fool yourself about it. And such extreme, such persistent desire, it could only mean the one thing, she couldn't help but believe.

Walking past the rank of dented mailboxes on the ocher stucco of her downstairs hallway, she thought, No mail, then remembered it didn't matter anyway, since Frank was back. Not that it had ever mattered, considering the brevity and emptiness of the letter and postcard she'd gotten. She was still in her sexy clothes when the phone rang.

All week, each time the phone rang, she thought it was him. She had managed not to call him.

She let the first ring finish, still arrested in the act of bending a leg to remove a shoe. It would be indecent to pick up on the first ring. It won't be him, she warned herself, gripping the edge of the dresser. She listened to the second ring as though its tone could tell her. Please, she prayed, her hand above the receiver; I've gone to *church*.

"Hi. It's Frank," he said in a sleepy voice. As though she might not have recognized it.

"Hi. It's Ella," she said. He laughed! She had made him laugh! He did love her.

And, indeed, he wanted to see her.

He started kissing as soon as she shut the door. He put his hands on each side of her neck and shot them into her hair, ripping her head back. He withdrew only to grab her face again and press his own to it. One of his hands caught in the big bangle of an earring. She pulled it off. We worship hoops. Her hand followed its practical task of setting down the golden hoop while the rest of her was swept into kisses. She could kiss him without going further. She was determined on this. Maybe then he would call again, sooner.

He walked her backward to the rug, lifted her body and laid her out upon it. He stood regarding his achievement. Up and down, from the hair billowing over the pattern she lay on, to the vivid scarf fanned out like an advertisement for her, and down along the violet causeway of her dress, the shimmering stalks, down to the heels that suggested twin erections. She lay impassive, the cool expression refusing to yield comment, or rather commenting: Do your worst, you won't get anything out of me. Or so she imagined.

He pushed a smoothly shod foot between the sueded heels, the gleaming ankles, and quickly knelt between her knees. He pushed his glasses up his nose, serious, staring. "Boy, are you beautiful. You could"—he smiled, staring—"you could really go upscale if you wanted." And he laughed, at the word "upscale," at the idea that he got to have such a dish from the rich man's table.

She let him lie on her. Let him! It was everything she had ever wanted. He was the world, and he was the escape from the world. But she was not going to give him everything he wanted, or she would lose it all. Nevertheless, he had not yet come to the line where *everything* was, so he could not yet know she had drawn it. Leaving her free to luxuriate in his kisses. She didn't let him know she did. She lay passive, her arms limp. But her body lifting to him, her mouth opening and opening on his kisses, pulling him in, did not exactly say Get off, sucker.

In short order he was doing what men always do when they start kissing, their hands turning advance men sussing out the territory, infiltrating, preparing the way. She heard the zing of nylon. All but tumbling him off, she shot up to pull the stockings down herself. "I don't want my stockings to run," she said, throwing them in a ball a cat ran over to sniff. She didn't look at Frank. Those were the first words she'd spoken.

She didn't want him to get the wrong idea.

He kept his eyes right on her, drawing aside but with an

arm possessively spanning her, as cautious as though he were dismantling a ticking bomb. But he ran his hands over her bared legs with a sexual groan, sinking down once again.

Soon her dress was up around her midriff, under her arms. He was kissing her belly, he was kissing below the elastic of her chaste white Lollipops. He kissed the bristling hairs, looked up, checking; she gave no sign; he kissed and looked up again, more briefly this time, gaining courage. He had, after all, worked photographing the world's zoos; he had, after all, liked stroking the big cats, seeing how far he could go. He hadn't gotten clawed, he'd gotten asthma.

He pulled the purple dress over her head. For moments she was trapped in its tent, but she wouldn't help, however long it meant lying in the dark, feeling like a horse being led through fire, an animal that has to be tricked into guidance. He got the thing off; stared with what might have looked like anger in other circumstances and, actually, looked like anger; then darted, plunged, with a kiss that was the osculatory equivalent of an attack.

It wasn't long before the low-cut black lace bra circled one wrist, and the little white pants had been palmed. Then he fell back to his knees and pulled off everything he wore on his upper half, not bothering about buttons, his eyes fixed on her. He stood to let down the pants. And that was where he revealed his really big surprise. Really big. It was as if, all these months, her desire had diminished his. Well, she had his true measure now. Just hate him enough. My God, was that thing going to go into her? That hybrid yam? That suckling pig?

Well, she wasn't getting her diaphragm. Let him make her pregnant.

Make me pregnant, she silently prayed.

"Are you pro-tec-ted?" he asked in soft minced syllables.

She raised her eyebrows.

He sighed heavily. He took off his glasses, always the last thing to go. He hung back a moment more, then plunged heavily into her, a porpoise released from captivity into brilliant aquatic bliss.

She gasped. The bliss was far from one-sided. Not only was this everything she had ever wanted, there wasn't anything else.

After some time, he said in a soft purr, "I'm going to withdraw."

Like hell he was.

With the power of her pelvis she followed. High in the air, until he couldn't help but plunge downward again, burrowing, run to earth. But then back and arcing away, as though he thought he were allowed to leave that place.

"Baby, baby," she breathed half-articulately. It wasn't an endearment.

He couldn't help but come in her. It was getting more difficult, also, for her not to come. But she could hold out. She would not give that signal a gentleman requires before politely withdrawing.

Her lips pressed, her whole face stiff like someone hefting the strongman's weights, she managed not to make a sound. But she couldn't stop the almost dizzying stillness that followed the convulsions. And then there he was, beached, springing, in a tide pool of his own spume on her belly.

27. All the way uptown

Burton had an arduous day ahead of him. Meeting Stephen at Maurizio, of all places; packing up stuff at Cynthia's with Ella; and then dropping off something Ave had wanted at her new place uptown, which he hadn't yet seen and had no de-

sire to see, as he had no desire to do any of what he was doing or see anyone he was doing it with.

The shafting, oblique sunlight of November pierced his
eyes, striking like punishment. He hoped that coffee would
help him cast off the lead cape that weighed him down and
muffled everything. He could not walk at normal speed, as
in those dreams where epochs pass while you try to take a
step. As he arrived at the café, he could see Stephen already
inside.

"Maestro!" Stephen rose from the toylike marble table.
"Yikes! When'd you shave it?"

Burton's full face had emerged for the first time since high
school. "I thought it was time to come clean."

"Jesus shit. You're like another person. I'm not kidding, I
thought who is this guy when you said hello." Stephen shook
his head to dramatize his amazement, his delicate fingers to
the hard stubble of his own cheek, and shook his head again.

My hatred will go away when I drink my coffee, Burton
assured himself. "I am another person," he said. He passed
his hand over his shining face as over a childhood abrasion
that you have to keep touching for a sensation more potent
in its novelty than in its sting.

Stephen took his words as a joke, tossing his head back
and hooding his eyes in a kind of mime of laughter. Burton
recognized the gesture as Ella's. It was impossible to remember who had stolen it from whom. It was eerie that a person
might live on that way in someone who had once loved
them. That the very memory of that person might die while
her traces lived on, forever. People thought things were so
inconstant, so tragically ephemeral, when the tragic truth
was that nothing changed. That neuroses clung with the per-
sistence and vitality of viruses; that Stephen made love to
Melody while wearing Ella's face; that when Burton heard
Cynthia's Thorazine-slugged voice, what he saw was his
mother with her lemonade gin and the orange shag carpet

that smelled like damp dog scattered with cigarette ash.

And yet he was a different person, a new person. Or at least something that was always there had shifted, toppling an immensity of the familiar into darkness. As soon as could be managed, Burton heaved this shiny-faced heavy man out of his seat, to drag him on to the next errand on his round. He counted out a tip for the pretty waitress, with whom Stephen had pointlessly flirted. Wavy needles of electricity shot along his upper arms; that was as much as the coffee had done for him.

When he got to Cynthia's apartment he heard music coming from inside. Time slipped; it seemed possible that she was there; it seemed to him he felt something like joy in the shock of his surprise, but it was fear. He entered on a cresting surge of guilt. Ella had gotten there first and turned on the radio, so that a string quartet sawed like insects. She appeared in the doorway, touching her eyes. "There are all these poems," she said.

On the double bed, where he had never paid Cynthia the kindness of spending the whole night, an open suitcase had folded into it neat squares of warm clothes. A sweater would keep her warm, a sweater would hold her, and he would not, because he was an unmitigated shit. Ella, turning from the closet, looked at his face and said, with that ability Cynthia and Ave had wondered at, "It's not your fault, Burton. You couldn't have saved her. Nobody could."

"Why did she turn against me? I mean, it was when I found out she knew, but she knew the whole time."

"Because—as long as she could contain the hurt, she wasn't on display as someone so desperate you could fuck her over. You didn't fuck her, you fucked her over."

As soon as he heard it put that way he saw that the pleasure had not been the sex but the inflicting of pain, without consequence. That was what he had loved her for. The freedom she had given him. And taken back. "But her hand—"

He found stinging water was coming to his eyes and looked at the wall as though, if he didn't see Ella, she couldn't see him. Remembering that he was angry at her helped, but he couldn't remember what he was angry at her for.

"She wanted something that would keep her from playing," Ella said.

Burton tried to object.

"No, it's selfish to think of what we wanted for her. You have to think of what she could stand."

For a glorious moment Burton was able to summon his fury. "You're talking about her as though she was dead."

Ella sat on the edge of the bed, stroking some satiny cloth folded in her lap. They both knew that the person they had loved had barely been holding on for as long as they had known or loved her, and that recovery would not recover her. Burton had talked to doctors, but he knew the most absolute form of this truth in his own sense of foreboding, in the thunderous misery that beat at and nearly blinded him. People on the street or subway must think he was crazy when he clutched at his middle with a gasp. Burton sank onto the edge of the bed, the end away from Ella. "I'd like to be locked up too."

He could feel Ella's hot eyes on him. He had heard her say the same thing.

"I just realized what's different," she said, putting the black satiny thing in the suitcase. "No beard! I knew something was different, but—"

He tried to bear up under her inspection. "Well?"

"Huh." She seemed to find new information in the naked skin. She looked at his face as though he were not inside it.

"What?"

"You're still you."

"Is that good or bad?"

"Oh, good. Too kind. Sad," she added.

He grabbed her shoulders. They felt crackable. "We should

run away somewhere together. We should go to the Midwest and take assumed names and live normal lives."

"Oh. Like normal people."

"We should. You wanted to do this, Ella, you used to talk about it."

"'Which way I fly is hell; myself am hell.'" She disengaged herself. "*Paradise Lost.* Appropriately enough."

"Ella!"

She kicked his instep gently with her shoe. "I'd like to. If I were a different person. But that's just the trouble, isn't it."

That was just the trouble.

He asked if she would at least go on with him to Ave's.

"Ave! We *have* been out of touch. Oh no. I'm through with—I suppose she's gotten you to do her some favor."

His eyebrows shot up as he lowered his lids.

"She's never, there's always something more she can get out of you. That *bitch*."

Something stirred, like a little hand in his heart, freed from shackles. "But she's pitiful," he said.

"She's pitiless."

The little hand was joined by another. They clapped. "Please come with me."

Ella shook her head, smoothing the last things in the suitcase and pushing it closed. As a result, she was the second-to-last person he spoke to in his life.

28. Foul play

At the end of the 1970s, black was still the predominating color at funerals. Ave had never seen Stephen in a suit, but

didn't comment, since her role as widow called for falling
into his arms, as his called for falling into hers. He was to give
the eulogy. They had discussed it in detail. A large sector of
the music and theater communities turned out. Ave unconsciously sought the sight of Ella in the crowd. She and
Stephen had agreed that they were mad at her, since she
hadn't even made the ritual sympathy call. Only once everyone was seated and the music was started (unusually good
music for this sort of thing, naturally) did Ave catch a glimpse
of her, in the back, alone. In black. But not in a magnificent
black hat like Ave's. No one else wore a hat.

A dead person is always a celebrity, at least at his own
funeral.

There were other star-fuckers there, people who had done
Burton out of jobs, who had had nothing but horrible things
to say about him for years, people about whom, if you had
asked did he want them invited to something, he would have
said, Not over my dead body.

Everyone had seen the picture. It was in the tabloids:
CHORAL CONDUCTOR FALLS TO DEATH. Not much more, not much
more than a caption: rescuing cat from ledge, apartment of
Ave Shulamith O'Shaughnessy, recently resided with the de-
ceased. Ambulance, police; cat okay. Photo credit: Ave
O'Shaughnessy; neither foul play nor deliberate intent suspected.

Ave wasn't so sure about the deliberate intent part, or
rather pretended to be sure: "Of course he killed himself," to
which she would add, with a purposefully brutal laugh, "After all, I had left him. What else could he do?" Stephen at the
wake the night before had engaged in the most complicated
maneuvers of lips and eyes at this. "See Ave and die?" he had
said, rolling his eyes but pursing his lips with disapproval,
and at the same time smiling in his friendly, good-natured
way. She wore that great onyx brooch and those jet earrings
that were actually called funerary jewelry. People got drunk

and talked about what a great guy he was. It was definitely in her interest to come down in the great-guy camp. Well, he was a great guy, she wouldn't have been with someone who wasn't.

Ella hadn't shown up at the wake either. Neither had that Cynthia person, but Stephen said she was in the bin. Good place for her! To think Burton had been ready to dump her, Ave, for a nutcase. Actually, it made you kind of queasy to think of it this way; it bracketed you with mental illness: if he could love one cuckoo, he could love another. Though he really hadn't loved her, Ave.

It was useful to think of this. It made her cry. It is well to cry at a funeral. At Bergdorf's she had lucked into linen handkerchiefs hemmed in black.

Words drifted from the podium or pulpit, where a minister who didn't know Burton and various of those who did were speaking—"tragic waste" was a favored phrase. Perfect pitch, exceptional ear, natural gifts combined with wide command of the literature, and in addition to this myriad wealth of musicality and wisdom about his art and craft, his wisdom about the players, his sensitivity in rehearsal and performance—whereupon followed anecdotes of same, along lines to make you think, Oh that such a light has passed from the world.

He wasn't that great, Ave thought, at the same time feeling she'd missed something—that all these people had gotten to have a much better time with her lover than she had. At the bottom of this sour mud parfait was the fear that at her funeral, no one would find such things to say, and hardly anyone would show up. Many there, less well prepared than she was, wiped noses on wrists and sleeves or on balled-up Kleenex. They all loved him, *loved* him; so what was wrong with her that with the fairest of opportunities, she had been unable to?

If she really wanted to make herself cry, she had only to

think of how she had behaved when he came over for his fatal visit.

She couldn't be blamed. Really she couldn't. She had been frantic. The cat had just refused to come in. And then his reproaching her with not having food to lure the cat in with. So she had no food in the house, big deal! It wasn't like she starved the damn thing. And screens—the way he went on and on about not having screens. Who expected to have to open the windows in November!

He had looked so sandbagged, so reluctant. As if he had gained a tremendous amount of weight. He did look different, but not that way. She hadn't been able to put her finger on it.

She was distracted by music in between speakers, piano and soprano—*Why must the beautiful ever weep? Why must the beautiful die?* It didn't make sense, did it—beautiful? Sort of insulting for a boy. Or was it *dutiful?*

Ave had leaned out the second window to watch Burton inching along to get the cat. Out on the ledge, the high air carried the sound of distant traffic and of its own whistling movement around the corners of the tall buildings of the housing project she'd gotten into. Off to the west the sky was streaking with one of those early-gloom end-of-the-year sunsets. Close to where the ledge went around the corner, the half-grown cat lifted its head back for the full view of its rescuer, with a familiar, trusting look. "Harris," Burton called in the high voice the cat liked. It stood, plumy tail straight with pleasure. It rubbed against the brick, then, remembering, cast an anxious look downward. "Harry-Harry-Harris." He held a hand out to it. It promptly sat back, drawing its prim paws close; stared a moment; and let out a howl. "Babycat, what do you want me to do?"

"Pick him up, for God's sake," said Ave from the other window, where she was photographing the transaction.

As Burton reached for the cat, the kitty, with a sudden

frightened bound, leaped over Burton's shiny shoes. Burton had seemed to teeter. Ave was so sure that he was all right—this was a guy who liked rock-climbing—that she snapped away, to catch the comicality of his skewed, unbalanced movements. She had a number of stages of the fall. But not that moment when he had looked directly at her, both hands free as if in surrender.

She had run in and thrown up.

Stephen was shaking hands with the minister up on the stage, jerking at his suit jacket, clearing his throat. He was going to tell anecdotes from college. Within moments laughter rolled through the crowd.

She had had the presence of mind, after calling nine-one-one, to offer her pictures to the *Post*. And now this gallery dealer wanted to put one in this show of New York pictures and had asked if she had others in this vein . . .

She drifted in a fantasy of acclaim, of going from success to success; and of course an adoring man—this gallery owner, for instance, if he wasn't gay. She could go for someone really conservative, a man who even for ordinary occasions wore a suit.

She was dressing herself congruently when she was tugged out of her daydream by the sound of Stephen choking at the end of his talk. He stumbled from the stage moving his hands as though polishing a windshield, indicating that he was all right, even if he couldn't speak. Of course everyone was very moved, and lone maladroits here and there brought their hands together in inappropriate private claps.

Though people filed out after the funeral, they didn't seem inclined to move from the sidewalk outside, collecting in murmuring knots, rushing up to one another. She heard, "He had just shaved his beard . . ." That was it, that was what had looked so different. How embarrassing not to have noticed. Maybe she couldn't be a good photographer, she began to think, but the thought with imperceptible immediacy began to transmute itself. Of course she had noticed, just not consciously, she was an artist, she operated on her instincts.

Stephen was thronged, but when Ella appeared before him, he threw himself into her arms, the little traitor. Ella offered feeble pats to his nattily suited back. Ave watched Melody looking on coolly, her pregnancy not yet showing and officially still a secret. Ave would have been glad to share it with Ella, if Ella had acknowledged her presence.

Part III

. . . . .

AFTER LONG SILENCE

Speech after long silence; it is right,
All other lovers being estranged or dead,
Unfriendly lamplight hid under its shade,
The curtains drawn upon unfriendly night,
That we descant and yet again descant
Upon the supreme theme of Art and Song:
Bodily decrepitude is wisdom; young
We loved each other and were ignorant.
                                    —W. B. Yeats
                    "Words for Music Perhaps," XVII

29. The end of the day at the end of the year

"Take, eat": the Jewish part of the service. It was impossible for Ella not to hear Christ's words, spoken through the vehicle of his upright Anglican priest, with the inflections of a Yiddische mama, as if they were to be followed by the words "fix yourself." Every week, same old joke.

But the part she cared about was the Prayers of the People. She couldn't bring herself to stand up and say their names, but she silently threw Burton's and Cynthia's into the pot in hope of some kind of spiritual synergy working with everybody else's prayers. It was possible: the blue-haired ladies in millefleur silk suits didn't blanch when the externally displayed keyrings of the boys in black leather clanked as they ostentatiously genuflected.

Not that Ella really believed in any of it, unfortunately. She took the approach she had taken to loving Frank: it would be a great idea if it happened to be true. In church she thought, a Jewish boy, God? are you kidding? Did these nice gentiles know their communion wafers were matzohs, that they were drinking Passover wine? Same thoughts every week. She was so sick of herself!

Chantez à Dieu chanson nouvelle

That was probably what she really came for: to sing, and to cry. Hey, it was practically like having a love affair.

She wondered if Burton had ever conducted this song in the days before they worshiped hoops, if Cynthia and Burton had played it. Cynthia, Ella had just found out, had re-

cently been found living on the street. Her parents had
whisked her into one of those rich people's drying-out
places. That would do her a lot of good. Ella kept meaning
to get the number or address; but maybe she didn't mean to.

When the service ended, letting out from the gym into the
church-school's paved playground, Ella walked around to
the garden to inspect from that side the progress, if any, in the
church's reconstruction. She wandered over the paths, sniffed
at the last roses, felt the brittle earth under her proper and unnecessary pumps, allowing memory to overcome her with all
the perverse pleasure of probing a wound. A couple of congregants sat on a bench, arguing about the architect's latest
design for the reconstruction. Why, she wondered, couldn't
they just put it back the way it had been? Was it so impossible
to restore or retain anything? Well, what did she care; she'd
never been inside the damn place before the fire anyway.

She walked home along the river, where gay men cruised,
prostitutes and peddlers solicited, and a permanent holiday
air prevailed. Tropical plants offered for ten dollars per; soon
there would be Christmas trees. Maybe she would get a tree
for herself this year. Stephen would never let her have one.
She could make stars and angels for it.

It would be a relief from her illustration work. She had
been so pleased to be hired to draw—professional ratifica-
tion at last. But she discovered she hated the work. It had
been more fun to hang out with Mona-and-Groana. It paid
better, though. It left her more time for her own work.

The sky was clouding up in the west, as the weatherman
had promised. Everything in her life was so predictable. Even
the weather reports were right, as if nature itself had been de-
natured, become a meek apprentice to the television screen.
It was like the mistakeless performances of recorded music.

Yet it was habit that had made her, if not happy with her
life, able to move smoothly within it. Even Frank had been
reduced to a habit, as harmful and as hard to break as smoking, a habit of waiting and unfulfillment. She looked forward

to no longer sleeping with him the way she used to look forward to happiness. Already she could anticipate the more
solitary loneliness that her liberation would be.

When she got home she first checked on the yahrzeit candle she had left burning for the anniversary of Burton's
death. It made her nervous to leave it flaming while she was
out, she had such a horror of setting fires. Theoretically it
was safe in its ugly little jar. That was the trouble: Christianity
had all the aesthetics. It was easy enough, after all, to make a
candle beautiful. In fact, it had to be deliberately punitive to
make it this ugly.

The cats more or less ignored her. All four of them—her
own two, plus Queenie and Pinky—forming a kind of pride,
mercifully unto themselves, so that Ella could take note of
their private laws like an ethologist in her successfully tamed
New York apartment.

The painting wall was covered with a canvas in progress.
She had thought it would be too kitschy to do a sunset ever,
but had discovered that including ugly bits of landscape
made it acceptable.

More than ever, she was aware that what she painted
wasn't this or that, but light. This was what Frank always
liked to talk about as making his pictures. The difference
was, he spent half his life in the darkroom, in the dark.
Whereas the darkness from which her pictures emerged was
the secret interior of the mind lit by imagination. And that
was secret enough; the paintings, she had found, didn't have
to be. In fact, as far as who saw them was concerned, she
couldn't give a flying fuck.

She put on the country and western station as she
changed into paint-hardened pants that practically stood up
by themselves. "The only country in New York," the jingle
went. "Are you cryin', lovin', or leavin'?" said the announcer
so that all three merged as a joke. As well they might: it
made Ella laugh out loud. After an inane exchange with a
caller who was "cryin'," they put on a countrified version of

"I Cover the Waterfront." Oh, for God's sake, thought Ella, can't they leave anything alone?

Before Ella went to bed, she checked that the candle had burned itself down to a puddle, and looked at the calendar for Monday appointments. The optometrist, at four, to pick up the annual new lenses. She would probably have to wait hours, she thought.

But as it turned out, she was in a fairly mellow mood as she left his office the next evening. It was dark, and the headlights racing past Abingdon Square sparkled with the brightness that was always surprising with fresh lenses. It was like the first time she wore them, when she walked out of the office and had a glimpse not only of how bright and sharp the night could be, but of how she too might become part of the beautiful world.

Gorgeous and vivid as the night had been—those yellow car eyes, the white streetlights, the ziggy curling neons and bits of people's softly lit lives through their windows—the picture that had beckoned had come from the night inside, where her pictures came from. It had been of Frank, that smacked expression after he'd first tried to kiss her that showed not his shame at what he'd done but his disappointment and humiliation in being refused. She'd thought he was angry, but in the grip of that naked expression she'd felt such a desire to comfort him that even as her feet carried her over the bricks of the park walkway, over the sidewalk glittering with mica and trash, toward Stephen and her then-home, it had been Frank she was walking toward, who filled her imagination from then onward like the lights with which the doctor professionally dazzled her eyes.

Ella blinked. The drops made her eyes sting. Down at the ends of the blocks, over the river, the rich sky was still stained a murky yellow. The doctor had kept her waiting. Though often enough she painted right through it, here she was, out, she who lived for color in the sky, and she had missed the sunset.